Ballad of the Northland

Ballad
of the
Northland

JASON BARRON

ART BY HARMONY BARRON

Kanabear books may be purchased for educational, business, or sales promotional use. For information, please write Kanabear Books Box 996 Suite 011 Lincoln Montana USA 59639
www.kanabearenterprises.com

ISBN: 978-0-578-06822-0

Library of Congress number pending

Kanabear Books
a division of Kanabearenterprises
Box 996 Suite 011
Lincoln, MT, 59639

Text Design & Layout: Jonathan Gullery
Cover Art & Interior Art: Harmony Barron
Printed by RJ Communications

This book is a work of fiction; all persons, characters, and events are a product of the author's imagination. A resemblance to any real persons or events is purely a matter of coincidence.

First US Edition

To my wife Harmony,
for holding hands with me
during this journey;
And to my brother Laird—
he alone knows how much
of the following story is true…

Acknowledgments

As many of you know, writing a book is a huge undertaking and not a task for one man alone. Thankfully, I had a great deal of help with this project.

Sherry Sutherby, Amy Breakey, and The Wang family helped 'focus test' the material every step along the way.

Shawn Strannigan not only edited, but also gave me a new set of tools to evaluate my work; without her help, this manuscript would have suffered immeasurably.

Phil Whitmarsh, Jonathan Gullery, and the rest of the team at RJ Communications; for all of their help on the layout & design of this book.

Gordon Shafer, for his unconditional support.

My brother, Laird Barron, for writing the introduction.

Last, but most certainly not least, my wonderful wife Harmony; it is her fabulous art which graces the cover and all of the chapter headings.

Thank you all, from the bottom of my heart…

Introduction

LIFE in the north is hard. Those who've traveled Alaska's rivers and trekked across her mountains will attest the land radiates an aura that at times feels sentient. She is ancient and she does not suffer fools. For many who dwell on the fringes of the Last Great Frontier, far from the major population centers, daily life is purely a matter of survival, of eking out a hand to mouth existence upon the back of frozen wastes or along windswept shores.

A handful, however, seek a deeper, more profound equilibrium with the primeval land and her savage moods. Jason Barron is such a man. *Ballad of the Northland* is his expression of that essential yearning to strike a balance between the needs of our species' primitive core and the drive to create, to test one's limits even at the cost of blood and sorrow. His tale is an articulation of a pioneer spirit for the modern age. Just as the pioneer existence is not for the faint of heart, neither is this novel. It is not a true story, nor are its characters based upon any real persons, living or dead. But, without question, this harrowing account of The Boy's journey to adulthood is *inspired* by the persons, places, and events that marked Jason's tumultuous early years. I know this to be true, because I was there.

My brother was raised in rural Alaska. He spent many of those years in the deep wilderness. His was a youth of want and rigor. Our family dwelt in a rude cabin and subsisted by hunting and fishing, running traplines, and racing teams of huskies in middle and long distance events, including the legendary Iditarod. Those were lean years. There was hunger and privation borne of poverty;

a sense of isolation and melancholy engendered by the remoteness of our surroundings. Winters were as harsh as anything you'd care to imagine. We survived perpetual hardship by making a kind of compact with our dogs and the land itself. The Iditarod, that thousand mile long endurance race from Anchorage to Nome became the Holy Grail of our communal dream, and those trapline huskies carried one Barron or another to honor on many occasions. The Iditarod was the crucible that forged Jason's character. His relationship with his huskies perfected it.

Others have written odes to the great northern realm and its peoples. Robert Service did not tarry long in the Land of the Midnight Sun when he made his way throughout the territories — first as a bank clerk, then a famous poet. Such was the conviction of his voice, the power of his vision regarding life on the frontier during Gold Rush days, readers can be forgiven the mistaken belief that Service was a grizzled citizen of the Yukon rather than a keen-eyed tourist. The music of his poetry, the melancholic edge of his wit is undiminished by provenance, but said provenance bears note, for there are layers and layers to be peeled from the bark of truly great literature. Authenticity of character, authenticity of experience — these are layers possessed by Jason. They make an indelible impression upon the narrative of Ballad of the Northland and imbue its scenery with a verisimilitude that can only spring from a life fully lived.

There is something of the epic *Beowulf* in the grandeur of the landscapes and the poetry of language of this book. However, *Ballad of the Northland* is first and foremost a bildungsroman in the honored tradition of *Catcher in the Rye* or *Blood Meridian*. *Ballad of the Northland* is a celebration of man's eternal struggle to survive in an inhospitable world — and more than that: to triumph. It is also a paean to the bittersweet glory of wild Alaska and her amazing children, the huskies; a sincere and grateful acknowledgment of their loyalty and courage, an acknowledgment that the beasts don't truly belong to their human masters, but that we belong to one another now as we have for millennia.

This isn't the story of Jason's youth, or mine, or yours. Rather, this story speaks to all of us who've ever shouldered too much too soon, who've braved the storm and emerged changed, rarified, spiritually ennobled.

—Laird Barron, author of The *Imago Sequence*

August 25, 2010

Ballad of the Northland

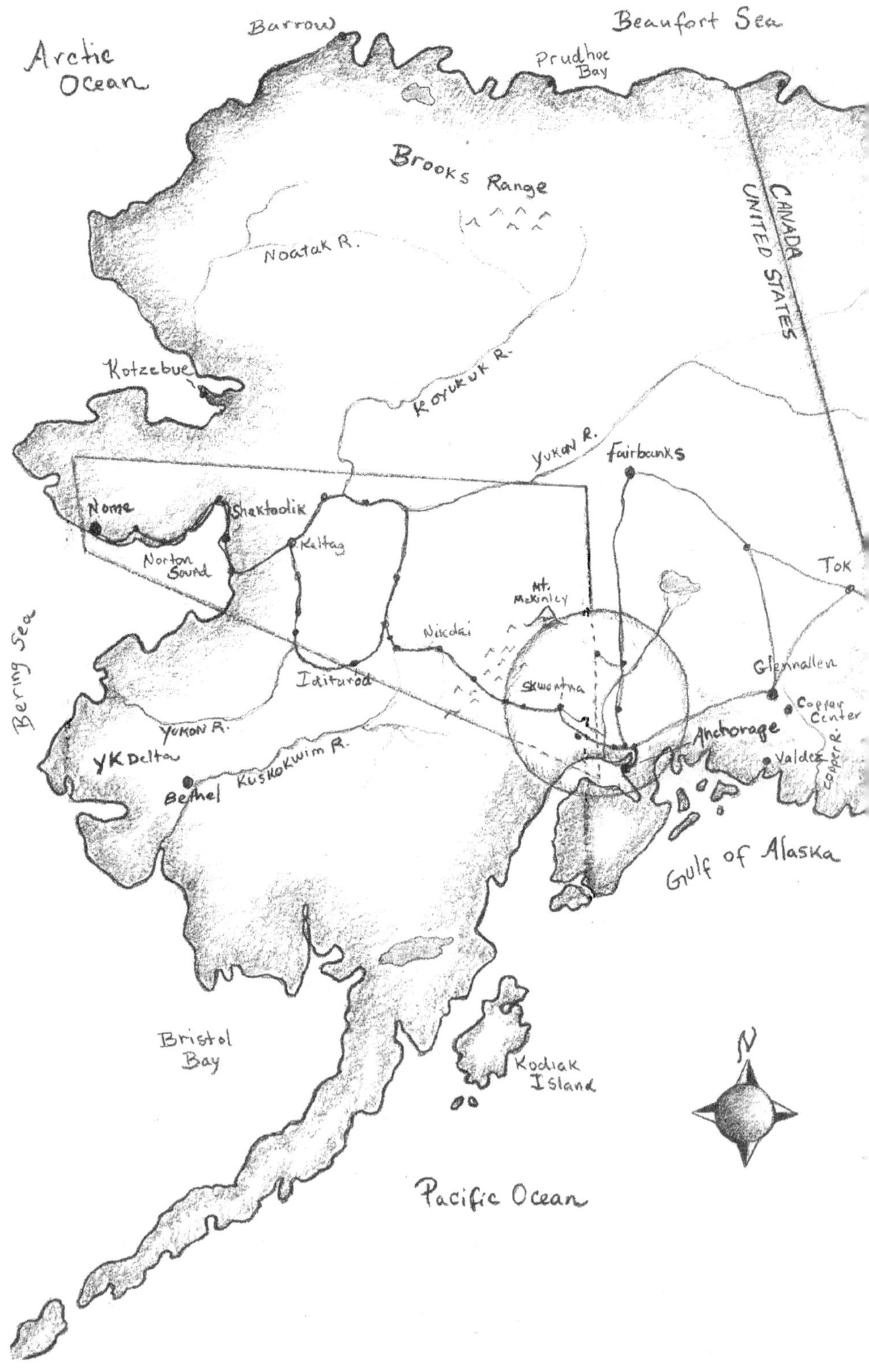
Barrow
Beaufort Sea
Arctic Ocean
Prudhoe Bay
Brooks Range
CANADA
UNITED STATES
Noatak R.
Koyukuk R.
Kotzebue
Yukon R.
Fairbanks
Nome
Shaktoolik
Kaltag
Norton Sound
Tok
Mt. McKinley
Bering Sea
Nikolai
Glennallen
Iditarod
Skwentna
Copper Center
Yukon R.
Anchorage
Copper R.
YK Delta
Kuskokwim R.
Valdez
Bethel
Gulf of Alaska
Bristol Bay
Kodiak Island
N
Pacific Ocean

INSET ONE

Nome, Wh. mountain, Elim, Koyuk, Nulato, Galena, Ruby, YUKON R., Shaktoolik, Norton Sound, Unalakleet, Kaltag, Eagle Island, Cripple, Grayling, Anvik, Shageluk, Iditarod, Ophir, Takotna, McGrath, Nikolai, Alaska Range, Dalzell Gorge, Farewell Burn, Rohn, Rainy Pass, Skwentna, Finger Lake, Rabbit Lake

YUKON

INSET TWO

Petersville, TrapperCreek, Susitna R., Parks Hwy, Finger Lake, Skwentna, Yentna R., Big Bend, Willow, Susitna Station, Rabbit Lake, Wasilla, Knik, Anchorage, Alaska, British Columbia

INSET ONE: Great Race Route

INSET TWO: Matsu Valley &
              Yentna River Area

Prologue

1

TRUST me when I tell you there is a place where the wind never stops blowing.

We are on the coast of the Bering Sea and very near the town of Nome, Alaska, at a small Eskimo village known as Shaktoolik. We are arranged in the lee of the orange metal box which serves as the town's armory; I, huddled down behind my sled, those few of my dogs remaining in the team crusty eyed lumps curled nose to tail against the blow. All around us the wind howls its black rage, a mighty bellow of sand, ice, and splintered dreams sucked from the body of the earth and flung into the hungrily waiting maw of Norton Sound. Numb and frozen, I can imagine Mother Nature herself bending down to scream her inarticulate fury directly atop my shivering body, her face made twisted and terrible by the offense of my hubris.

Funny thing, hubris. After the last number of days, there is no courage or bravery left, only a brittle shell of fearful despair, and the distant memory of pride is but a pale joke. I have been locked into a particle accelerator and smashed down to my lowest common denominator, a handful of atoms thrown into the cold to burn like tiny meteorites before fading down the long, dark throat of eternity.

And maybe this is even funnier, but whether by destiny, fate, or simple brutish determination, now that I have come to this place at the end of all creation where almighty God himself has seemingly turned his gaze away, I realize that my life has finally come full circle. It was here that my story began, and very likely it is here where it will end. The sands of time are running from the hourglass as surely as the heat is cooling out of my bloodstream, so I guess I had better get into the meat, what little there is, of my story. Oh, but beginning a story is such a very hard thing to do.

First off, my name is unimportant. My ghosts are my own, and to tell you my name would only serve to make them yours. And second, I came here to win. No excuses, no complex agenda; just the primal need to test myself against the legendary Great Race, the 1000 mile sled dog race from Anchorage to Nome, and come out the victor. I came armored with youthful determination and a gutful of talent and ability and accompanied by a collection of my finest dogs, warriors one and all. Only to be smashed and broken, the wreckage of my foolish desires scattered from one end of the mighty Alaskan wilderness to the desolate coast of the Bering Sea where onyx waves crash upon the seawall and ravens spin against the firmament like fragments of ash on sackcloth. My primary adversary takes his ease inside the Armory, cool blue eyes glittering with calculation and stern appraisal above an unsmiling beard as rough as steel wool; he has championed this race for the last six years in a row, and it is clear to everyone that he intends to make it seven. I and my pitiful group of nine tired dogs pose no real challenge for him…or so some would say.

Looking past my team, I gaze out to the Sound where the detritus from the shoreline has been launched into a perfect black wall, and I understand that the battle taking place out there between Odin and his brethren to subdue the Great Wolf is literally shivering the ice apart and carrying it out to sea. I am suddenly and completely tired. In an effort to keep my mind from considering the frozen gray horror lurking in the depths of my boots, or the grim plan which has been ticking over in the back of my head, I think instead about those distant memories of my family, that long ago day when we had all lived in this tiny village together for the very last time; the beginning of my story.

2

My Mama and Papa were schoolteachers; they brought my baby brother and I here to Shaktoolik when we were both very small, to teach the ways of modern western civilization to a timeless people who may have been better off having never met a white man. I remember nothing before this point, and all of the people and places from this section of my history are faded, sepia toned clips out of a dusty album salvaged from the ruins of a neglected childhood; disjointed and jerky, hiccupping impressions only loosely based on reality.

I remember that my Mama's eyes were soft and gentle, and that her long, dark hair would hang down in front of her face whenever she would laugh at something that she thought was funny. Her bosoms were large and full, and looking at them made me think of warm dough rising in the leaf patterned bowl next to the old soot stained cook stove. When she bathed my brother and me in the galvanized tub also used for our laundry, she would tie her hair back with a faded pink bandana and roll her flannel sleeves up to the elbows to keep them out of the suds while the two of us boys frolicked like seal pups and generally made a sopping mess out of things. Not every time, but often, she would sing to us an Irish ballad of love or loss, her voice sweet and husky and reminiscent of swift flowing streamlets and fields of feathered tundra.

I miss my Mama so bad sometimes.

I don't remember Papa as well. He was tall and bearded, his voice rough and smelling of liquor and tobacco. He was as hard as Mama was soft, though I don't really recall why I think this. He was never punishing or cruel, but there must be some reason that I do not miss him as much. His hands were very big and calloused, and I can visualize them with perfect clarity holding the barrel of a graphite pencil and making marks and symbols against smooth unlined paper while his breath made my eyes water like I needed to cry.

My little baby brother…he was no more than two years old on that last day, lengthening out and leaving his baby chub behind, and I like to think he would have grown to be a very strong man. God knows he was smart. He would sit there cross legged and chocolate faced, already out of diapers, frowning and crooning with concentration as he sorted out the nine block animal puzzle on the floor.

'Me buf-lo,' he would announce. A few minutes later, after building the buffalo, he would say triumphantly 'Me done!' than 'Me Ea-gle,' and so on.

We were playing on the floor together, using our set of colored blocks to build an elaborate animal corral, when Papa burst unexpectedly through the door full of excitement and smelling of cigarettes and alcohol. The wind that came in at the heels of his work boots was raw and hungry. I can remember his excitement, red eyed and loud voiced, almost shouting at Mama. He had an idea, a plan, but I know that Mama did not like it. She tried to talk him out of it, hand on his arm and gentle toned.

Time shutter steps, lurches a bit, and now me and my brother are bundled into fleecy thick snowsuits with heavy scarves smelling of the morning's cooking wrapped about our little faces, standing outside in the blistering teary eyed cold, the funny little houses of the village standing in rows two by two and marching off into the Sound where we had been told never ever to play. Every other house sported a furry husky on an extraordinarily long chain, long enough to allow the dog to perch on the rooftop like a misshapen spiky furred bird of prey.

Papa's yellow snowmobile is idling and he is pouring gasoline from a red plastic jug, slopping fluid onto the seat and cowling in the process. Mama stands with us, and I can't see her face behind her scarf, but I can tell by her eyes that she is very unhappy.

Memories stutter, grainy black and white, and now we are on the Sound in a little sled being pulled behind Papa's snowmobile. I can't see much, because I am buried with Mama and brother under heavy blankets in the basket of the sled, but I can see the sky which is a clear, hammered blue stretching from horizon to horizon and impossibly huge and empty. To either side is nothing but a flat white blank for miles and miles without end, uninterrupted by feature of any kind whatsoever. It makes me feel small and squirmy, so I quit looking. It is cold cold cold, and my mouth is rank with the exhaust fumes from the snowmobiles engine. Brother moves against me, his little body shivering, and Mama hugs us both really tight.

Now it is silent, save for the sounds of Papa softly cursing and a subtle wind whispering at our feet. Baby brother is sitting on a pile of blankets and fussing, tired of this trip and wanting his puzzles. Papa kneels against the snowmobile, and his big hands rustle senselessly at the exposed and muted engine. His bushy beard is a mess of dangling icicles and he looks scared. We are grains of sand sandwiched between the great white pan of the Sound and the gunmetal gray cap of the sky. The sun is a silver nickel on the horizon. Off in the distance, I can just make out the blocks and rectangles of the village of Koyuk, and then they mysteriously disappear behind a gauzy curtain of snow. Fine cold flakes suddenly pepper my stinging cheeks.

Old stilted black and white film; overexposed. Memories jump and skip, and the soundtrack is interrupted by a throaty gush of wind.

The dark of night is almost upon us, and it is snowing and very windy now. The sled has been overturned against the brunt of it, and we huddle miserably cold and desperately afraid as the needle points of ice drive and swirl about us. It is so loud that I cannot hear myself think, but I can clearly make out my baby brother sobbing with terror and pain. I, too, am sobbing. Papa hunkers down with the only form of light left in the world, an old battered electric lantern producing a feeble orange glow.

'It's no use,' he says. 'It won't go.'

'I know,' Mama responds.

'Koyuk is close.'

'No it's not.'

'It's our only chance. I'll get help.'

'Don't you dare leave us,' Mama says.

'Got to,' Papa replies.

'Please don't. Please don't leave us.'

Papa stands, turns from us. He puts his head down and begins to walk away. It only takes a few seconds for the wind and snow to render him a wraithlike silhouette lit by the faint arcing glow from the lantern. I never saw him again, and I will always remember his big, solid hand carrying that lantern into the night.

It is full dark now. The wind is alive; a howling beast, ravening and slobbering to be fed. Mama is holding us really really tight, and she is singing something sweet and warm. It has been a long time since my little brother quit his crying, or maybe I just can't hear him anymore. It is dark, dark like the inside of a well, and I'm starting to not be so cold.

The wind is howling.

I squeeze brother as tight as I can, but he doesn't squeeze back and Mama has her face as close to mine as she can get and she is singing something, something, sweet and warm, and I'm no longer cold at all, not even a little bit. The wind is howling and Mama is singing, Mama howling and the wind singing. I can't tell one from the other now. Howling and singing.

Please believe me when I tell you that there is a place where the wind never stops blowing…

River Rat

Chapter I

1

AT twelve years of age, The Boy was lean and hard, and bore his scars in silence. He looked onto the world with an eye much older than his paltry count of seasons would imply, and his mouth seldom, if ever, curved in an upwards direction. The day his little cousin was attacked by the wolf, the two of them were walking down the narrow mud path to the spring to fetch water in greasy five gallon buckets. There was no warning save a little barking from the dog lot back up the hill. One second Little Cousin was chattering happily at The Boy's heels; and the next he was not.

Hearing a scuffle, The Boy stopped and turned. Little Cousin, a lad of four, was face down in the mud. Straddling him with paws to either side of his skinny little shoulders like a beast about to mount a bitch, was Bo-Dog, a mangy wolf hybrid that had been living in Uncle's dog lot for the last few months.

The Boy's testicles had only recently dropped, and now they crawled back up into the warm cavity of his pelvis. His bowels loosened and he could feel the hairs on the back of his neck stand erect. Bo-Dog regarded him lazily through amber slits while his prey moaned sluggishly beneath him. The long shadows of afternoon pooled, and a slow rain sizzled from a leaden sky to hiss against dead brown birch leaves and bead upon Bo-Dog's sallow fur.

Little Cousin put his hands down splay fingered in the muck and raised his chalk white face. His eyes were like doorknobs with a slender thread of scarlet running between them, and in a very calm voice he pleaded for the beast to not eat him.

With one smooth motion, Bo-Dog sank his fangs into either side of Little Cousin's skull and yanked him back into the dank under-brush as if he never was.

The Boy was aware of his heart pounding and cold wet soaking his back and shoulders; the gurgling of the nearby spring and a trio of camp robbers bickering from an overhanging branch. Then he was moving, running, diving headlong into the willow and devil's club and screaming his lungs out like a madman. Wet branches tore at his face and chest and stinging thorns slashed his legs and outstretched hands. A thick, unreasoning panic that tasted of vomit clogged his throat.

He caught up with them very quickly. The beast had dragged Little Cousin only twenty feet or so into a clump of dead alders and was working to bury the length of his powerful muzzle into the boy's neck, grunting and chuffing with the effort. Little Cousin for his part had curled into a silent ball. The Boy reached out and clutched Bo-Dogs collar, heaving backward with all his might.

It was like trying to yank quicksand. Bo-Dog had been trained to pull, and he weighed as much or more then The Boy; he hunkered low and surged forward, catching Little Cousin by his muddy pant leg as the boy flipped over and attempted to crawl away and into the thicket. The Boy lost his hold and fell back on his rear. Little Cousin began to shriek, terrible whooping gasps that shivered the underbrush. When The Boy regained his feet, he grasped the gnarled length of a birch root wad that felt almost too heavy to hold, even using both hands. He was very careful, knowing now that this was his last chance to save the child before the beast had his throat out. He stood at Bo-Dog's shoulder, close enough to smell the creature's sour undercoat, the odor of blood and urine soaking his littlest cousin's pants.

'Hey boy,' he said as he drove the club down into Bo-Dog's face.

Bo-Dog yelped and lunged back. Little Cousin got on his hands and knees, still wailing hysterically. Bo-Dog's hackles were up, and he swiftly darted around and came in from the side, closed his jaws around the child's ankle and yanked him back down. Looking right into The Boy's eyes, he began to snarl while pulling his prey backward in explosive heaving motions.

The Boy swung again and made solid crunching contact. Swung once more, and this time forced the beast to release. Very quickly, he reached down and grabbed Little Cousin's shirt collar and yanked him up into a rough embrace. Bo-Dog had quit his snarling, and now began to circle the children in wary arcs, his eyes never leaving the screaming four year old.

Blood flowed in a dark sheet over Little Cousin's face and white bone gleamed through his mussed hair. 'Make him quit make that bad dog quit,' he pleaded.

'It's okay. I've got him,' The Boy answered, feeling the little heart thundering against his own. 'I got him.'

The brush banged and crashed and then Middle Cousin was there, yelling in a panic. 'What is it, what's happening?' He stopped dead in his tracks, eyes popping as he tried to understand what he was seeing.

The beast ignored both of the older boys, the one with the club and the one with the tousled bed hair and powder blue corduroys. He kept circling and looking for an opening to get to the little one.

'Take your brother. Hold him real tight,' said The Boy.

Middle Cousin did as he was told, and The Boy caught Bo-Dog's collar as he tried to dart past, giving it a sharp yank. Bo made a funny little bark in the back of his throat; then relaxed and became a dog once again. Middle Cousin took his little brother up to the cabin and inside. The Boy brought Bo up to the dog lot and put him back on his chain, ignoring the rest of the pack as they lunged and spun on their pickets. Old Tang cans rattled and plastic barrel dog houses rolled frantically as they barked in anger and excitement. As soon as the brass snap clipped shut on Bo-Dog's collar ring, the dog leaned against The Boy's thigh and wagged his tail. He attempted to lick his hand, and The Boy roughly pushed him away.

Uncle and Auntie were coming in over the mudflats when they heard the lot go crazy. They ran up the hill and into the yard, ponchos flapping, rifles wrapped loosely in Hefty trash sacks dangling from shoulder straps. When Auntie saw what had happened to her youngest, she began to shriek almost as loud as the child. Uncle just stood there as if frozen to the spot, mouth agape and eyes burning holes in the gloom of the approaching evening.

It was very dark in the cabin by now, even with blackened

kerosene lanterns going. Little Cousin was on a pile of dirty blankets, mewling in his mother's arms, blood dripping down his neck and turning his hand me down bibs into a sodden mess. A stream of it soaked through the blankets and pattered like thin syrup against the splintered hardwood floor.

Uncle crouched down, stroking his son. 'What happened?' he asked after a time.

'One of those new dogs got off his chain. Tried to eat him,' The Boy explained.

When Uncle finally turned his attention away from his mutilated baby boy, his hands were red and his face was hard.

'Why'd you let this happen?' he asked harshly.

The Boy could say nothing. He looked down at the floor.

'You let this happen,' his uncle repeated.

Uncle stood suddenly, shucked the plastic cover away from his rifle, a stainless steel Mini-14 outfitted with a Leopold scope and a banana clip that held fourteen rounds. His fingers dug into The Boy's slim shoulder and he dragged the lad into the rain and near dark. In the lot, about a hundred yards distant, the dogs were all whipping around on their pickets, tails up and tongues out, still visible in the last failing light of the day. It was almost dinner time.

'Which one?' he asked.

The Boy pointed to where Bo-Dog was standing on his house in the middle of the group. His tail was up and he had a look of frantic expectation about him, sure that he was about to be fed or ran.

'You sure?'

'Yes. It was Bo,' The Boy said.

Uncle thumbed the safety with a dry click. He raised the rifle to his shoulder and squinted through the scope. 'Get back in the house,' he said.

The Boy went back in and sat down on a stool at the far end of the living quarters. It was very dark, and when he looked out the window he could see nothing of the trees or bushes of the dooryard. Long seconds passed, and just when he had decided that Uncle was going to relent, the window pane lit up like a flashbulb going off. This was followed by two more popping flashes of white and the dog lot erupting in frenzied barking. The next eleven rounds were unloaded in a great squirting rush, and The Boy was unaware of squeezing his eyes shut or pushing his fists against his ears until it was all over.

Uncle came back in and slung his rifle on a peg over the door and the smell of it was overpowering in the small space.

Nobody said a word.

2

Rain splattered against the tin roof all throughout the night and The Boy could not sleep.

He lay in the dark near Middle Cousin, listening to water drip into pots and pans placed to catch various leaks coming down through the cotton candy pink insulation; Little Cousin whimpering softly and chattering with fever; the fire softly crackling in the barrel stove.

Somewhere in the dark, as he was drifting off, he heard Auntie's low voice, 'What if he gets sick? He's going to be sick!'

Bed springs squeaking, settling. Then Uncle's voice: 'Shush now, honey, it'll be all right. Just come to bed.'

Auntie's stifled sob. 'My little baby!'

The Boy drifted away.

3

Dawn smudged the sky into gradually lightening tones of grey, and a chill rain continued to fall. The Boy knelt in the mud and squalor of the dooryard amidst a flock of emaciated Cornish Cross chickens and starving Toulouse geese, all honking and gabbling desperately to be fed. He had gathered a little pile of the driest alder sticks that he could find and was now trying to set fire to some old crunckled up dog food bags covered with sap-sticky handfuls of dead spruce limbs. The plastic lining of the bags started to sizzle and black coiled upwards. He immediately began to feed the smallest of the alder sticks to the growing blaze, and soon had a modest cook fire going under the chopped down 55-gallon drum that served as the dog team's cook pot.

Heaped in a sticky pile on a tattered blue tarpaulin was the catch of chum salmon that Uncle and Auntie had gill netted from the previous day; a glassy eyed, hook nosed jumble of dull red flesh and toothy grins. The Boy shooed the chickens away, then dumped the fish into the pot. Up in the lot, the dogs watched silently from their houses. Once the water reached a hard boil, he added several Tang cans of dry rice to the steaming mix and more wood to the blaze. He had a long stick which he used to keep the mess stirred up.

The day warmed and the rain let up. His clothes began to steam from the fires heat, and he became aware of his own dull hunger. Auntie would be in the cabin making breakfast. When the rice had thickened to the point where he could not stir it anymore, he let the fire die out and ladled the mix into a series of five gallon buckets; gluey kernels and heat slushed chunks of chum mixed with a little dried kibble. He placed an old piece of plywood over the buckets to keep the birds out of the scalding soup.

At the cabin, The Boy found the family gathered around the table, heads down to their plates. The smoke from burnt sourdough greased the air and the smell of salmon frying in the pan nearly drove his stomach into convulsions. Little Cousin sat wrapped in towels and hunched over, his plate untouched, his face blackened with bruising and his eyes slotted nearly shut from swelling.

The Boy sat down and Auntie looked away, face shuttered and cold. Uncle grunted, tossed his fork down on his empty plate.

'Here,' he said, sliding Little Cousin's food in front of him. 'You finish his. He can't eat it.'

The Boy stared at this for a while and they all sat in silence.

4

The late afternoon sky was faded to azure and the sun hung like a copper penny just above the western horizon. A cool breeze smelling of the approaching winter gusted in from the north and thick bellied clouds swollen with rain simmered away in an uneven line to the east. Despite the last day's drizzle, the creek was down and the mudflats were exposed, a mottled slick brown like the hide of a fresh water pike. Gulls cawed while the last of the summer's Arctic Terns wheeled in a loosely morphing cloud over the surface of the river, about a hundred yards from where Auntie and Uncle beached the two Coleman fiberglass canoes and the 24 foot flat bellied john boat which served as the family's primary source of summertime transportation.

The Boy and Middle Cousin walked onto the muck, each dressed in shabby hand me down denim pants and filthy button up shirts of indeterminate color. They each carried a number of sodden burlap sacks scaly with old blood. Mud like soft tar sucked against their cheap rubber boots and came free in long furrows. In the belly of the first canoe, they found the last of the night's before catch of chum, stiff with rigor mortis and loaded with the delicate lace of fly blow about the gills and eye sockets. The boys loaded all seven of the swollen fish into their sacks and lugged them back to the foot of the steep hill leading up to the cabin.

They went back and stood at the bank of the creek, now little more than a thin brown trickle less than a stone's throw across. Though the water was very low at present, both knew that it was likely to come up overnight, perhaps enough to float all of the boats and carry them away. The two exchanged sidelong glances, and then began the chore of hauling the canoes across the glutinous surface of the exposed flats. They were both reed thin and scrawny from undernourishment, little more than scarecrows in flapping cloth, but they were both strong in the manner of small wild animals, and they managed the task with the grunting efficiency of those accustomed to drudgery and toil.

They each chose a side and wrapped stiff little fingers around the fiberglass sidewalls and half carried, half dragged, planting one foot solidly before pulling the next step out of the muck. Working steadily, they had both canoes at the foot of the hill and tied off to stumps and both sat panting in the damp, colorless grass that marked the high water line.

The boys rested for a while in companionable silence, leaning back on damp elbows and listening to the distant gurgle of the river. An outboard motor droned softly, two, maybe three miles out on the Big Bend. The rain clouds had disappeared from the sky, leaving it soft and unbroken save for the sun dipping low over the tops of the naked alder thicket that demarcated the entrance of their creek to the main channel of the river. As they watched, the sky low to the west kindled in a buttery soft orange glow and the sun bloated from a penny to a sagging pumpkin. The alders screening the far bank of the creek ran together thick with sudden shadow, and quick golden light flared over the boys' thin and dirty faces. At their feet, the mudflat rolled away like a sheet of gently pocked crepe paper.

'Do you think it'll dry out by tomorrow?' Middle Cousin asked.

The Boy slowly shook his head. 'Nope. Maybe the next day. If the water doesn't come up too high tonight and cover it,' he said.

'Hope you're right. I'm ready to play some football. Figure Mama and Papa will play with us?'

The Boy shrugged. They both fell silent.

After a time, Middle Cousin said, 'You saved him. I know you did.'

The Boy could hear tears in his cousin's voice, but when he looked sharply to see, shadows had bloomed over the other child's face and he couldn't be sure.

'Why didn't he try to eat you and me?' the younger boy asked finally.

The Boy could only shake his head. He had wondered that, too, and felt that the answer would be too terrible to bear if he ever managed to grasp the nub of it.

'I don't know,' he said finally. 'It doesn't matter.'

'Yes it does.'

The Boy shrugged again, a brief hitch of stick-skinny shoulders. From above and behind, up past the brow of the hill, they both heard Auntie's strident voice yelling for them to come on in for supper.

5

The dogs' supper came first; the buckets of cereal The Boy had cooked earlier in that morning. The dogs leaped and spun on their chain pickets, splattering mud and frantically barking to be fed. The food was ladled into rusty No. 10 cans that used to contain things such as stewed tomatoes, broad beans and dried juice mix. The dogs hit their meal with heads disappearing up to the ears and gelled rice and fish chunks slopping over the rim. They were hardly more than throat gulping, tail wagging smears of brown and black against the darkening of nightfall. Blue stars prickled overhead and the white plastic barrels of the dog houses seemed to hang in empty space. Bo-Dog's silent spot was like an empty socket in a jaw bone.

The family's supper was chunked king salmon battered with Krusteaz pancake mix and dropped in a pot of rolling oil, and fat yukon potatoes boiled so hard they fell into tasteless mush under the bent tines of a fork. Two Coleman lanterns hissed and surged from hooks over the grease-varnished plank that served as a dinner table.

Little Cousin's fever had passed, and he was chattering and happy at his end of the table, his scrawny little buttocks perched on an upended plastic bucket, gulping food like an animal. His face was still darkly bruised and his head was wrapped in a turban of thick toweling, red flower pattern on stained beige. Though bloodshot and still swollen, his quick brown eyes were bright with imagination and humor.

Silverware clinked and scraped against porcelain as the meal was consumed in the absence of conversation. Towards the end, Uncle pushed his plate aside, stood up and crossed the uneven creaking floor to where the old transistor radio nestled between two stacks of paperback books on a low plywood bench, long silver antenna jutting up and tipped with a wad of dusty aluminum foil. He flipped it on and they all listened to the garbling pop of static as he worked the tuner to get the one available channel to come in clear.

The static cleared up and a deejay's voice came through the speakers. They all listened to the Bush Pipeline; a five night per week public service rendered by the far off Big Lake based radio station. It was an assortment of short messages read aloud by the sandy voiced announcer, messages logged by folks traveling into town to get supplies who wanted their families out in the bush to know what was going on, when they would be home, delays and the like. People whom they had never met, but who felt like family nonetheless.

When it was finished, normal programming resumed and the twanging chords of classic country music filled the little cabin.

Auntie made a stack out of the dirty dishes and cleared the table with a damp cloth. After, she and Uncle took one of the lanterns and went to their bed at the far end of the cabin, one corner blocked off by a bed sheet strung up like a wide curtain. The boys remained at the table with a jar full of green dice and a pad of paper. The Boy unscrewed the jar lid and sent the dice clicking across the table surface.

Little Cousin put his tiny hand on the bigger boy's wrist. His face trembled like a small earthquake was taking place just under the surface of the skin, and then he broke into a smile that was nearly heartbreaking in its sweet fragility.

'Thank you,' he whispered.

Outside, the dogs broke into song.

6

The rains did not come back for a time. The weather cooled a bit, mornings becoming crisp, afternoons pleasant. The mudflats dried, then hardened to a composition like dusty gray concrete. The spine of the creek remained a sluggish artery smelling of algae and spawned salmon. Auntie stayed in the cabin sucking on her seemingly endless supply of Rolaids and reading her paperbacks, while Uncle went into the woods with his chainsaw and jugs of oil and gasoline.

The three boys stood out in the middle of the wide span of dried up creek bed, staring down in awe at a line of tracks that originated from the brush near the mouth of the creek and wandered down-creek and out of sight. They were bear prints, bigger then Auntie's porcelain dinner plates. They left only broad smudges on the hardening surface, but were still perfectly identifiable.

Middle Cousin whistled in appreciation while Little Cousin looked nervously in five directions all at once, like his head was mounted on a spring. The Boy laughed and squeezed the young boy's shoulder. All three of them could tell just from looking that the bear was hours gone, but for boys of this age there was still a gripping thrill in the fact that there had been a meat eating beast the size of a car wandering about on their prospective football field.

The field was laid out in the widest spot on the flat; a series of marks rubbed into the chalky surface with the heels of their rubber boots; gnarled lengths of drift wood laid down where the surface of the dried mud refused to score; de-limbed alder trunks denoting the end zones. Their ball was a battered plastic one gallon syrup container filled part way with small rocks and handfuls of dirt to give it some heft. This was a big step up from their previous ball, a leaky No.10 can that some dog had chewed a serrated edge about the rim and was no longer safe to eat from. It had been hard to throw, even harder to catch.

The boys spent the afternoon free from chores, racing from one end of the field to the other with reckless abandon; running options, going out for short drops and long passes which were promptly dropped from fingers stung by the unyielding plastic, full tackles with no mercy shown or expected. Little Cousin was fast like the wind and evaded the larger boys' clumsy attempts to stop him if he had the ball, juking left, then right, spinning like a dervish until crossing the end zone for a score.

At one point, The Boy, who was easily the largest of the three and constituted his own team most of the time, took the ball for a long run up the middle of the field and could not understand why the two smaller boys just dropped back and seemed to make no effort to stop him. They parted way before his charging advance, which was probably a good thing because by now he had his body at a dead run, almost floating on the air with raw unbridled speed. They exchanged glances and quick knowing smiles. As one unit, they both knelt down and reached across his path, locking hands just as his blurring ankles met their obstruction.

The Boy flew for what seemed like forever; just sailed and

sailed, syrup jug tucked under the crook of one arm and free hand outstretched like a superhero. He knew it was going to hurt when he hit the ground, and it did. He hit so hard that he bounced back skyward and threw up a small cloud of dust. The ball flew out of his boneless grasp and tumbled across the field end over end.

'Fumble!' Middle Cousin screamed in triumph, and both of the younger boys were on it like cats on a mouse.

And so on.

7

Later, when afternoon had lengthened into early evening, Uncle descended from the hill. His flannel bibs were covered with wood-chips and he smelled richly of gasoline and two-cycle oil. His checkered wool cap was pushed way back and sweat gleamed on his face. He called the boys over, noting their bruised and limping gates as they trotted up obediently. A faint smile etched his tired face while he listened to his sons recount their games on the field.

The smile went away when he turned to look at The Boy who was standing back and off to the side, head down and unkempt brown hair hanging in a curtain over his face.

'You two, get back up to the house and get the dogs fed and cleaned up,' he said. He nodded to The Boy, inclined his head in the direction of the canoes. 'I need you to help me with the net tonight.'

The Boy noticed that Uncle was carrying the Mini-14, the gun he had shot Bo-Dog with, and could not suppress a shiver. Uncle nodded again, seemingly at nothing. The two of them trudged to the canoes without either saying a word. They pushed all eighteen feet of the fiberglass hull out to the channel and The Boy held the nose steady while Uncle clambered onto the rear bench. Once Uncle was seated and had his paddle held tightly in both hands, The Boy pushed off with his rear leg and jumped in as the craft rocked away from the shore. He took his seat quickly, grabbed his paddle, and together he and Uncle cruised out of the creek and into the river beyond.

The water made soft sucking sounds against The Boy's paddle as he dug in long, even strokes. Small whirlpools curled away to either side of the blades passage. The narrow mouth of the creek opened onto the flexed elbow of the Big Bend, rich brown mixing with the darker gray of the Yentna River. Steep crumbling banks of clay and topsoil to the right, the beached whale hulk of an exposed sandbar looming ahead.

They stroked upriver against a gentle current, following the bank and only veering into deeper water when the shaggy branches of deadfall forced them to. The sky was overcast and sullen, sketching the last of the day in various tones of charcoal on graphite. Naked alder gave way to stout cottonwood and a scattering of stunted black spruce as the shoreline rose from floodplain to low hill, then climbed swiftly into a steep ridge choked with a dense forest of old growth Tamarack and heavy white spruce. There were sounds all around, but the loudest was the slap of water against the hull and the pull of laminated paddles as they dipped and churned through the water.

They reached the next creek upriver, a mile from their own inlet. Here, the hill to their right plummeted sharply to a tangle of alder and devil's club on floodplain. The features of the east bank continued like this around the great oxbow of the bend and out of sight. Careful to avoid the tip of a snag undulating in the current, they guided the canoe into a narrow cut between two muddy embankments and ran it ashore. The Boy swiftly jumped out and again held the nose steady while Uncle followed after with his rifle slung over his shoulder from a broad leather strap. Together, they heaved the canoe up and halfway out of the water. Uncle took the faded yellow nylon rope and looped it around the slender base of a nearby willow.

The net was strung across the mouth of the creek just a few feet from where it let into the river; a series of rough wooden bobbers strung out and holding the leading edge of the webbing upright just a few inches below the surface. It was secured on either side by a thick poly rope emerging from the water and half buried in the muck of the shore, further camouflaged by leaves and grass and a subtle scattering of brush. Each end of rope went up the bank and fastened around the trunk of a stout alder to keep it from drifting away.

The Boy clambered through the thicket, careful to avoid the sagging brown leaves and bristling stocks of dying devil's club, and quickly unwound the rope and let it fall loose. Starting with the end nearest shore, Uncle squatted down and began to pull the net up onto the bank. The Boy scrambled down and lent his hands to the task, and within moments they had the glistening green webbing out of the water and exposed on the mud.

It was empty, save for two small flat bellied sucker fish tangled near the bottom. Uncle swore under his breath, and The Boy could hear the desperation in the words, more so than any anger. He was just reaching down to untangle the fish when they both heard an outboard motor making its way up the river, on their side. They both froze in place, hunkered down in the cold muck, listening.

It was a dual setup, medium horsepower under heavy throttle. Chugging beneath a heavy load and moving slow in deep water. The boat was hidden from sight behind the bank of the creek mouth, but The Boy guessed twin Mercury 55s driven by propellers, piloted by somebody who knew the river well enough to avoid the shallows on the other side of the bend. After a time, it drew abreast of their position, then away and upriver. They listened to it until it finally droned out of earshot.

When they could hear it no longer, Uncle freed the scrawny fish and slung the net back into the water. His knees popped when he stood up with a groan. He sighed.

'Going to get awfully hungry this fall,' he said.

The Boy could think of nothing to say, so he just nodded.

8

Night was coming on fast as they returned.

'Let's go out to the bar,' Uncle instructed.

It took just a few moments to cross the channel and run the canoe ashore on a stretch of sandbar that sloped smoothly away from the water's edge. Both of them got out, repeated the process of pulling their craft out of the current and stood looking down the long expanse of exposed river bottom. The surface was mostly granulated sand and little shells of smooth rock. About a hundred yards distant, a lone tree lay on its side, tremendous skeletal root system lurching skyward, trunk shorn of branches by a summer spent underwater.

Uncle un-slung the Mini-14 from his shoulder, held it out. 'You ready to learn how to use this?' he asked.

In answer, The Boy quietly took the gun. It was heavier than he had expected, and smelled strongly of solvent. Its walnut and stainless steel length felt oily and pitiless in his hands. His stomach contracted into a hard hot ball and the skin of his arms humped into tight gooseflesh. He could not have made his throat give voice even had he wanted to, for his mouth was suddenly as dry as the bottom of an ashtray. He was hyper aware of the soft breeze ruffling his shabby clothes, and the sound of a loon calling; the river gurgling softly and dogs barking up in the distant lot.

'What do I do?' he asked.

Uncle pointed out the slide, the scope. Explained the clip and how it worked.

'I don't care about aiming right now, tonight. I just want you to feel it and understand how it operates,' he said. 'Do you want to fire it?'

'Yes,' The Boy lied.

'Good. Okay. Hold it up to your shoulder like this,' he took it back and demonstrated. 'Chamber a round like this, then sight through the scope. Remember, squeeze, don't pull the trigger. Ok?' he handed the rifle back.

The Boy was so scared that he nearly dropped it. Hardly able to see in the gloom, he held the rifle awkwardly to his shoulder and attempted to work the slide. It took him several tries, and he nearly dropped it twice more, feeling Uncle's exasperation mounting like a cloud of fumes. He could taste WD-40 in his mouth, coating his teeth and gums. He felt like he needed to evacuate his bowels.

'Stop!' Uncle suddenly barked.

The Boy froze, terrified. Uncle reached out and grasped his hand where it was wrapped around the stock. Very carefully, he removed the hand and guided it forward a bit.

'If you had squeezed the trigger like that,' Uncle said softly, 'the slide would have ripped your thumb off.'

The Boy gulped thick bile, and began to tremble. He pulled the stock in tight to his shoulder and squinted through the opaque scope, seeing nothing but a smooth, dark wall.

'Take a deep breath, let it out. Take a breath, let it out partway, then hold it.'

The Boy pulled the trigger and was rewarded by a brief cracking yellow muzzle flash and a solid kick against his shoulder. Sand spurted about twenty yards distant. The tension instantly began to drain out of his body. He raised the muzzle slightly, pulled, felt exhilaration as fire and copper jacketed lead leapt from the barrel and the sound of the report rolled across the sandbar. Ears ringing, he lowered the weapon.

Uncle took it from him, ejected the clip and jacked the chambered round into space, catching it before it reached the ground.

'That's enough for tonight,' he said.

9

Auntie took the news with no outward expression. They all knew that it was near the tail end of the fishing season.

She and Uncle sat apart from the children, sipping tea from chipped mugs and reclining on folding lawn chairs. It was full dark outside, and a fierce wind was whipping the trees and causing the roof to groan. Dirty supper dishes were cleared and stacked neatly in the plastic tub that served as a sink. Only one lantern was burning and the radio had not come on to conserve battery power.

Uncle had dragged the table over and laid out a small arsenal of weaponry. He was stripping rifles down to their component parts, thoroughly wiping each piece with an oily rag.

'We can hold out for awhile on dry goods,' Auntie said. 'But we're going to need meat.'

'I know.'

'What about going to town?'

Uncle gave her a sour look. He didn't need to say anything. They all knew that there was no money for such things.

Chapter II

1

THERE came a day when the rice barrel emptied save for a few small handfuls of powdery yellow meal and small pieces of grit scattered at the bottom. The last of the summer's salmon had run out the week prior, and the dogs were all growing skinny and weak, tottering about their pickets on sore paws like a collection of old men. Auntie gathered up the hens that she wanted to remain as layers throughout the coming winter, and then had the two older boys butcher the rest. There were very few of the scrawny birds, and not a one of them seemed to have enough meat on its bones to amount to anything resembling a decent meal.

Late on one morning, Uncle came out of the cabin and stood in the litter strewn dooryard like a scarecrow in overalls and sweat stained cap. He called the boys over and explained that they were all going on a trip; to gear up with their warmest clothes and trash-sack ponchos. Auntie packed a basket with leftover Spam casserole from the night before, pilot bread crackers, and two mason jars full of sweetened black tea. Uncle had his long range shooter, a Winchester bolt action 7mm Magnum, wrapped in plastic and slung over one shoulder, and a heavy rucksack loaded with a 12 gauge Remington pump action, Mini-14, and a Colt .41 magnum. He handed this pack to The Boy, and the five of them made their way down hill to the mudflat and their john boat tied up at the mouth of the creek.

They all clambered aboard the narrow wooden craft and fastened on bulky orange life vests while Uncle moved gas cans around and got the Mariner outboard ready for use. He pumped the rubber bulb on the hose connecting the motor to one of the gas tanks, and then pulled the starter cord three times in rapid succession before it coughed to life in a cloud of rich blue smoke. He nodded for The Boy to shove them away from shore, and when the boat had slid far enough out to deep water, he twisted the tiller handle and guided them into the main channel of the river.

2

The sky wore a brooding cap with the white disk of the sun glaring low from the eastern quadrant. The river and surrounding country-side rolled out before the nose of the boat like a magic carpet of rippling gray water and musky spray. The east and west banks were covered by alder and towering cottonwood, with regular intervals of birch and spruce topping low hills, and the occasional narrow mouthed creek and wider expanse of slough curving away in lazy detour.

They travelled for many miles upriver without seeing another boat, Uncle keeping them close to the bank as much as possible, his keen blue eyes glued to the water and looking for the signs of deep current; roiling undertows that came up out of the murk and mushroomed like fluid blossoms, darker in tone then the smoother surrounding surface. In contrast, shallow water was very light in color and covered by choppy little ripples, a sign that it was less than two feet deep, sometimes much less. The outboard motor was driven by a propeller that required a minimum of eighteen inches when up on step at cruising speed, so this difference was crucial.

The children were hunkered low near the bow, faces screwed tight against the wind and constant fine shower coming off of the prow as it cut against the river. They felt the water knocking through the thin wood beneath the soles of their feet and slapping the laminated hull mere inches from their buttocks. Wet and miserably cold, fingers cramped and teeth chattering, the boys found it easier to look back the way they had come and watch the river unspooling like a long steel tape behind the foaming rooster tail thrown up by the Mariner. Uncle sat squint-eyed and resolute with the tiller handle held firmly in one hand, other hand locked around the sidewall for balance; a rock, seemingly impervious to cold, wet, and general discomfort.

Without warning, Uncle cut the throttle and let the boat settle down into the hole. Muddy water surged up nearly over the side-walls while the current caught them and took control, working to spin them out and around. Uncle kept the motor at a low rumbling idle and twisted the tiller handle to the side to straighten them out. They bobbed, cork-like, and began to gently float back the way they had come. Keeping one hand on the tiller, Uncle half stood up with his eyes carefully scanning the eastern shore where a sizeable stream opened up in a gush of chocolate brown.

'What do you think?' he shouted to Auntie.

In answer, Auntie just nodded. She reached down and pulled Uncle's long rifle out from where it lay on the floorboard, covered by a blanket, and began stripping the plastic wrapping away. Uncle increased the throttle a bit and got the nose turned around and pointed at the inlet. Moving slowly, he guided them into the channel between two steep brush choked banks. One hundred yards in, the creek crooked in a brief dogleg and abruptly widened to a distance of maybe a football field in width. To either side, the bank sloped up to a floodplain dense with alder, willow, and mature cottonwood which formed an impenetrable curtain that foiled the eye with a tangle of limbs, sinuous trunks, and dying brownish red foliage.

3

They putted along for a while through deep, still water, breathing in exhaust coming from the Mariner mixed with the cloying smell of spawned salmon rotting in the shallows. Once, a beaver slid down the bank and swiftly swam downstream and out of sight. The creek, Uncle called it Moose Creek, twisted round and around in a dizzying series of oxbows and doglegs.

They had just cleared the length of an ancient spruce tree leaning drunkenly over the channel, when Uncle's eyes suddenly widened and he cut the engine to let them drift. Bent at the waist, he stepped forward and grabbed the rifle from Auntie's lap, flipped the rubber lens covers off of the Leopold scope and threw it up to his shoulder. He was sighting down a straight stretch of the creek, at least a mile long.

At first, The Boy could not see what Uncle had spotted. It was early afternoon, and the no-color light confused his eye, made everything farther than a hundred yards away seem blurry and indistinct. He blinked furiously and rubbed at his eye with dirty knuckles.

Uncle lowered the rifle, eased down onto his bench. 'A big blackie. Maybe five hundred yards,' he said to Auntie, speaking in a low voice. His fingers worked a dial on the side of the scope. 'You boys stay low and plug your ears.'

Carefully, slowly, he worked the bolt action and levered a round into the 7mm's chamber. He worked his way up to the nose of the boat and knelt on the wet wooden surface, again raising the heavy rifle to his shoulder and lowering his head to the scope.

The Boy laid on his belly, his chin propped on the sideboard of the hull. Now that he knew where to look, he could see it; a small black dot on the eastern bank, half in the brush, impossibly tiny. While he watched, it seemed to shrink back in the undergrowth. A moment later, it emerged fully and stood in the clear, looking like an ant in the distance. The boat slid softly against the muck on the shore, branches scraping the hull, gently rocking up and down with motions of the water. Uncle looked like a statue, breathing slowly, evenly.

The Boy felt sharp pressure against either side of his skull before he registered the shot, which came a moment later with the flat, atonal boom of a fighter jet breaking the sound barrier. The black dot tumbled down the embankment and disappeared.

Uncle turned, clicking on the safety. Swiftly, he handed the rifle back to Auntie and restarted the Mariner. After a quick thrust of reverse, he gunned it forward.

4

It took them a long time to reach the spot where the bear had been standing.

They tied off the boat and walked the last few hundred yards along the bank with Uncle leading the way. The bear was long gone. His tracks cris-crossed back and forth all along the bank and the marks where he had slid down to the water's edge after being shot were clearly visible as a long sloping furrow carved in the mud.

Uncle knelt and pointed. Gleaming in the muck was a length of blue-white intestine. He stood up, scanned the thick underbrush for a time with his rifle held at port arms.

'Okay,' he said presently. 'Let's all eat something. Give him some time to bleed out.'

They went back to the boat and retrieved the basket Auntie had packed. Gathered around at the foot of a naked birch tree, they spread the contents on a green diamond patterned handkerchief. They took their time with the rough meal of elbow noodles, Spam chunks and Velveeta cheese heaped on stale Pilot Boy crackers, careful to avoid backwash while swigging black tea from a mason jar. As they finished up, a thin drizzle began to spatter the ground.

While Auntie and the boys unrolled and donned their garbage sack ponchos, Uncle reloaded his 7mm with fresh cartridges, three for the magazine and one directly fed into the chamber. He carefully eased the bolt closed, and when he looked up to regard his family all standing huddled in black plastic bags with frigid rain water slicking their faces, it was like he was seeing them for the first time that day.

'Honey, I need you to stay back here with the kids,' he said.

'No,' she said, without a moment's hesitation.

He looked over his shoulder at the wall of brush, then back at her. 'It's too dangerous for the kids.'

'I'm coming with you.'

He just stared at her for a while with the muscles of his jaw knotted. 'Okay,' he said finally. He looked at The Boy. 'You handle the Mini?'

The Boy nodded.

'Okay. Get it. And bring the shotgun, too. When we go, I go in front; you all follow me like little ducklings. And keep your mouths shut.'

By the time they made it back to the spot where the bear's prints led into the brush, the rain was coming down hard, buzzing against a carpet of fallen red and yellow leaves. Overhead, the sky was dark like the underside of an ash bucket. Uncle walked in front, refusing to wear a hat even though Auntie practically begged him to. He said it would bother with his hearing. He moved in a kind of bent over crouch with his rifle held in both hands and the muzzle pointed at the ground, lens covers flipped shut to protect the scope. His head swiveled like it was mounted on ball bearings—down to check the ground, pause; up left to right to scan the brush, pause; down at the ground and back again.

The Boy followed right on his heels; next came Little Cousin, then Middle Cousin, with Auntie toting the shotgun and bringing up the rear. They moved in fits and starts through the thicket, working their way around, over and under the tangled growth. They zigzagged in an easterly direction where the tops of a great old spruce forest could be seen, perhaps a half mile distant. The ground under their feet was deeply cushioned by wet sand and fallen cottonwood leaves the color of bloody lemons.

The Boy's eye was quick and perceptive, more than capable of tracking an animal the size of a mature black bear, but even he was having trouble spotting its sign in the steady rain and failing light. The ground cover was a sopping mess, and the bramble they were fumbling through seemed to defy his senses. Here a broken branch, a bent clump of grass. There a folded devil's club and a puddle of scarlet. Water was running freely down his back, and his pants were long since soaked. The Mini felt like an anvil cradled in his numb grasp.

Suddenly, Uncle froze.

They had come to a narrow washout running north south, its edges choked with a scrub of cranberry bushes and willow. Uncle stood there looking into it, his head turning slowly back and forth. Finally, he crouched down and summoned everybody to gather round.

Little Cousin's cheeks were turning pasty blue from the chill, and Auntie crouched to warm him in her arms. Middle Cousin's eyes were dull with fatigue and fear.

'Something's wrong,' Uncle said.

They all waited for him to elaborate.

'He crossed right here, but he's doing something different now.'

'He was moving hurt before,' offered The Boy.

'He was scared. But now he's not.' Uncle agreed. He wiped his face with his forearm, looked over his shoulder. 'Now he's got a plan.' He looked back at Auntie. 'He's hurt bad, but not so bad that he shouldn't be miles gone by now. He's not, though. He's in here with us.'

Auntie said nothing, but the sharp lines of her patrician face paled and she held her youngest a little tighter.

The rain whispered against their garbage sacks and dripped down their collars. They went down and across the gully, grabbing handfuls of grass and willow branches to pull themselves up the far side. The bramble closed down so tight that they could only see a few yards ahead and to either side. Uncle paused next to the exposed bulk of an old downed cottonwood tree to the party's left, its ragged system of roots and dirt wads looming higher than his head. He ran one hand thoughtfully over the sopping trunk. He looked back briefly to make sure everyone was together, and then continued.

The Boy took two steps, which brought him to where Uncle had stopped, and reached out to touch the rough bark himself. He knew instantly that something was dreadfully wrong.

The bear came out of the ground right next to him from where it had been hiding, like an avalanche in reverse—a screaming mountain of gut-shot fury. Sounds erupted, muted blips popping from an old eight track; Auntie, something about her babies; Little Cousin, a sharp screamy intake of breath; Uncle shouting to get down dammit get down; the reaching bear, shrieking in rage and fear.

And The Boy just stood rooted to the spot, his shooter forgotten in his arms, looking up up and up into the slobbering mouth of certain death towering above him. Sudden pressure hammered his eardrums. The bear went down on its back and seemed to go crazy. Hissing like a giant kettle, its arms worked in a frantic blur to send a shower of dirt and shrubbery flying in a rough cloud. It bounded and rolled over and over in frenzied motion, and then finally lay still in a softly mewling heap, sounding not unlike a weeping child. Moments passed, and gradually the beast fell silent. Save for the sound of rain crackling against the forest floor, there was absolute silence all around.

They all stood in frozen montage, faces slack and mouths painted on with a careless brush. Still smoking, the 7mm hung from Uncle's bone pale hands with water pooling against its optics.

Later, when they butchered and ate the bear, they were only a little disappointed to find that it was tough and stringy, and tasted exactly like the spawned salmon which it had recently been feasting upon.

5

Winter hit, hammer and tongs.

The wind came blue and hard out of the north, stripping the last of the leaves from the trees and leaving them shriven and naked. Almost without warning the river was clogged with automobile-sized cakes of ice, grinding and groaning their way downstream. The sky yawned open and the snow began to fall, first peppering the already frozen ground, and then covering it in a thick blanket of white.

The dogs became restless, then frantic, as the weather turned. Inscribing long looping circles around their pickets, they raced in constant motion interrupted only to leap up and over their barrels, snow thickening their shaggy coats and crusting their whiskers. They knew that their time had come.

The Boy thought that his time had come, too. He had never been allowed to run Uncle's dogs before, but he felt that this year would be different. He spent all day going into the forest to fetch armloads of bristly spruce boughs to freshen up the dogs bedding. His feet grew wet, and then numb in cracked and leaking rubber boots; fingers long since devoid of feeling in cheap cotton monkey gloves three sizes too large for his hands. As he marched along, intent on his self appointed chore, it occurred to him that perhaps he was not tough enough to withstand the elements inherent to dog mushing.

As he stooped to fill each house, the occupant darted out to cover his face with an excited tongue bath, then dove back in to stretch luxuriously and roll, relishing in the feel of fresh spruce needles combing his or her body. This brought The Boy almost as much pleasure as it did the dogs themselves.

It was getting dark by the time he finished this chore, and he sat on top of Golo's house and allowed the old gentleman to leap into his arms and rub his frosty muzzle against his open jacket collar and naked throat. Golo was Uncle's main leader, an old Tanana river husky right out of the villages, a ruggedly built animal with thick black guard hairs tipped with a dappling of gray, and an undercoat as tight and water repellant as a spotted seal's. His muzzle was broad and short, housing a mouthful of broken teeth gained from a life spent idly chewing on rocks and sticks. His faultless blue eyes were ringed by sockets gone gray from age and one ear jutted from his skull like a torn and weather blasted sail, giving him the look of a good natured junkyard mongrel.

He wondered which dogs he would choose to run if it were his decision to make. Which ones would be the best for pulling hard and hauling firewood out of the forest, which ones had the most endurance for really long runs.

A thin snow fell through the night, and by the first gray light of morning it laid knee deep on the mudflats. Off in the distance, the watercourse could be heard grumbling and snapping in tormented protest against the freight of ice clogging its arteries forcing it to gasp and crawl. Seen from the banks of the creek mouth, the river undulated like a great torpid serpent, its hide mottled blue-white and mucksome brown. The children stood shivering, knock-kneed in the early morning cold, watching as the last visible expanse of water seemed to sigh and suck back into the channel, allowing the flotillas of crusted ice to grind together like giant engines mindlessly driven by some unimaginable force to squeal and splinter and finally heave themselves into a crude sculpture of overlapping jagged ridges and glowing spines of translucent crystal.

It became very quiet and a fog began to seep forth from pores in the ice, quickly rising to treetop level and coating everything it touched with perfect flakes of frost almost dripping with moisture. Behind them, up on the hill, the dogs began to call for their breakfast.

When the day warmed a bit and the fog burned off, Uncle opened the door to the shed where he stored the dry kibble, traps, and mushing tack. First, he pulled out several large crates filled to overflowing with an assortment of black and rusty orange ironmongery; leg-hold traps each with a dangling length of chain. Next came his heavy wooden toboggan sled with its basket loaded full of lines and harnesses for the dogs.

He pushed the crates aside with a grunt and set to work unloading the sled, laying the harnesses on the ground and fumbling with cold fingers to unknot the frayed coil of braided poly rope and jingling brass snaps that would serve as the means of keeping a team of energetic huskies attached to the sled. When it was untangled, he tossed it out with a casual offhand flick of his wrist, making sure to hold onto the last section, the wheel dog section, so that when the line struck the ground all he had to do was feed the back loop into a metal carabineer hanging from the bridle under the sled's nose piece. Next came the snowhook, a black piece of wickedly hooked and cruelly sharp metal meant to function in a manner similar to a boat's anchor. This, too, was affixed to the sleds nose by means of a long shank of sturdy climbing rope. A crude bag of oiled green canvas sewn together with lazily looping strands of whale gut thread functioned as a carryall in the toboggan's belly.

The sled itself was also of a rough construction, built by Uncle two summers before atop a pair of rickety sawhorses; sawn lengths of poorly dried birch fashioned into the necessary pieces and bound together with strips of vinegar soaked moose hide. Its sturdy runners rested on a pair of thick iron slides to protect the wood and provide resistance.

Into the bag went the chainsaw and fuel jugs, ice pick and two axes, one with a broad double bit and the other something like a slender hatchet on a long wooden handle, its blade honed to a chrome shiny sharpness. All of the tools had long lengths of rope attached to their handles.

Together, Uncle and The Boy dragged the sled and its load of tools to the mouth of the creek.

Leaving The Boy on the bank, Uncle hefted the spear like ice pick and carefully stepped onto the river. He took several curiously sliding steps before halting on a perfectly flat section of caked ice with smoothly polished surface showing a fine trail of silver bubbles winding just beneath his feet. He stood motionless for a time, small clouds of steam escaping through the tangled briar of his beard at regular intervals. A low wind ruffled the hem of his parka and moved small runnels of granular snow about his feet.

Stooping, he carefully placed the weighted tip of the pick against the ice, scoring it just a little, then drew it back and brought it sharply down. A puff of powdered shavings flew up and the brief cracking sound was immediately carried away. He struck several times in this manner, driving the pick into the ice with the precision of a needle in a sewing machine, until dark water gushed in a quick geyser. It spread into a wide pool, and then subsided.

Uncle nodded to himself and continued on. He moved about fifteen feet out from the bank before repeating this process, working slowly and cautiously. As he struck with the pick, The Boy could read the sure knowledge of certain black death waiting just inches below his feet in every swiftly violent movement of his shoulders. Another small geyser spurted, fell back.

Working like this, Uncle felt his way to the sandbar across from the creek mouth. It was less than a hundred yards distant, but by the time he stepped from the river and onto the snow and sand mixed surface, the sun was well past mid-day and sweat glowed on his ruddy face and dripped steadily from the ridge of his nose. Once across, he hunkered for a while, resting and not wanting The Boy to see how badly his legs were shaking. After a time, he stood and walked back.

'We'll be ready to cross all the way tomorrow,' he informed The Boy.

Chapter III

1

SUB-ZERO temperatures settled in and gradually froze the land all around.

The little seep where they fetched their water during the summer slowed to a thin trickle and finally glaciered over completely. On the river, the ice grew so thick that Uncle had to get his saw going and cut a hole almost as big around as a half sheet of plywood and nearly as deep as an axe handle could reach. After carving several massive chunks out of the hole, leaving just a thin dry shell on the bottom, he put the saw aside and took up the ice pick, making sure to toss the loose end of the safety line to Middle Cousin.

Several blows drew a long rent in the bottom of the hole from which crystalline water began to boil. Several more in rapid succession turned the narrow opening into a long gash and water rushed in until the hole was completely filled. Ladling with a battered cake pan from Auntie's kitchen, The Boy and Middle Cousin filled up the dog buckets and plastic five gallon drinking jugs and loaded them onto a long fiberglass sled designed for pulling behind a snowmobile, and began to drag them back to the cabin. They had to stop several times on the way back to stamp their feet and blow on their numb fingers. When they began to ferry buckets two by two up the steep climb to the cabin, they were well beyond discomfort and into the land of pain. After setting the last of the buckets on the porch, they trooped into the oven-warmth of the inside to crouch low at the side of the barrel stove, stretching out their feet and splaying their fingers. The Boy's toes gradually came back to a feeling of normalcy in radiating degrees of stinging agony.

Uncle, who had departed after cutting the hole, was already drinking tea with Auntie on the other side of the room. He looked at the boys with stern eyes.

'Did you two cover the hole?' he asked.

'No,' said The Boy.

'I'll tell you what. After I go through all that trouble to cut you a water hole, you had better take care of it. I don't plan on going down there again to cut you a new one,' said Uncle.

The boys ducked their heads and remained quiet.

'You heard your father,' said Auntie. 'Get down there and cover it up before it freezes. And get a start on bringing the firewood. It's going to get cold tonight.'

Little Cousin watched them from where he lay curled under heavy blankets, reading from a comic book.

Carrying a shovel and thin sheet of tin siding, the two older boys trooped back down and carefully covered the hole, first laying down the tin, then sledding loads of snow from shore until the hole was buried. Then they walked back up and out to the woodlot which lay on the other side of the property. It was on the edge of a swampland, dotted thinly with stunted black spruce, feathered moss and cranberry bushes. Birch trees and old growth white spruce came down from firmer high ground to form a stark demarcation. Here, Uncle dropped half the forest in the late summer, bucking it up and splitting it while the boys layered it into long stacks and covered them with broken spruce boughs to keep off the winter snow.

It was much warmer off of the water, away from the river's bone chilling humidity. The boys wasted no time loading their sled with wood and ferrying it back to the cabin and stacking it high on the porch. On their third trip, the smells of cooking layered the air in the outer yard and their stomachs began to convulse with hunger; they hadn't seen food since a meager breakfast of dry sourdough pancakes and cold macaroni. The dogs, too, had smelled the cooking's and begun to come out of their houses and patrol the area with heads up and nostrils quivering.

The boys got the last of the wood stacked as a drab twilight overtook the day and the mercury began to plummet. That evening's dinner was fried Spam, boiled potato, and crusts of sourdough bread lightly coated with generic peanut butter.

The night grew very cold, just as Auntie predicted. The Boy lay sleepless on his cot, shivering under a thin blanket and aware of his breath frosting in the air. A dim light came from the glowing sides of the barrel stove and the window panes creaked.

'You awake?' Little Cousin whispered.

'Yeah. I'm too cold to sleep,' said The Boy.

'Me too,' said Middle Cousin.

'You think you'll run some dogs this year?' asked Little Cousin.

'I heard Pa talking about that with Mama. Said you were gonna help him train this year. Said that he was gonna work real hard and win some money in this year's race,' said Middle Cousin.

The Boy shrugged in the dark.

'Do you want to?' asked the youngest.

'Yeah. I do. But only if I get some better clothes. I got pretty cold today,' said The Boy.

'Didn't notice Pa out there much today. He pretty much let us do all the work while he sat in here with Ma drinking tea and talking all day,' said Middle Cousin.

There was nothing new in this evaluation. Uncle only did the things that the kids could not do, like cut firewood and drive the boat, and once they were big enough for that he would have them doing that, too, they reckoned.

Much later, The Boy drifted into fitful sleep and dreamed the strange and unsettling dreams that had haunted him since his earliest memories.

2

Uncle and The Boy stood in the outer yard examining Uncle's collection of traps. A light snow showered them through the overhanging branches of the trees and the sky had the look of burned clay which meant warmer conditions and heavier snow to come. The Boy hoped this change in the weather pattern would hold for a while.

Uncle demonstrated the use of his assortment of leg-hold traps; number two and four for marten, mink and fox, number six for beaver and possibly wolf or wolverine. He held up a boxlike rectangle of thin metal rods coupled to heavy springs.

'This is a conibear trap,' he said. 'It may be too much for you right now, but I want you to know it in any case. It's for beaver mostly, to set up at their ice holes when they come out of the water. They stick their heads through and it snaps shut around their neck. Not enough to break if it's a big one, but it'll strangle them or force them back in the water to drown.'

He looked down at The Boy's feet. 'I got something for you in the house. I meant to wait until Christmas time, but I think you had better have them early,' he said.

Inside, The Boy found a large cardboard box labeled Sorrel on a bench next to the stove. It contained a new set of pack boots, brown rubber soled with heavy leather leggings that came up to the knees. Careful to keep his socks out of the melt water pooled on the floor, he tossed his old wellies aside and donned the new footgear. Though a little too big, they were the best things which had ever touched his feet. Sudden tears of gratitude welled up and clogged the back of his throat. He felt about a foot taller when he trooped back out, nearly tripping over the door stop in his excitement to try them in the snow. He already knew that they were going to keep his feet warm no matter how cold it got.

They hitched up a seven dog team with Golo and Quincy in the lead. Uncle took his spare toboggan and hooked it up to the front sled and showed The Boy how to stand on it.

'I don't care if you tip over or fall off, just don't let go no matter what. And don't run into me,' he said over the dogs barking. 'Never let go.'

Uncle pulled the hook and the sled nearly leapt out from beneath The Boy's feet. Even with his fingers tightly wrapped around the driving bow, he could feel the wild power thrumming back from the dogs. Golo loped through snow drifts that reached up to his chest, while beside him Quincy nearly disappeared in the deep snow. After a few minutes, they slowed from a crazy, all out run, to a slow trot, all of the dogs leaning heavily against their tuglines. A rooster tail of snow whipped up from Uncle's drag mat and covered his face, forcing him to squint and scowl against the stinging grit.

Their sleds made almost no sound as they shushed along in the well created by the dogs passing, except for muted jolts from ground debris transmitted through the sled's runners. Necklines jingled and canine breath came like the chugging of a freight train. The Boy's heart raced and the melting snow and mucus dripping from his nostrils tasted of raw metal.

Once clear of their creek, they came across fresh snowmobile tracks laid in from the night before. Here, the snow was packed down and only a little punchy, enabling the dogs to run much faster. Uncle stepped on the brake bar and drove the sharp steel teeth into the pack, immediately putting The Boy into a furious blizzard. He looked back, grinned. The Boy turned his face away and hunched his shoulder against the spray.

At the mouth of the creek, they turned off the snowmobile trail and plowed through fresh snow. Golo and Quincy led them between the narrow embankments at the inlet, and after a few windings, they found where overflow had come up and refrozen in an ochre colored shell, steam rising from seeps soaking at the margin where ice met buried dirt. After anchoring off the sled and leaders, the two of them carefully made their way off of the ice and along a narrow path through the crouching alders, Uncle stooped from carrying his rucksack in his arms, The Boy having an easier time of it with the long axe and plastic handled bucksaw.

Uncle stopped them in a place where the ground folded in a runnel from the top of the bank to the creek below. He dropped the rucksack and began to forage for pieces of dried alder sticking up from the snow. The Boy joined him and soon they had a large armload between the two of them. Uncle hunkered down, withdrew a number two trap and some baling wire from the rucksack. He used the wire to affix a section of alder as big around as a coffee mug to a live tree, making sure to point its tip away from the runnel, then bound the trailing end of chain tightly to the trunk. With a sure economy of effort he held the trap between two rough hands and forced it open and locked it, placing it delicately on the stub furthest from the ground. He looked at The Boy as he began to fashion the remaining sticks into a crude cabin around the trap.

'Marten and mink are very curious,' he said. 'They love to explore little cubbies and bolt holes. With this hut, they have no choice but to climb the pole and cross the trap to get to whatever bait we leave.' He cut a strip of moose meat from a hunk kept in his parka, and this he wired onto the pole just out of the reach of hungry paws.

'How long before one comes along?' The Boy asked, timid but curious.

Uncle shrugged. 'Don't know for sure. Probably pretty soon, I would think. Not much for them to eat out here.' His eyes hardened. 'Not much for us to eat out here,' he said to himself.

They backtracked and found the dogs curled up sleeping in their traces. Their heads immediately whipped up and they watched silently as their humans approached. They leapt to their feet and began to bark as soon as it became clear that they were going to be moving again.

The team crossed the frozen portions of overflow in a straddle legged rush, slacking off to let the lines drag only to skirt some unfrozen areas, then charged on breaking their own trail. Uncle and The Boy built four more marten sets before they reached the place where the creek widened out and low forested hills slumped away from the floodplain. Uncle halted the team near a willow thicket overhanging the dimple of a cart trail leading up in shadows. Further down the creek, a large hump of mud and sticks blistered the shore, and off in the distance the zigzagging wall of a beaver dam blockaded the creek as it tapered again into swampland.

A gust of warm wind brought fresh snow splattering in large clumps, and the dogs shook their bodies and pawed at the drifted snow, searching for shrews or mice. Uncle rustled the axe and his rucksack out of the sled and made his way to the beaver hut while The Boy fetched a small plastic bag containing the last of the dried bear meat and fed the dogs from it. The dogs were so hungry that the snacks never even got close to the ground.

When he finished, he stuffed the empty sack back into the sled bag and joined Uncle at the hut. He watched, trembling and cold; his new boots had finally soaked through, and his bibs were wet up to the knees. His gloves, too, had been damp and then refrozen so many times that they now fit his hands like slick armor.

Having found the smoothly polished ice hole at the foot of the hut, Uncle carefully inspected it before setting one of the conibears at its mouth. The trail the beavers had made from this exit was perfectly clear, even with fresh snow covering it; a gently winding trough mounting the bank and disappearing into the willow thicket. It was plainly obvious what would happen to the next one to come along on a food gathering mission.

Uncle saw the worry in The Boy's face and turned away with a scowl.

'This is going to be your job,' he said with his back turned. 'Your line. You need to check it every day, bring back what you find. If you can handle it, you can put in more of your own traps up the trail.'

He pointed at the cart track. 'That way is fine; but you're never to go up to the dam. That's how people die.'

They turned the team around retraced their steps home. That

night, Uncle filled Auntie in on the day's doings and talked about his team's chances this year in the upcoming race season.

3

Uncle gave him five dogs to use, the ones that were not fast enough to make his own crew, but would serve him well as a trapline team. The Boy had his own sled, harnesses and lines, as well as a small backpack loaded with extra traps and fixings, a summer weight sleeping bag, a tarpaulin, and an old single shot twenty-two rifle with a handful of extra cartridges.

His lead dog was Quincy's littermate brother, Apache; a roan-colored male with long legs and curved range of knobby backbone. He was sweet and smart, but too submissive for Uncle's taste. The other four were small females and only good for the team positions. When the Boy hooked them up for the first time, though, he was surprised at their power. They wrenched him and the sled out of the yard and fairly flew up the river. It was still warm and gray, but the snow and wind had died down and the man on the radio had said the weather was supposed to stay this way for a while.

He quickly realized that the all out run they were traveling at was much too fast a speed for them to maintain for any length of time without exhausting themselves or damaging their feet. These dogs were bred to give it their all no matter the consequence to their own bodies, and only training and careful management would ensure that they ran safely and to the best of their ability. This knowledge came to him on a gut instinct level, and he wondered briefly if Uncle possessed this insight. As the miles ticked by underneath the runners, something very strange began to happen. The ever present feeling of miserably cold discomfort fuzzed away and a feeling like being wrapped in a blanket of wet cotton slowly began to replace it. He was still aware of the physical sensation of cold, but it no longer seemed to be of any relevance. The trail leading to his trapline passed by on his right and the open white expanse of the river rippled and stretched out before him like melting taffy.

Funny to be thinking about candy, he thought. Though it was not yet noonday, the sky deepened, became dark. The dogs dimmed… sharpened…dimmed, then steadied out as jerking cardboard cutouts against a monochrome stillness, glowing faintly around their edges. He was aware of pressure building at his temples, in the back of his head. A tremendous surf boomed and crashed and he saw a rich weaving of colored threads bleeding from the backs and legs of the dogs; all of the hues of the rainbow radiating from the tips of their ears and out of their open mouths when they turned their heads to look back at him.

I can see what they're thinking, he realized, and for some reason this filled him with a sense of dread. He could smell bread rising, not Aunties, Auntie never made bread like this, no, and he heard singing and felt arms around his shoulders holding him singing into his ear over the roaring of the surf.

'Come back,' said she, the singer of distant lullabies. Pain like he never dreamed existed exploded behind his eyes, both the one open and staring and the scarred empty socket, a great white supernova that ripped the cheese cloth fabric of his mind away and blew the breath from his lungs like a candle flame exposed to a storm wind.

It was a dog licking his face and open mouth that woke him, made him aware of his stiff body and freezing limbs and blood that drooled from his nose and flooded the back of his throat. Also, he thought that he could taste tears, but he couldn't be sure.

I know how this story is going to end, he thought, and the taste of tears grew much stronger. This thought lingered for only a moment before fading like the afterglow of a dream upon waking. He sat up, hocked and spat; found that it was Apache standing over him. He hugged the dog, and for a time he buried his face in the fur around the dog's collar.

The sled lay on its side in the middle of a stretch of river that he did not recognize. The dogs had turned themselves around and now were all gathered around him in a loosely tangled pile, panting and playing with one another, watching him with some curiosity.

'It's okay,' he said, his voice rusty. 'I'm okay. Sorry guys.'

4

By the time he got them straightened out and turned around, the memory of what had occurred was utterly gone from his mind. He did find it puzzling to have travelled so far past his turnoff, but the dogs covered the ground so fast on the way back that he hardly had time to think on it.

He found the first two traps untouched. The third was sprung and empty, trap dangling from its chain, cabin exploded. The bait was gone and a tuft of orange fur showed in the bite of the trap's teeth. He rebuilt the cabin and reset the trap. When he got to the next set, he found that this one, too, had been raided. He made sure to build the cabin a bit smaller then Uncle had shown him, and placed the open trap and hunk of bait closer together then before.

When he and his dogs made it to the beaver hut, he could tell before he even brought the sled to a halt that the conibear was sprung and down in the hole the beavers used as a front door. The hole was lightly crusted over, the conibear's safety chain disappearing down into it. Using his axe, he carefully chopped it open and pulled on the chain. It was heavy and unyielding.

With a feeling of revulsion mixed with adrenalized anticipation, he slowly fished it up. It came out in a sopping brown haired mess, a big male with a tail nearly as long as his own arm and a body as wide as a sack of grain. It was frozen with rigor, mouth gaping absurdly with long orange teeth and small eyes dull under beetled brows.

It was almost too heavy to carry. He staggered with it back to his sled, the extra weight pushing him down through the fragile crust of the trail. The dogs watched him intently, mouths open and tongues lolling. Again following his instinct, he pulled his fixed blade cutter out of its leather sheath at his belt and severed the tail from the creature's body and hacked it into five large chunks. He threw these to the dogs and watched as they devoured them.

Fumbling, and twice almost closing the trap on his own wrist, he got the conibear reset and in place. He stood up from his task with wet knees, looked up for the sun. It was growing late, but he thought he had time to put some more trail in, and even build some new marten sets. The dogs were perkier then before, and he knew that the fatty snack had done much to refill their fuel tanks.

Also, he could tell that they liked running and pulling for him. He made sure to check all of their harnesses for a good fit and ruffled each ones face and head, and when he asked them to continue on up the unbroken cart path, they were eager. He went less than a mile before turning around, but it was mostly uphill and much of it was through heavy wet snow. He was able to find spots for three more traps which he set with increasing proficiency, taking vague pride in his ability to perform the task.

He got back to the dog yard just before dark. As he unhooked the dogs and put them back on their houses, he realized that Uncle was still out with his team. Auntie's face was a pale oval at the door screen. Middle Cousin and Little Cousin came out to watch him, stopped in awe as he flopped the beaver carcass to the ground.

Middle Cousin muttered an expletive, gave it a kick. 'Did you kill it?' he asked.

'No, he was already drowned when I found him,' The Boy said.

'Holy cow,' said Little Cousin. 'That's the biggest one I've ever seen.'

'How many have you seen?'

'Enough to know this one's big.'

The Boy fetched a bucket of feed from the cabin and was ladling a thin mixture of rice and kibble into pans for his group, when Uncle's team came trotting up in the gathering gloom of nightfall. Uncle stepped off of the runners and shouldered the bushy armload of his day's catch, three fat marten and a bundle of chocolate brown mink.

'Unhook these dogs,' he said without looking back. He stalked into the cabin, and soon the Coleman lanterns were pulsing white-yellow against the window panes. The Boy slowly stripped away harnesses, hesitating when Golo cried out in pain when his foot was raised and folded back to pull it free. He realized that Uncle's dogs were very tired. They walked slowly by his side when he led them back to their houses. When he fed, some of them would not eat, just curled up nose to tail and fell asleep.

Inside, Uncle was bent over the kitchen table. Bone handled skinning knife in hand and shirtsleeves rolled up past the elbows, his bloodstained hands were already shucking the skin from the third marten, pulling the hide free from the blue red cords of muscle and tissue like someone in a hurry to get their socks off. Darkened water sloshed in a tin can at his side and the lantern hanging over the scene threw his shadow long and hard across the room. The odor of emptied musk glands overpowered even Auntie's cooking.

The Boy knew that hides such as these were fetching upwards of sixty bucks each in far off Anchorage; the minks, if they were blue enough, maybe thirty or thirty five. Beaver like the one he had caught went for over a hundred, and their meat was rich and fat for the cook pot.

5

That night, The Boy lay awake for a long time listening to the wind sigh against the roofing and thinking about his mother.

Chapter IV

1

THE days on the calendar clicked by like a train of dominoes. Uncle pushed his trapline south and overland to Rabbit Lake, bringing in daily loads of marten, mink, and often times red or cross fox. His dogs grew wishbone thin and dull eyed, their winter coats coming in a fuzz of perpetual shed. He took his rifle with him everywhere that he went.

A few days before Christmas, a prop driven Cessna buzzed the house, droning like an angry bee. It put down in the creek and taxied up to the bottom of their hill in a cloud of snow. From the plane emerged a pilot in a red and black checked vest and heavy woolen cap—and old Saint Nick himself with an armload of grocery bags and a pillow for a tummy. Little Cousin did alright until he saw that big man all in red with his great white beard and belly laugh of *ho ho ho*. The little boy's face became stricken with horror and he fell on his rear in his haste to back away. He fled on all fours up to the safety of the cabin.

This time Santa Claus laughed a real laugh though a bit strained, and pulled down his beard to do it. His face was stubbled with whiskers and his teeth were the color of weak coffee. He and the pilot talked to Auntie and Uncle like they were old friends, and soon they got back in their plane and flew away and became a gnat in the sky. At the sound of the receding engine, the dogs broke into song.

The grocery sacks Santa had left contained a twenty pound turkey and cans of candied yams and cranberry sauce, a double handful of tootsie rolls and small bag of hard candy. There were also some prayer pamphlets, which Uncle tossed into the firebox. When he looked the other way, though, Auntie scooped them up into the folds of her apron and went to start butchering the tom.

2

The Boy pushed his own line further out to the big swamps east of the river where the moose sometimes liked to collect when there wasn't too much snow. One day, he took a bag full of unused conibears and no one made comment. He fashioned crude snowshoes from bent willow limbs and scraps of rotten bike tubing and put a trail around the dam (the one Uncle had forbidden him to go beyond), to the series of steaming ponds on the other side. He crossed weak ice a couple of times, his heart in his throat, listening to it crack and settle under his weight. The overhanging branches of brush on the shore were well beyond reach, and he knew full well what would happen should he go through.

He knew that the ice was weak here because the water collected underneath was warmed from the beaver swarming about on their various tasks. He found their huts, and in the days that followed, began hauling them out by the sled load. He did so well that Uncle never once asked about the missing tails, and maybe didn't even notice how The Boy's five dogs became thick and sleek, in stark contrast to his own.

Christmas morning dawned and the three boys were fit to bust with excitement. It did not matter that there were no tree or lights or crinkling colored paper, or that the only presents were few and poor, placed in small bundles on the kitchen table and surrounded by open number two traps as Uncle's idea of wit. Little Cousin got a small stack of funny books and box of crayons with paper. Middle Cousin and The Boy received lady's plastic Casio wrist watches with faces that lit up green when their buttons were depressed. In his pile, Middle Cousin also found a country music cassette of a kind that Uncle and Auntie favored and a pair of woolen socks that rolled up to his knees.

Later, while the boys read Little Cousin's comics, Uncle saddled a small team and took his rifle with him and mushed into the woods. The sky was fair and held little cold and Auntie put an apple cobbler on to bake with the turkey and the smells they made filled the cabin with the feeling of festival. In the distance, they heard the faint liquid popping of a rifle shot. A few moments passed, and then they heard two more, one right after the other. Uncle's 7mm only held three rounds in the magazine, and The Boy knew that he was busy reloading. When enough time went by without more firing, he knew that whatever Uncle had shot had either gotten away, or was down for good.

Uncle was back within the hour. He sat at the table and broke the 7mm down into parts and he worked to clean these with an oily rag.

'It was an old bull and two cows,' he said. The cows were alright because they fell down in the brush, but the bull was going to be a problem, he was just right out in the middle of the swamp right where God or just about anybody in a plane could see him.

Later, Auntie cleaned the table and brought the food to it; the turkey, yams and cranberry sauce with potato salad the color of mustard and lightly sugared flatbread. The meal lasted for less than ten minutes, but they managed to pretty much wipe out the entire spread, including a pitcher of hot tang and a full platter of stuffing.

3

Uncle waited until the sun pooled orange against the horizon before loading his and The Boy's sleds with tarpaulin, axes and bucksaw, Coleman lanterns, cutters and whetstone. He connected the two sleds and hooked up the same team which he had used earlier. Bundling Auntie and the two smaller children into the baskets, he and The Boy took their positions at the driving bows and set forth to where the moose lay under hastily-mounded blankets of loose reddish snow.

It was full dark by the time they arrived and the stars glittered overhead like diamonds cast in a darksome well bottom. Coyotes yodeled from out in the scrub, self righteous from being driven from their supper. Scavengers had uncovered parts of the bull and pulled out a length of whitish intestine from a gash in its abdomen. Raven prints and tufts of bristly moose hair circled the scene of industry, and when the lanterns were set afire to pop and hiss, they rendered the tableau in a morphing island of shadows and pitiless yellow light.

Uncle made short sure work of the bull with Auntie and The Boy holding various limbs and flaps of hide away from the path of his cutting. Golo crouched near the antlers, lustily stripping off the nostrils and other soft tissues of the face. The gutsack flopped out in a steaming rush behind a careful unzipping of the belly, followed quickly by a red-handed yanking of the edible organs. The great, bruised loaf of liver lay quivering and leaking in the snow, and Quincy whined and strained to get at it. Meat parted under a glint of razored knife edge; occasionally, there would be a pause in the cutting for Uncle's blade to shush against the whetstone before continuing on in its tracings.

When the first piece of butchery was finished, Uncle stood straight with a soft groan and heavy popping of knees and surveyed the scene with steam rising from his wet hands.

'You two get this one started back to the house. We'll stay back and get on those cows,' he told the two older boys.

The sleds were overloaded with hindquarters the size of fuel drums, but the boys managed to also find room for the heart, kidneys, liver, and all of the back-strap. They had to jog alongside the sleds and it was slow going as the old freighters groaned and sagged, leaving tracks that swayed drunkenly from side to side. The team was incapable of hauling the cargo up the hill, so they dumped it at the foot and went back for more. With one mostly-dead headlamp between them, they got the last of the meat out of the swamp. On their last trip, the sky paled over the eastern bank of the river as Little Cousin slept, exhausted and bundled inside a thick down sleeping bag and tucked inside a sled with the last rectangle of rib rack.

Only a meager offering of backbones, scattered entrails, and the bull's mighty antlers were left for the scavengers to pick clean.

4

The dogs strengthened with the rich new moose meat and Uncle started making longer and longer runs, sometimes pulling two truck tires behind his sled on a long chain. Once, The Boy met him on the way back from checking his traps and had to pull over to get out of the reach of those tires as Uncle's eighteen dog team boiled past like a furred freight train leaving a vapor trail in its wake.

Shortly after the New Year, Uncle hooked up his team and was gone for four days to Anchorage to sell furs and bring back supplies. When he made it back, he and the dogs were cloaked with wet snow and his sled was filled to the brim with all of the necessities of Aunties larder—plus several forty pounders of kibble, too. He spent the next week making round trips to the landing on the Big Su seventy miles away, and by now there was a lot of talk going around the kitchen table about the Great Race coming up in March.

Auntie spent most of her days hunched over an antique sewing machine which was powered by a manual foot trestle, cutting out dog booties from swaths of trigger cloth the color of pale lemons and sewing them together and packing them away in burlap sacks. There was some barely realized excitement building in the house. This could be the year things came right, and they all knew what a big finish in Nome would mean; more and better food, warmer clothes, and gas for the generator. Every day, Uncle brought back reports about how much stronger his team was then the year before, how much faster. Golo and Quincy were looking unstoppable.

On a day in early January, Uncle came back late from a run, bent nearly double over his handlebar like a man sick from too much drink. He toppled over from the sled when it came to a stop in the dog yard and they all ran out to him. His face was sweat-streaked and ashen, lips thin and blue and eyes flat with pain. Lurching and stumbling, they got him inside and to his bed. Auntie fussed about getting him undressed and under some blankets, snapping at the children to get that stove cranked up dammit!

'What's wrong, what's wrong!' she moaned over and over, until finally Uncle reached up with a shaking hand and touched her face and she began to weep. The Boy and his cousins stayed well out of the way and as small as they could make themselves. They heard a hoarse scream during the night, but by morning, Uncle was feeling better. Auntie had bandaged his ribs and set him propped up in bed, and now she hustled about the house as if nothing was wrong.

Uncle said his team had been going at an all-out run when one of the tires had caught something under the snow and stopped the whole train dead in its tracks, sending him flying over the driving bow and crashing down slantwise across the sled's side rail like a child's toy doll, smashing a number of his ribs like seasoned kindling.

Uncle saw The Boy shivering in his pajamas and motioned for him to come closer. The Boy could see pain squinting his eyes and thought, for the first time, that he did look sort of like his long lost Papa. Uncle coughed up rusty phlegm and hocked it into a crusted bowl at the bedside. His chest hitched when he breathed and his voice was hoarse.

'This is where things start to get tough,' he whispered.

The Boy said nothing, but nodded in reply.

'You've been doing a good job with your team,' said Uncle. 'And your trapline.'

These few words started a coughing fit that doubled him over and made him retch. 'Better than most grown men,' he continued, once he had his body back under control.

He looked at Auntie who had come to sit at the foot of his bed. 'Honey, I can run the dogs, after I rest up for a couple of days. If all I have to do is stand on the runners and not jump around too much.'

Auntie nodded, eyes swimming with tears.

'I need you to run my trapline,' he told The Boy. 'All the way down to the mouth of the Yentna and over to Rabbit Lake. It's long, maybe thirty five miles one way, not counting offshoots. It'll take you more than a day to do it. Do you think you can?'

'Yes,' said The Boy, with only a little hesitation.

'The snow is getting deep out there. The moose might start being a problem, so I'm sending you with a gun that can put one down if need be.'

'Okay,' said The Boy.

5

Two mornings later, Auntie, Middle Cousin and The Boy went out and Auntie watched as the two of them harnessed up Uncle's team. The boys fumbled the new trigger cloth booties onto the dogs jerking paws, clumsily binding their tops with black electrical tape that had almost no stick in the cold. When Uncle came out of the cabin and limped to the sled, his face was the color of oatmeal and he panted like a dog that had just galloped a long mile. When Auntie helped him don his parka, he made not a sound, but made her stop several times so he could rest, leaning with his full weight against the handle-bars. Sweat dripped from his beard and his hands shook. When this was done and the last of the eighteen dogs were hitched to the gang-line, he looped a cord around his wrist and attached it to the driving bow. None of them had ever seen him do this before, and it was a measure of his discomfort that he should resort to such a precaution.

After finishing up with the wood stacking and water hauling, The Boy saddled up his own team. He packed his sled more carefully than ever before, adding all the necessities for camping out; extra dog food and cooker, sleeping bag, canteen and .41 magnum. He had to boot his own team, too, because of the extra mileage and uncertain conditions, and this time his hands were more proficient in their task. As he pulled the hook and his team rolled out of the yard like a shot from a canon, he caught a brief glimpse of his cousins watching from the door of the cabin, unsmiling stick figures.

His longest run before this had been no more than twenty miles, and he knew that this new adventure would pose a difficult challenge for his small team. Right away, he brought their speed down to a precise trot, careful not to put too much pressure on the drag, instead using the influence of his soft voice and even tempered body language to calm the dogs down. They were all very strong from the last two months of training and eating the rich diet of beaver and moose meat, long powerful limbs and muscles rippling under slick coats; eyes shining and bright. A fuzzy black coated bitch named Pilot had joined Apache in the lead. She was short and stocky and not very fast, but The Boy sensed in her a mental toughness that would never waver in the face of adversity; a heart that would always beat for her master's command.

They traveled downriver on a narrow trail barely the width of a dogsled, through country he had only before seen in the summer months. Stands of giant cottonwoods were arranged like mute sentries on the west bank; a great bluff with bands of olive and tan striping the exposed stratum stood to the east. The features of the surrounding country maintained for several grand sweepings of the river, and the trail was hard and fast under the runners. They reached a place where a broad slough snaked away from the main channel and a number of small creeks let into it at regular intervals, and they saw fresh moose tracks zigzagging across in a multitude. The team climbed to a sandbar covered by a miles-long collection of old stripped trees, polished smooth of bark and welded in place like soldiers left scattered on a field. Through the haze, a mountain range grew in outline to the southwest; gentle lines describing a long waist and full hips, half turned shoulder and slender throat, all in pastel blues and whites. As they mushed towards the elegant figure of the Sleeping Lady, the sun settled orange and full behind her back and limned her outline in a flare of spun gold, blanketing the rest of her in a stark black shadow that dazzled The Boy's eye.

Several well beaten snowmobile paths intersected their own and the trail widened and grew crusty where they joined. Far ahead, through waves of shimmering air that promised a night's cold bearing down, was a great opening where two major rivers merged and several broad sloughs let off from the main channel. Light winked from distant window panes, and he could see a bank of steam rising from a place where he knew there must be open water. Faint wood smoke scented the air. He stopped the team and, one by one, went through their feet, inspecting for telltale signs of blood or damage to the booties. Some of them were missing, and all the ones that remained were blown through. He stripped these off and threw them into the sled bag. When they got moving again, the sky had deepened to purple and a handful of stars flickered above; the brightest of them was pinned a few degrees below the tail of Orion's electric kite, oscillating between red and cyan.

Steam came from the mouths of the dogs and The Boy's hands grew very cold. The only sound they made was the jingle of brass snaps against collar rings and a dry squeak trailing from the steel runners; the dogs steady breathing. As it darkened, the lights on the far shore resolved themselves into squares of steady orange and then they were passing close to a collection of cabins that made up Susitna Station; some used, others darkened for the winter. A small generator clattered and the smells of gasoline, two-cycle oil and food cooking mixed together in the evening air. The dogs ran with their heads up and noses sniffing as they passed this assortment on the high bank.

Then they left the small island of light behind.

The Boy had his headlamp strapped over his cap, but the batteries were near dead and he was loath to waste the power. Finally, he was forced to switch it on just to look down at the ground, trying to spot Uncle's old sled tracks. He had never before been to this place, but he knew from Uncle's talk that the overland trail to Rabbit Lake had to depart the river from somewhere around this confluence of the

Big Su and Yentna rivers. Little more than a weak candle glow, his headlamp beam was hardly any help at all. Uncle's old sled tracks were lost in a confusion of windblown snow and overlapping of fresh snowmobile tracks, and the light merely cast this into a brownish haze that hurt his eye and baffled his senses. They would have been forced to stop but for Pilot putting her nose down and running stiff legged, head practically dragging on the trail while she sniffed out the correct passage.

The Boy felt cold steam on his face that chilled him down to the bone, and by now his hands were so stiff that he wasn't sure if he could make them release the handlebar. The trail soon narrowed and the river bank reared up before them, twice as high as the team was long and snow-covered except where the passage of numerous snowmobiles had worn it down to dirt and ice near the crest. As they labored to its top, The Boy warmed a little from the exertion of pushing the sled, and he was aware of some pain pulsing along his toes to the tempo of his heartbeat.

He stopped and looked back the way they had come, saw the distant lights of Susitna Station twinkling, the searching beams of a set of snowmobile headlights probing the mouth of the slough off to the northeast. He turned his own failing headlamp beam to the trail ahead of his leaders. Its steep sides reached up as high as the top of the sled bag, and he could tell that it was punchy soft from the way the dogs sank down into it even while standing still. The dogs looked tired, but he knew that he couldn't afford to stop here for very long; Rabbit Lake was still over twelve miles away, and if he did not reach it tonight, then he would not be able to make it home by the following evening. And he still had all of Uncle's traps to find. His stomach was an empty hole in his middle, and he decided that the dogs could at least take a short break before continuing on.

He was suddenly aware of how far from home he was, and the

knowing of it made him feel very small. He fed the dogs each a handful of kibble dropped right on the snow in front of their noses. He fished out his own foam wrapped canteen and took a long pull of slushy water that stung his teeth and scalded his belly when it hit bottom, then sat on the nose of the sled while the dogs curled up in tight balls and went right to sleep in the trail. Later, his feet became so cold that he had to get up and walk around to build up some body heat. After walking down to the river and back again a number of times, he got the dogs up and on their feet and started down the trail, his own body so stiff that he wondered how he was going to make it through the night.

They moved at a crawl, dogs pulling hard and falling through the thin crust with every other step, mightily tugging the sled through loose snow the texture of dry sand. Old shaggy trees crowded around and soon laced their branches together overhead to blot out the sky, and it grew much darker then it had been back on the Yentna. The trail took them in a series of tight looping whorls that constantly tried to suck the wheel dogs into the soft banks, and progress became glacial. The Boy ran behind the sled punching in past his knees. His breath came in quick hard gasps that burned like hot syrup in his lungs and seared his throat on the exhale.

At last, they broke from the clutch of the forest and came into wide open swampland with a lake on its far boundary. The constellations had changed their positions since first dark, swung across the sky in a lazy arc; now their sons and daughters and beasts of myth lay scattered in the vast like a giant's hoard of precious gemstones burning against a hard pane of coal black. He stopped here, and his fire when he got it going blazed in its deep cave and sent up its own offerings and the smoke from it warmed him as much as the flame itself.

He and the dogs ate a meager supper and each bedded down

for the last stretch of the night; the dogs in their melted holes, The Boy shaking and rattling in his thin sleeping bag arranged on a bed of spruce boughs and covered with a crackling tarpaulin. His breath sent up a plume of frost and he lay awake for a cold eternity.

6

He broke camp before sunrise. It was so cold that when he arose to stretch and do his daily, his urine exploded into vapor immediately upon leaving his body. The noncommittal light of predawn rendered the lake and surrounding shoreline in a hazy outline of softening gray shadow; a snow covered surface that was long and free of blemish and a ragged band of black spruce encased in frost jostling for space at its limits.

The fire was out and long cold, but he rekindled it and prepared a thin breakfast of hot soup mixed with kibble and strips of frozen moose meat. The dogs watched anxiously and gulped the food when it came. He refilled his canteen with the dregs of water slopping at the bottom of the small aluminum pot which he used for melting snow, and when he drank from it, he had to strain bits and pieces of rubbish from the warm liquid. After warming his hands in his armpits, he tried to reboot the team, but gave it up as impossible when the tape just fell in useless spools at the dogs feet, too cold to stick.

He found that the trail had set up after their first crossing, and the return trip was much faster than the outgoing. Even with stopping to check Uncle's traps on the way back, releasing the long dead catch in some cases and re-baiting in others, The Boy thought that they would make it home before dark.

7

The month of January passed in this manner; The Boy running to Rabbit Lake on every third day to check traps, Uncle wheezing and gasping and clutching his handlebar in an attempt to keep the miles up on his own team. Uncle slowly got better, and by early February he was almost back to moving normal. Some of Auntie's geese starved to death, and these were baked in the oven without ceremony. It stayed cold, bottoming out the thermometer almost every night, and the old cabin creaked and complained and even under the thickest blankets, the family nearly froze. The three boys took to sleeping together in a pile, combining their covers and pillows into one big pallet on the floor. The stove blazed and snorted up wood like a fire-breathing dragon, but did little to stave off the cold since the house had poor insulation in the roof and none at all in the floor or walls.

The Boy's team had become so strong that he could leave in the early morning hours and make it to the end of the trapline and back within the space of a single day, and as he did this, his confidence grew. He was on just such a return trip, nearly back to the banks of the Big Su, when the moose attacked. He never really saw it, it came from his blind side, just heard a strange crunching of snow and complaining of parted brush, and then there was a wall of brown hair and frantic barking from the dogs. The world spun and he was down on his hands and knees trying to get up, trying to claw the .41 from the sled bag out of simple blind reflex. Something struck his head, and now it was just wind in a dark tunnel. Mama's hands were on his shoulders and baby brother was in his arms and it was dark and the wind was like something from a nightmare and Mama was crying and trying to tell him something but the wind was too loud.

What Mama, what?
Come back come back.

How? Where?
The ravens will show you.

He shook his head like a dog trying to dislodge a gnat from its ear and watched as a swarm of meteors crossed his field of vision. His hands were a throwback to a bygone era and the cold grips of the .41 were in his fist long before he could actually see anything clear enough to shoot. He was alone in the forest. He stood on shaking legs, gun in hand and skin ringing like a hollow shell. There was no sign of the moose, just a meandering track where it had come and gone. He carefully bundled the pistol away in its holster and terry-cloth towel wrapping. He got back on the sled and whistled for the dogs to take off.

When he got down on the river, he saw that there were people on the edge of the bank, at Susitna Station, a man, woman, and a young girl about the same age as himself. They watched with smiles on their faces, all except for the girl, and for some reason this made him stop just below them, immediately feeling foolish and awkward for doing so. They invited him up to their cabin and made him sit on a low couch and take helpings of hot chocolate and peanut butter cookies; a bowl filled with steaming soup and crumbly hot cornbread soaked with real butter.

The couple had tons of questions for him, but the girl just sat and stared. Her eyes were dark and her cheekbones sharp and her chestnut hair fell in a soft wing against her slender neck. He could smell her even from across the room, and the smell reminded him of summer. For the first time in his life, he became aware of his own smell; his filthy clothes and hands. He could not bear to look at the girl, so he kept his eyes trained to the floor and answered questions in monosyllables and tried to get away just as quickly as he could.

As he went back to his team, the man followed him. He looked in the direction of Rabbit Lake, then up the Yentna. 'How far did you come, did you say?' he asked.

'The Big Bend of the Yentna.' The Boy told him.

'And you went all the way to Rabbit Lake?'

'Yessir'.

'All by yourself.'

'Yessir. All by myself.'

The man frowned, looked back up to the bank where his wife stood listening. She gave a slight shake of her head. He turned back to the boy standing before him, stick thin and dressed like a raggedy man from some farmer's field.

'Son, I want you to make me a promise. Whenever you come this way, I want you to stop in here and catch a meal with us. Can you promise me that?'

The Boy could not keep the doubt from his face.

'It'll worry us if you don't. Especially my wife.'

The Boy looked at the mother, then the girl, then quickly away with a strange lump forming in his throat. 'Ok,' he said. 'I'll stop by.'

'Anytime, day or night. You promise?'

'I promise.'

'Ok.'

They shook hands just like grown men do, and when The Boy reached the far side of the river, only one tiny figure stood watching his departure.

8

Uncle, Auntie and Little Cousin left late in February, in preparation for the Great Race. It was warm, verging on thaw, and they harnessed up a team of twenty-two dogs and left without looking back. There was extra wood stacked in the woodlot and Uncle had carved a fresh ice hole out on the river. Before leaving, he told the two boys to behave themselves and not to fight, to go upriver to Lake Creek if they needed any help; there was plenty of dog food to go around, but don't feed too much because we won't be back until late in March.

'We'll send you messages on the Bush Pipeline, so keep the batteries charged up, but don't go burning up all the gas.'

They had embraced Middle Cousin and said their goodbyes, but not a tear was shed; at least not until they were out of sight and Middle Cousin went inside and shut the door.

The Boy stood there in the middle of the mostly empty dog lot, feeling as empty as the dog barrels scattered about him. Uncle had taken Apache and Pilot with him, and this made his heart ache and he thought maybe he would cry after all. He turned a slow circle, taking in the cabin slouched and swaybacked under a load of snow, the twisted wire chicken coop still full of ducks and a few geese and all of the Cornish Cross that had managed not to freeze their toes off over the winter; a ramshackle sprawl of tin siding and flapping blue tarps that served as storage for the generator and dry dog food; wood smoke fogging the air and fluttering bits of loose garbage and debris. A sudden mute horror stole over him as he recognized the meanness of it all.

Not knowing what to do, he went inside. It was warm, and Middle Cousin was sitting on the floor going through the cupboards. A heap of Auntie's sundries lay piled on the floor next to him.

'What are you doing?' asked The Boy.

The younger boy looked up at him, and his face was much too young to be so thin and haunted.

'I'm looking for sweets. I know there was some in here some-where. Mama wouldn't have left me without any sweets,' he said. He was holding a long box of Pilot Boy crackers in his lap. He looked away and his skinny shoulders hitched. His effort to stifle a sob sounded like a frog croaking.

The Boy hunkered down and put his hand on the hot little shoulder. 'We'll make some cookies,' he said. 'Would that be sweet enough?'

Chapter V

1

ON his last trip to Rabbit Lake, The Boy had left all of the traps sprung and dangling from their chains. Now, he struggled to pull in his original beaver pond line; this was especially challenging because he had been left without a single lead dog, and it was almost impossible to get the team to go without at least one. Finally, he trudged out on foot. It took him all day, and when he made it back just after dusk with three stiff chocolate brown mink and a pack filled with ironmongery, he was surprised to find the man from Susitna Station waiting in the yard.

The man was garbed in blue Refrigawear from top to bottom and sitting astride a battered old Skidoo snowmobile, chatting with Middle Cousin like it was the most normal thing in the world.

'How did you find us?' The Boy asked, stupefied.

The man smiled. 'I followed your tracks. Your brother and me were just having a visit.'

'What do you want?'

'My wife thought you boys might like some of her cooking,' he said. He produced a large cardboard box from a carry rack mounted behind the seat. Nobody moved to take it until The Boy nodded and Middle Cousin grabbed it from the man.

'I'll be going now, but I just want you boys to know that if you need anything, you just have to give a holler,' the man said.

The Boy did not bother to tell him that they had no way to give him a holler.

'Thank you,' he said, somewhat stiffly. It occurred to him to ask the man what his daughter's name was, but he could not make his mouth form the words.

The three of them stood for a time in awkward silence, until the man finally fired up his Skidoo and left the way he had come. Inside, the lanterns were burning and the damper on the stove was turned up. The harsh cords of bluegrass music twanged from the radio. The Boy left his coat by the door and hung the mink to thaw in the corner, well away from the direct heat coming off the stove. The box that the man from Susitna Station had brought them was sizeable, containing an apple pie with perfectly scalloped edges; a long Tupperware container packed with lasagna, paper plates, forks and napkins; a canister of Tang, four tins of Spam, and a bag of half frozen nectarines. The boys hardly knew where to start, and ended up gorging on apple pie and drinking Tang made so thick and sweet that Middle Cousin got sick and threw up during the night.

With most of the dogs gone and no more trapline to check, there was very little to keep the boys occupied. They mostly stayed indoors, which was all for the good because the weather was shifting into warmer spring patterns which brought heavy wind and often wet snow driven before it. There were no messages on the radio for them until one night in early March. They could tell by the way that the deejay read it that it was Uncle's words.

'The dogs look fantastic. We're all good here. The race starts tomorrow. Wish us luck.'

The words sent gooseflesh rippling along The Boy's arms, calling out to him from a barely understood distance across lakes and rivers, vast swamps and epic mountain ranges. The Great Race. One thousand miles from Anchorage to Nome, twenty five thousand dollars in gold waiting for the first musher to reach that fabled shore. A legendary journey peopled with near mythical figures. Uncle was going to compete for his fourth time; a year's training and hardship, and it would all be put to the test tomorrow. Uncle had said that this year would be different, that life would be better after this race because he was going to win it this time. Golo and Quincy, Apache and Pilot, would see him through. The Boy knew nothing of God, but now he wished so hard that it was very much like praying.

The morning of the race, the sun arose to a cloudless blue sky the shade of faded denim. The reports came to them over the radio, broadcast from a station in Big Lake that specialized in public programming. Static and faint banjo music, then dogs singing, an entire chorus of canine throats begging to be let loose; people talking in the background, more static. Then, the music faded and the announcer came on.

During the next two weeks that it took for the Great Race to play out across the northland, time contracted for the boys. They stayed glued to the speakers, leaving the house only to do chores in between the hourly stories and reports. They both listened to the unfolding drama as the days thawed and the nights chilled; as rain tattooed the exposed tin roofing above their heads, and then cooled and covered it again in a blanket of white; as the flows of winter waxed and waned around them. They heard about the players, both major and minor, the folks who had come from all over the state and even some from as far away as distant Norway; champions both old, new, and those waiting to be crowned. Some held back while others rushed to the front and pushed the pace harder than it had ever been pushed before.

The field was packed with sixty-five drivers; more than ever before. Most of them were going for the experience, but a small handful of them were out for blood. The man to beat was The Outdoorsman, last year's champion, and also the winner of the very first Great Race; he was a rugged competitor known as much for his crusty attitude as his ability to race. The Tinkerer, also a multiple time champion; this man hailed from the mountains of the Alaska Range, and he and his team had been hammered and forged at the very gates of the mighty Denali wilderness. The Woman, the driver whom many dismissed, but none to her face; it was she who had battled The Outdoorsman nearly to a draw between the banks of the Yukon River the year prior, and who had chased him like the devil from there to Nome in one of the most hotly contested race finishes in the history of the event. It was said that she had assembled a team of dogs that were near machinelike in their perfection, and that her goal this year was to shatter the overall speed record.

The Cowboy, a champion musher up from the ranchlands of Montana; The Silver Fox and The Whaler, both natives, one from the villages of the YK Delta, and one from a country so far to the north that God himself was rumored to turn his back on it come winter; both sly competitors and grizzled veteran of many a campaign. The Old Man, the one they called the father of the race; The Fisherman from the beaches of Seward; The Preacher and The Longhair. Some talk about The Norwegian whom had finished fifth place as a rookie the year before.

Of course there were others, but it was around this handful that the early talk revolved; The rivalry between The Outdoorsman and The Woman; Last year's mad dash to the interior by The Cowboy, the possibility of him trying it again; if there was weather on the coast, then maybe it would be the year for The Fox, or perhaps The Whaler. The Tinkerer, too, was known for his savvy ability to wait for the best moment to strike, husbanding his dogs' energy and unleashing it only after his rivals had wasted their teams on fruitless struggles to dominate the lead. And so on.

It came from the boys' radio in ragged bits and pieces, hour by hour, day by day, but to the boys, it played like one continuous narrative.

2

All the drivers safely to the first checkpoint at Eagle River, The Cowboy with the fastest time as usual. Trucks packed, a mad rush to Wasilla, and then chaos as the race officially restarted late on that first afternoon. Late that same night into the first checkpoint of Rabbit Lake, reports of heavy snowfall and punchy trail, The Cowboy is first in, followed quickly by The Woman and The Norwegian. Uncle, too, was one of the front runners. In a move of unprecedented aggression, The Norwegian does not even stop long enough to break a bale of straw, but instead continues on into the night. He is followed out much later in the early grey hours of predawn by The Outdoorsman, The Woman and The Whaler, and then by a steady trickle of drivers who were already behind the eight ball and desperate to catch up before the race had truly even begun.

The Norwegian is far out in the lead, stopping in Skwentna only long enough to make soup for his team, and then continuing on before the next team pulls in. There is a frantic pile-up of activity in Skwentna now as teams start to file in, The Cowboy the first of this group. Tragedy has struck back along the trail; The Woman is out of the race, her team massacred by a moose in a lonely stretch of forest. Four of her dogs are severely injured, and there would have been more but for The Outdoorsman who arrived and shot the beast with six shots from his .44 magnum.

How are the drivers feeling? reporters want to know.

'Tired, tired, and more tired.'

What do you think of The Woman's problems with the moose?

'Heartbreaking.'

What do you think about The Norwegian?

'He's pushing too hard. Way too hard.'

The Cowboy thinks that the man from Norway will be walking before he makes it to the interior, probably already is; this thought a consensus amongst the elite.

But he's so far ahead; you're not worried about that?

'It doesn't matter, his dogs will quit if he keeps pushing like that. Nobody can push like that and get away with it.'

Not even two days into the race, and already the competition is beginning to form up; The Norwegian already through the pass at Puntilla and down the craggy winding of the Dalzell; The Whaler, Preacher, Uncle and The Cowboy, are the next group struggling to make it over the summit in a vicious ground storm that has wiped the trail and knocked down markers, and it is The Outdoorsman who dominates here and leads the party into the checkpoint of Rohn, only to find that The Norwegian has long been gone and still with all of his dogs. The various drivers are getting spread out pretty thin, some drivers already into the interior Athabaskan village of Nikolai, while the tail enders are still struggling out of the steaming heat of the Matsu Valley. Uncle is somewhere near the front, The Fisherman and The Fox keeping company, but there is word that his sled has broken and that his dogs have caught sick. The Cowboy is the fastest and he is the one to give chase, perhaps realizing that The Norwegian is not really showing any of the signs of slowing that were forecast earlier, may even be speeding up in fact, seeming to never need rest.

The Tinkerer breaks from his own tradition and gives chase as well, but The Outdoorsman refuses, insisting that they are all fools and letting a train of panicked drivers on by before following in their wake. Uncle tries his best to hold on, but it is no use; as he drops dogs, he slips further and further behind until the reports seem to lose him altogether, and that part is over even with hundreds of miles to go.

The race reaches the halfway point at the long abandoned gold mining town of Iditarod, once home to a thriving crowd in need of saloons and saddlery, stock and supplies; now, long since dead. It is The Norwegian who takes this prize in the subzero hours of the early morn, bedding his full team and declaring his mandatory rest almost half a day before The Cowboy and The Tinkerer are to arrive.

'It is called the blitzkrieg my style of racing,' says the man from Norway when quizzed by reporters. His voice is softly lilting, but steely with confidence. 'I go slower than other teams, but need less rest.'

'You must be feeling pretty good,' The Tinkerer later says to him. 'You haven't seen us for the whole race 'til now. That's going to change.'

It has been fairly warm up until this point in the race; this changes with a howling wind that churns the trail over the foothills leading into Shageluck and turns the surface of the Yukon River into a storm blasted battleground with temperatures plummeting off of the mercury. It is here that teams and hearts begin to fail. As The Outdoorsman has predicted, to some degree at least, it has been foolish to chase after The Norwegian. He is unstoppable. Nobody knows how he is doing it, but as the other teams grow weak and tired, his seem to get stronger. The Cowboy and The Tinkerer fall back, their teams drastically diminished in both size and competence, and now The Outdoorsman re-passes them and it is he and The Whaler from the north-country who will give futile chase through the worst of Mother Nature's savagery.

From here on, there is very little racing being done; mushers are now concentrating primarily on survival, putting their heads down and one foot in front of the other and only looking up when absolutely unavoidable; frostbite and windburn, blown headlamp bulbs and sinking spirits; so long on the trail that the concept of civilization has become a faint joke, so far gone as to be unimaginable.

There is some word of Uncle, desperately holding onto the coattails of the top twenty, his team now a ragged band with only seven tired dogs left to pull the sled; still clawing and scraping with everything they had left to give.

The race reaches Kaltag in a howling windstorm, and then a harrowing passage to the checkpoint of Unalakleet on the wild Alaskan coastline. Now the real brutality of Mother Nature's fury is chronicled on visages made gaunt and pallid except for where the cold has burnt them to black. As The Norwegian makes his last push up this legendary coast, it is The Whaler who proves to be the last man standing at his back, perhaps the only man in the field who truly understands what it means to be tested by this vast, uncaring wilderness.

The Whaler runs behind his sled with his teeth bared in a burnished grin and his dogs are heroic in their pulling. But it is not enough. White Mountain looms just shy of Nome, and it is The Norwegian who reaches it first, as he has every checkpoint for the last nine hundred miles. It is this team from Norway that is first to breach the gold fields of Nome on a record pace in the afternoon of the second week, his dogs charging out of the storm and onto

Front Street looking as fresh as they had at the starting line so many days before. He has earned the gold of victory and the momentary stunned silence of his competitors.

He has won.

Next in and almost a full day behind is The Whaler. Then The Outdoorsman, with The Preacher and The Fisherman close behind. Weary. Wind burned. The Cowboy and The Tinkerer stagger to the finish, and then one by one and scattered over the space of a week, the racers tough enough to withstand the elements come on in to take their positions. Considering his problems, Uncle is lucky. He makes it to the finish in the last spot in the top twenty. It's not much, but there is a paycheck waiting to be cashed.

All in all, only a little over half of the starting field has survived the Great Race.

3

Uncle, Auntie and Little Cousin returned on a rain-blustery day near the end of March. Several nights before their coming, Uncle sent a message over the Bush Pipeline.

'Made it to Nome with Apache and Pilot in lead. Not much money, but we made a little. Be back in a few days.'

The boys had been on hard rations for the last two weeks. The weather had been so warm that all of the extra beaver meat had thawed, and The Boy didn't trust it but to feed to the dogs. The chickens had not laid an egg since December and their meager supply of powdered milk, Spam, Velveeta, and pasta had all been used up. They were down to one can of garbanzo beans and a few cups of boiled long grain rice per day.

Slick coated and sopping with wet, the team that trotted back into the yard numbered only sixteen; they had departed a month before with twenty two dogs in harness. When Uncle saw The Boy counting the dogs, his eyes hardened. He was freshly shaven, and his face was raw and peeling with windburn.

'Where's Apache and Pilot?' asked The Boy.

'Left them up in Nome,' Uncle said, starting as if to turn away.

'What do you mean you left them in Nome,' said The Boy, though he knew exactly what his uncle meant.

'Let me ask you something,' said Uncle, stopping in his tracks. 'Do you like to eat?'

'You said they got you there. They got you to Nome.'

'That's right. And that made them worth some money. Enough to buy food for your ungrateful belly.'

The Boy did not answer.

Uncle turned and disappeared inside the cabin, leaving the team for The Boy to unhook. He stood there for a long time with his heart choked up in the back of his throat and a red anger beating between his ears and rain running down his face. When he got this under control and his chores done, he went back inside. He could see rage on Aunties face when she looked at him, but he didn't care why, just stomped to the room he and his cousins shared. He could hear Auntie downstairs complaining about how dirty the house was… how he was like a swine at the trough, what the hell had they been doing all this time?

Later, when the lamps had come on and food and supplies unpacked, the mood was much lighter. The Boy sat in the shadows in the corner and listened as Uncle recounted the tale of his race with Auntie supplying details as if she had been the one standing on the runners, Little Cousin chiming in excitedly now and again. Dull red spots burned high on Middle Cousin's cheeks; a whole person now that his family had been reunited.

All The Boy could think about were his two lead dogs, and the misery of it made his arms and legs feel weighted as if by lead. Not one question had been asked of how the two of them had fared on their own these last weeks as the perishables ran out. Uncle had said that it was going to be different this year, but this is how it always was. The Boy knew that things would never change.

4

It had been warm for weeks. The creek had sloughed off much of its snowpack, and green overflow pooled in its channel. Water also collected on the surface of the river and an immense lead had opened up just past the water hole. The trees of the forest stood naked and shivering, stark without their coats of frost and snow. Limbs reached, trembled, waiting for the feel of spring's renewing touch.

Uncle stood on the brow of the hill, looking out over the Yentna and towards Mt. McKinley hovering in the distance. He was not the same man since he had come home from the race. Already lean before, he now looked like a figure configured from pipe-stems, and there was something brokenly stooped about the set of his shoulders. His face was nearly healed from the ordeal, but now it was as if all of the long days of winters worst cold could be seen leaking from the glacial blue of his eyes. He sighed often and sometimes muttered softly to himself words nobody else could quite make out, and he moved like a man twice his age, a slow dragging of steps and cautious trembling of hand. He turned from the view and shuffled back to the cabin, stood just inside the door blinking like an owl with his face in shadow. Auntie watched him, her expression a curious mix of longing and fear.

'We have to go,' said Uncle after a time. He spoke to no one in particular, though the entire family was gathered in the living area. 'We have to go to town. Breakup is going to be early, and it's going to be bad,' he continued. 'We don't have enough supplies to last through it.'

Nobody said a word, and Uncle just stood there blinking. Finally, he muttered something to himself and shuffled back out the door. Little Cousin started to titter, until he saw the look on his Mama's face, a face that held a lot of love for his Papa and not very much for anyone else.

They built a long sled from hewn cottonwood beams and two-by-fours cannibalized from the storage shed, covered it with pieces of scrap plywood and sheets of visqueen, and filled it with practically everything they owned. The barrel stove was left cold and empty, and boards with sixteen penny sinkers driven through were left over the door and windows to act as a deterrent to the four legged scavengers bound to come snooping.

They left in the early morning hours. Uncle and Auntie took the biggest team and load, Uncle on the front sled with the new sledge behind, Auntie on a third sled tethered with a braided mooring line. Little Cousin was safely lodged in his Mama's sled, barely a bump wrapped in towels and a sleeping bag. The Boy and Middle Cousin shared The Boy's training sled with a team of eight dogs pulling. Towed behind them in the water sled were hastily built crates of lathe and wire, containing a frantic assortment of Auntie's poultry, all gabbling and warbling at the top of their throats. The dogs were sullen and without animation as they pulled out of the yard in a slow train, a warm wind upon their faces and a colorless sky pressing down to all points of the compass.

As they left the creek mouth, The Boy looked over his shoulder at the collection of structures huddled on the hill, abandoned and dark and small. He turned away and never looked back.

5

The Boy marveled at how much the surface of the river had changed since his last trip to Rabbit Lake, back in February. Then, it had been a firm highway of packed dry snow and crusted drifts and islands of rough ice. Now, it was almost melted completely smooth. The snow pack had turned rotten, knee deep except for where the trail crossed the occasional sandbar, and there it was soggy and mixed with brown dirt, coffee colored pools of overflow lining the perimeters. There had been no snowmobile traffic for weeks, and The Boy understood that what they were doing right now, traveling on the thawing river like this, was a form of madness.

The assemblage traveled through this landscape at a crawl; the dogs heaving mightily in their traces and the passengers pumping and running next to the sleds, their boot-prints filling with gray slush as they did so. The sun that climbed into the eastern sky was yellow and buttery soft, and soon steam began to rise from sopping fur and drenched gear. The faint slurring of trail brought them to a place where a great open lead yawned across their path, its edges gleaming and dark, black water rippling along its length. Turning the teams around in a tangled cursing mess, they backtracked to a place where the floodplain along the riverbank came down gently to a sandbar, and there they tied the teams off.

Uncle took his saw and snowshoes, and with The Boy following, he set off through the alder thicket along the shore. It was late in the morning before the two of them had finished cutting and clearing a winding path around the obstacle, and when they made it back, they were both red faced and soaked with sweat. Taking the teams through the new cut was a tricky piece of business, and they had to stop numerous times to cut more of the tangled alder as the ganglines hung up on gnarled trunks and outthrust limbs. The bank letting back down to the river was not as gentle as the one leading up, and they were forced to disconnect the sleds and take them down one by one.

They continued on and soon came to another lead, this one not quite as wide as the first one, and with only some backtracking were able to get around it. By now the dogs were getting tired, and when they reached a miles long length of sandbar completely uncovered and sifting in a gentle breeze, Uncle signaled for a stop and they pulled the teams over next to the exposed trunk of a massive cottonwood tree left stranded from the summer before. Low clouds scudded in from the north and cast the land into shadow. They quickly became chilled sitting around in their soaked clothing, and Uncle got them all moving again before an hour had passed.

The older dogs that had been on the race with Uncle were doing fine with the chore of pulling the overloaded sleds through the mess, but the younger dogs were beginning to fail, coming off of their tug-lines and looking back repeatedly with ears planed out and tails sagging. The Boy watched these young dogs very closely, willing them to stay strong, sending his own energies out and into their bodies. The steel sled runners were grinding, barely moving in the sand. Middle Cousin was in the basket, too tired to walk, but not to chatter along about his observations. Uncle and Auntie were just ahead, off their sleds and pushing. The chickens were cooing and gently squawking. The taste of pennies suddenly flooded his tongue, faintly at first, and then much stronger. The dogs began to glow, first bright and sparkling, and then darkened to a contrast of blackish-blue. The sandbar became a stark white plate and electric lines of color began to pulse from the dogs. These colors became those of a prism, and they leapt and flickered in a tangled assortment, and now the taste of copper was so strong that he knew it wasn't copper at all but blood, and he heard his baby brother crying and his Mama calling to him and he was afraid.

Come back come back come back, his Mama called.

The pain that stole into his skull then was deafening, drowning out everything but the crashing of some awful surf.

Then the pain went away, and with it, the tapestry of colors. Uncle stood looking down on him with an expression of disgust stamped into the sharp plane of his face. The Boy sat up, head spinning. He looked around. The teams were stopped and Auntie had her two boys gathered up close in her arms and her eyes were turned away. Uncle stood with his arms cocked and his hands fisted and violence in the set of his shoulders. The Boy groaned, too weak to puzzle this out. When he looked down at the sand where he had fallen, he saw that some titanic battle had taken place. The ground was furrowed and torn and he realized that it was he who had transcribed those marks. Blood drizzled down from his nose and the sand drank it where it fell. He knuckled his mouth clean and got to his feet and went to check on his dogs. Nobody said a word, but Auntie made Middle Cousin ride with them once they started on their way again.

It was late in the day when they reached the end of the long sandbar, and at its ending was a long span of still brown water with clots of snow and frothy scum floating on its surface. It reached from bank to bank and went on for as far as they could discern. The sky was heavy, and bits of rain spat down in brief showers. They parked the teams in the shadow of a stand of willows, and gathered up a pile of wood broken from the branches of downed trees left scattered from last year's high water. As the fire rose and began to flare skyward, Auntie arranged a number of sharpened sticks over the flame and spitted chunks of Spam and canned ham onto them. She cleared a spot in the coals and placed a cast iron Dutch oven full of cold stew next to the smaller embers. As they hunkered down and ate, the eyes of the dogs glowed from the depths of the dark like a pack of wolves. Later, it began to rain in earnest. They slept under a tattered square of tarpaulin and listened to the rain beating inches from their faces—their collected body weight causing water to seep up through the ground underneath them, soaking the last of their dry gear and stealing all of their heat away.

By morning, Auntie and her sons were like shambling zombies, moving with a kind of stiff-legged jerkiness as they went about the task of breaking camp. It was still softly drizzling and all of them wore trash sack ponchos gathered about their waists and belted with extra rope from unused tug-lines. They pointed the teams downriver and marched them into the overflow. It was shin deep to the humans, but the dogs were pushing a wake with their chests, forced to bound with their heads and muzzles up, frantically looking for dry land. Uncle and The Boy were obliged to grab the double necklines of their leaders and trudge along in front, feet quickly numbing beyond feeling. The miles unspooled and the day wore into afternoon, and they came at last to a place where the overflow ended and the snow pack became firm. It was a narrow slough that lay mostly in shadow. They stopped briefly to change inserts in their boots and put on dry socks, then had a quick lunch of pilot bread and peanut butter. The rain had quieted down, but the bruised sky still loomed with the promise of more to come.

Sitting on the nose of his sled and slowly eating his makeshift sandwich with hands wrinkled and as white as a fishes belly, The Boy didn't notice Middle Cousin staring at him until the younger boy spoke.

'What's wrong with you?'

'I don't know,' said The Boy.

'Papa says you have the epilepsy. That's it's going to cost us a lot of money.'

The Boy considered this, threw the last of his sandwich to the wheel dogs. 'Since when did Uncle ever spend any money on me?' he finally asked. 'Or you, for that matter?'

Middle Cousin looked down. 'Does it hurt?' he asked

'Does what hurt?'

'The epilepsy, dumb ass.'

'Yes. It gives me a terrible headache; like my head is going to bust open and my brains are going to come out. But mostly, it just feels…' The Boy trailed off, unable to put into words what he is feeling.

They sat together for a while, both aware of the sound of Uncle and Auntie murmuring to one another from where they too sat on their sleds.

'Mama and Papa don't like you much,' offered Middle Cousin.

'You think I don't know that?'

Middle Cousin shrugged helplessly. 'What I mean is, I don't feel the same way is all. I'm just trying to say that I think you're alright, and I don't care if there's something wrong with you or not.'

The Boy snorted laughter, ruffled the younger boy's hair. 'Yeah, I guess you're alright, too,' he said.

6

The slough brought them most of the way to the confluence where the Yentna and the Big Su came together. When they emerged back onto the river, they found a surface of clean wet ice covered with only an inch of overflow. Small holes were opening up all over and slow water came from these in sluggish fountains. They skirted a series of sandbars with leads opening from their tails and along their sides, and finally came to the great widening of the two rivers. The trail before them was a greenish track through knee deep slush and surrounded by a sea of rippling gray, all of it rotten and settling underfoot. It was getting dark again, and off in the distance lights twinkled from the window panes of Susitna Station.

A gap opened in the clouds above and a multitude of stars peered through and blinked down at them; the Pleiades, Cassiopeia. They toiled and splashed, and took out their headlamps and switched them on, and the weak light was bounced back at them from a hundred surfaces. Later, the sky burned clean and a low fog crept up from the morass as the temperature dipped below the freezing point. Auntie and the two younger boys couldn't take the cold any longer, and had to be wrapped into blankets and hauled in the sleds. The Boy did not know how he was going to take it much longer himself, for his feet and legs were wet up to the crotch and beginning to go numb. His breath came out in long, moist plumes. He lost sight of the station in the fog—even Uncle's headlamp beam was a will-o-the wisp flickering just ahead, but seemingly miles away. A sickle moon climbed the ladder of stars and grinned down at them from a posting at the foot of the great bear. The sounds of the sleds being pulled was like a wheelbarrow pushing through gravelly mud and the dogs breath seemed to be magnified to the amplitude of a piece of farm machinery.

Susitna Station emerged from the fog like an alien mothership and the dogs were at the bank before they even knew that it was there. The man who owned the station stood on the bank's lip holding a lantern and looking down at them.

'Is that you?' he called to The Boy.

'Aye. We're hoping we could stay the night?' The Boy called back.

'Do your chores, but send up the little ones so they can warm up in the house.'

The two youngest and Auntie climbed the steep bank on tottering legs and disappeared into the light while Uncle and The Boy secured their teams in the dirt which lay exposed from the crumbling over-hang. They fed the dogs a meal of dry kibble mixed with slush. After this, Uncle started up the bank, than looked back at The Boy with his headlamp.

'You coming?' he asked.

'I'll be up in a minute. I've got something to do,' said The Boy.

Uncle's shrug said suit yourself and he left without another word.

The Boy stood in the cold and the dark, shivering almost uncontrollably. With his light off, he could see the stars reflected from the glimmering sheet of overflow and the moon floating within it like an amber smile. He stripped off his parka, then his shirts and sweater, and stood half naked at the edge. His teeth began to chatter helplessly inside the framework of his jaw and he waded into the water until it reached up to his knees and became slick underfoot. He bent over at the waist and plunged the crown of his head into the frigid water and the shock of it nearly pole axed him. He began to knead his sopping hair and to scoop handfuls of slush against his armpits. He considered taking down his pants and having a go at his privates, but quickly discarded this notion, for he was already panting and almost incoherent with pain. He got back up on dry ground and fumbled his clothing back over his too long hair already frozen into a crackling mop atop of his skull. He was still dripping and shuddering with cold when he made his way into the cabin, and even though he tried to sneak unnoticed into some dark corner, all conversation immediately stopped.

'What the hell happened to you?' the man of the house asked him, incredulous. His wife just stared with her mouth hanging open.

'I just cleaned up a little,' The Boy mumbled into the carpet.

'Holy hell!'

The house was lit by small electric lights hanging from a wire running down the length of the living room, and the smells of wood smoke mixed pleasantly with those of the evenings cooking's. The Boy gratefully accepted a bowl of chili and mug of hot apple cider, and as he consumed these, his trembling subsided. He tried not to look around the house for the girl, but could not help himself. She sat across the table from her parents. Her eyes were on him, fathomless and unblinking. The elders talked on into the night, but The Boy took no notice, all he could think of was the girl and her dark hair, her smell of summer and clean growing things.

They slept on the floor under warm blankets with their clothes drying by the fire, and in the morning drank a pot of fresh coffee with a hearty breakfast of smoked sausage and scrambled eggs. They saddled up the teams, and as The Boy prepared to follow Uncle down the Susitna, the girl approached him and put her hand on his arm. She leaned her face very close to his.

'I know who you are,' she said, and these were the only words he had ever heard her utter. She kissed him softly on the cheek, then turned and walked away.

7

Three more days of blazing heat, alternating with freezing rain, got them to the landing on the Susitna Delta. The trip was much the same as it had been coming down the Yentna; overflow, opening leads and rotting ice; trails hacked along the bank to get around open stretches of river channel. Their food was down to almost nothing, and they'd had to slaughter some of the chickens. They trotted up and off of the melting ice and onto the long gravel ramp to the muddy parking lot where all the river rats parked their town vehicles, a motley collection of trucks, campers, beat up Econolines and old rusted cars. They strung the dogs out in the scrubland along the borders and Uncle went to warm up his old pickup truck.

The Boy stood blinking in the sunlight, turning in a slow circle, trying to remember how long it had been since he had been here last, here in civilization. A number of small buildings, some with placards and bright markings; a porch with some strangers in shorts and t-shirts who watched them in wary disbelief; a narrow dirt road exiting out of sight through a forest of tall birch and stately cottonwood; gravel and mud, trucks and a motley assortment of boats with outboard motors on trailers, all tarpaulined off for the winter.

Here is where town begins, The Boy knew.

Had it been years? Could it have been? He gave up the thought, walked down to the river. He knelt at its edge where the overflow met the earth. Their backtrail was a fading line of bubbles and floating slush, a faint scratching where the ice yet held. He reckoned that the ice might grip for a few more days, but winter was over and spring would soon have its say.

He thought then of many things, hunkered down like that with his gaze on the rippling water. Ice and snow and blowing cold and traps filled with the animals of the wild. The dogs and the miles, the feeling of well being that only filled him when he was on the runners behind them. The girl and her kiss which still burned like fire.

But mostly he thought of his long lost Mama and his little baby brother.

Come back, she had called. *Come back.*

I'm coming, Mama, he thought. *I'm coming.*

Dog Man

Chapter VI

1

M ANY seasons have passed since last we have seen The Boy, and he is now sixteen years of age. He has remained a ragged scarecrow of a figure, and his path is one that is both dark and littered with obstacles. Though he is still strange and awkward, his will has been forged into an instrument of iron and his knowledge of dogs has become great. He has spent the last four years honing his skills as a musher in junior racing, and has now come late in January to the barren tundra of Alaska's YK Delta to participate in his first professional sled dog race, the legendary K300. Racing against children has proved itself no real challenge for him, and the time has come to test his metal against some of the best professional mushers in the world.

2

When it is nearly full dark, they came for The Boy and his dogs; they had been sheltered beneath the floor of the Bethel college dormitory for the last several days, and now watched silently as their escorts arrived. Two Yupik Indians driving a beater Ford with sidewalls more rusted lace then clean metal. One of them sat in the cab with a foot on the peddle to keep the engine from stalling while the other shucked his mittens and scrambled like a hunch back amongst the concrete pylons footed against the deck of the building. Together, he and The Boy handed the dogs along, one by one, until the truck bed was full of wagging tails and open grinning mouths, and the sun's last rays refracted bronze plating across the land. The sled, bag, and gear were heaved right into the mix, and The Boy jumped up after and squatted in the cold surrounded by his mates.

Neither of the men offered to stay in the back with him, and he reckoned this to be a wise choice as they wound their way through the tangle of streets and side ways, between snow-berms with granular spray leaping in quick riffles from their crests and shuttered dwellings with fingers of light showing in fits of yellow and orange from gaps in their window casings.

The Kuskokwim is waiting for us, thought The Boy.

The truck popped and rattled and thrashed through town, and as they made their way, a plethora of taxi cabs shrouded in muffler exhaust and couples on the backs of snowmobiles stood aside to watch their passing. Soon, the last of the buildings were behind them and they were descending a steep embankment and their tires were crunching bare ice. The dark length of the fabled river yawned before them like the mouth of an abyss. An island of twinkling lights waited further on in the black, and that is where they headed now. There were trucks parked all over and people scattered and milled about with the harried energy of a carnival crowd. Their's was not the only truck-bed loaded with a freight of canine athletes, and they now pulled in between two other such rigs and took their place over a number spray painted onto the river ice.

The wind was picking up, and combined with the temperature, was cold enough to freeze bodily fluids before they could touch the ground. A fog of steam and exhaust was forming in tatters and dogs were beginning to whine in anticipation. A senseless gabble of voices overlapped and intertwined and at the far side of the staging area, a man on a podium tried the loudspeakers. Pennants flapped along guy-wires, and a steady stream of traffic poured by against the opposite bank along the road known by the locals as the Ice Highway.

The Boy jumped out of the truck, and from the moment his heavy boots touched the surface of the Kuskokwim, he knew that he would find his strength here. Moving quickly to keep his body heat up, he hauled out the sled and arranged it to point towards the outgoing chute. Only when he was finished preparing his lines and tack did he take a moment to check his time or survey the crowd for the faces of his competitors. His two guides leaned against the truck and rolled smokes.

The Whaler sauntered up in a cloud of steam. His broad brown face was bare and split to show a mouthful of square teeth seeming to leap from the framework of his jaws. 'Well, what do you say? You ready to freeze your butt off?' he asked.

'Yes,' acknowledged The Boy. 'Are you?'

The Whaler shrugged, looked over his shoulder at the press of mushers and bystanders shuffling and milling about. 'More ready than them.'

The Boy grinned. 'Aye, me too.'

'Let's take a walk.'

Side by side, they walked until the island of light was at their back. They stood facing into the wind and darkness, their boots firmly planted in the middle of the outgoing trail, and it was like no trail The Boy had ever been confronted with before. There was not one speck of snow anywhere, as far as he could tell, just a series of deep marks and wavering scratches going in every direction; imprinted upon the naked ice by studded snowmobile tracks and chained up four-wheeler tires. A faint star glimmered, faded, a reflective marker about two hundred yards out, lying on its side by the look of it. The cold knifed through his parka and began gnawing at his core.

'Nothing for the leaders to follow,' he remarked, and this made The Whaler laugh. 'How many markers do you think are left standing out there?'

'Not many,' said The Whaler, and laughed again. 'And those you won't be able to spot anyway, so they don't matter.'

'Why not?'

'Because of all of the headlights coming from traffic on the Ice Highway, right at your face. Too bright to see the reflectors.'

'So, how will we know which way to go?'

The Whaler shrugged again. 'Listen,' he said. 'Nobody follows the trail. You just go up the river and make sure to stay between the banks and not pass up the checkpoints.'

'Sounds easy.'

'It will be easy. For me, anyway.'

They extinguished their headlamps and squatted down together in the dark. The Whaler produced a strip of muktuk wrapped in stained butcher paper and a small mason jar of murky seal oil. The Boy yanked his cutter from the sheath at his side and cut hunks for both of them. They dipped the whale fat into the sediment at the bottom of the jar and ate it with greasy fingers. The Whaler carved himself another long piece and as he chewed, he pointed with the tip of his own long bladed cutter back at the proceedings under the harsh glow of fluorescent spotlights.

'You see them,' he said. 'What do you see about them, the ones racing?'

'They look cold,' The Boy answered. He was cold too, but already feeling the warmth of the fat spreading from his belly and giving new energy to his limbs.

'What else do you see?'

The Boy scanned the montage, some found, and others strange. 'They look out of place, worried. Some of them are scared,' he said after a time.

'Scared of what?'

The Boy shrugged. 'What's out in the dark, on the ice. What's out on the trail, up the river.'

The Whaler grinned and his naked teeth glinted with oil. 'We're out here in the dark. We're out here on the trail,' he pointed out.

The Boy stared at this savage, this mentor.

'Run and be true. Trust your dogs.' The Whaler told him. He gestured up the river. 'You were born to this, and the river knows you to be a friend. You know its ways, and there is respect. It will help you even while it's working to crush your enemies.'

'My enemies?'

'Everybody racing against you; everybody who would choose to place their hopes and dreams before yours. Yes, your enemies.'

The Boy considered this, and took another hunk of muktuk. 'Well. If you are to be my enemy,' he said, finally. 'I sure hope that you'll still share your seal oil with me out there. I forgot to bring mine.'

The Whaler laughed like this was the funniest thing that he had ever heard, and clapped The Boy on the shoulder with a hand cast from iron.

Together they rose from the ice and made their way back to their respective teams. The time had come to start harnessing up.

The time had come to race.

***

Before that moment in January on the bleak tundra of the YK Delta, came the rain and mud of earlier that September and a boy who was near the end of his rope.

He stood next to the open door of the truck cab looking up into the drizzle at where he knew the Petersville Mountains to be. All he could make out was a suggestion of rumpled hillside hidden within the gray clouds scudding just above the tree tops. Confronting him was the prospect of a narrow rutted track with a small river of brown water coursing down its glistening length. Old furred trees leaned in close from both sides, and a dense undergrowth of fiddlehead fern, devil's club, and cranberry bushes encroached with rough intent. The Boy's truck, an aged Chevy flatbed appointed with crude plywood sidewalls, was loaded full and covered with a shiny blue tarpaulin. The tires were bald and its engine clattered and wheezed like an old asthmatic. Attached at the bumper was a swaybacked trailer with a rickety dog kennel built along its topside. From this box came the sounds of dogs whining and grumbling, panting and barking, all wanting to be let out to play. Behind the boxes was the awkward shape of the Honda Odyssey, cinched down with ratchet straps and various bits of rope and line.

The Boy climbed back inside the cab and pulled the door shut against squealing hinges. It wouldn't close all of the way, but instead hung askew in its frame with rainwater pouring in through the gaps in its seal. He put the transmission back into gear and sent the truck lurching forward in a cloud of spent fuel and thrown oil. Lopsided windshield wipers worked fruitlessly to keep the windscreen clear, but only succeeded in smearing it into a senseless blur. Behind the truck, the trailer bounced from one side of the track to the other, foundering in the deep trenches cut by decades of four-by travel. He could feel the truck bogging down, and he gave it more gas from which it responded sluggishly.

All through the afternoon, he wound his way deep into the hills and through the slopping muck which reached up to the floorboards at times. Near dark, he finally reached a point where the truck could not go any further, but simply spun its tires in a raging froth of gravel and slurred mud. Gradually, he let off the gas pedal and the engine immediately stuttered and fell silent. For a long while, he just sat there with water coming in around his feet and heavy rain pounding the roof and spraying against his left shoulder. He stared out the blurred windscreen and his face was a pale oval in the gloom. Very slowly, he let his body sag forward and his head slump to rest on the cold plastic cover of the steering wheel. His body shook, small trembles at first, and then ragged, uncontrolled quaking.

No matter how far he drove, or how fast, he could not outrun the memories: that last day with Uncle and Auntie; the words spoken in a red anger that led to blows; the blood on his face and Uncle's hands and the rage and hatred twisting Auntie's mouth; his cousins, both cowering from that last explosive scene; he, a pale raggedy man fleeing from a world that was as strange to him as he was to it, fleeing from the jeering and the laughter and the cruel jokes concerning his clothing, his face, his inability to just fit in.

And the seizures, they were becoming more frequent, as were the things that they were showing him…

He sat with his head bowed for a long time, and when he finally raised his face, he saw that it was full dark and that the rain had stopped. He switched on the headlights and pushed open the door. When he got out, he found himself in cold, muddy water up to his crotch. He had his flashlight, and he now trained it along the length of the trailer, noting that the trailers' wheels were still thankfully on solid ground. He moved the beam in a large semi-circle to explore his surroundings, saw that there were graveled pullouts to either side, both bordered by impenetrable forest and dense stands of coarse shrubbery. Plenty of spots to anchor off tether lines for the dogs to get them out of their boxes.

He set about unloading buckets full of rusted chain and hauling them across the road, stringing their lengths between several likely birches and attaching cable tensioners to take up the slack. He pulled the dogs out, one by one, and carried them through the water, then led them to spots on the picket. They were all panting and eager, expecting to be harnessed and hooked up to go for a run. There were fourteen altogether, and when they were all safely unloaded and howling to be fed, he unpacked the feeding equipment and bags of dry kibble. There was a jerry can with fresh water in the bed of the truck, and he used this to mix up a solid meal for the group, and stood watching through the yellow beam of his flashlight as they went heads down in there stainless steel pans and gulped the food with unrestrained savagery. When they were finished, their eyes shined back at him like bright red sparks, eager for more food. He turned one of the feed buckets upside down on the ground, and as he sat, it began to rain again, fat icy drops instantly soaking him through to the core. He opened a can of chili with a church key he kept in his wallet and ate it cold while water ran down his face and dripped from the point of his chin.

It was a fireless camp, and in the end, he folded himself into a spare tarp and lay awake for most of the night on the mud listening to the drizzle pound and crackle above his face and thinking on days past. He wondered where the girl from Susitna Station was right now, and if she thought of him, too, when she lay down on her bed. He hoped that her sleeping arrangement was more comfortable than his, and this thought made him laugh out loud. It was funny, for had he not been responsible in picking his own bed? Whether it was one cold and hard, or one soft and warm, was a simple matter of his own free choice, and he was sleeping exactly where he chose. Besides, why should she think of him at all? He had nothing she would want, nothing he could give her. He would banish her from his thoughts, he decided. It would be only he and his dogs…and the ghosts.

4

He was up before the sun could do more than render the day in tones of dark gray. It had quit raining shortly before dawn, and the ground still bubbled and seethed with the liquid streaming from its pores. The sky was murky with low clouds, but they could be seen breaking up in the east where a mountain reared from the countryside and lumbered off to the north. It was darkly furred with timber, and its top disappeared in the mists. All around lay a dense forest of gnarled white birch and spruce shaggy with moss, most of whose trunks were creased and tracked with long streamers and flows of amber.

The dogs were curled up sleeping, and ravens could be heard gobbling in the distance. The Boy sat on his tarp listening and watching. The sound of dogs barking to be fed came from the north. More dogs sounded faintly from a westerly direction. He knew this to be dog country, that being the reason he had been directed to come to this locale in the first place. Somewhere in these hills The Old Man, the father of the Great Race, kept a kennel, supposedly the largest in the world.

His truck and trailer still hogged the middle of the narrow road, doors open and cab flooded. There were pullouts to either side, and one of these hosted a short series of trucks and battered cars, all four-wheel drive. One of these was a one-ton pick-up with a tremendous double layer dog box all lacquered and trimmed with fancy painted grillwork on its doors. 'Trapper Creek Kennels' said a placard on its tail.

The Boy got up stiffly, stretching and passing water. His dogs were still sleeping curled in tight balls, but he noticed that Titan's head was up and pointed right at him. The dog's body was tense and ready to spring to attention; The Boy looked back at him and slowly shook his head. Titan let out a brief sigh and lowered his muzzle to his paws and closed his eyes.

The Boy walked up the road a bit, his leather work boots sodden and squelching in the mud. The track was little more than a bottom-less quagmire, and it was obvious that there would be no continuing along it with his truck, assuming he could even get it unstuck. The old forest quickly thinned to a screen of stunted black spruce, and then gave way completely to a vast, open swamp of tundra and low swale. Its surface shimmered with pools of stagnant water and small birds fluttered and raced across islets sprinkled within its span. The far eastern horizon yellowed, and then flared orange, and steam leapt from the countryside as the sun's rays touched upon it. Overhead, the clouds scudded away to reveal the foothills of the Petersville Range in a rough tapestry of russet and charcoal. Further up, the slopes were craggy snow capped rock and loose gray shale. The wind was fair, but coming from the north, and winters first frost could be felt whispering on its breath. On the far side of the swamp, a cow moose and her yearling calf came into the open and hesitated, brown dots in the distance. They milled along the edge, and then slowly began to wade into the open expanse of marsh.

He turned back the way he had come and surveyed the borders at the forest's edge. The trees were gathered in a dense barrier and he knew that they would protect a camp from the wind, should he care to place one deep enough within their fold. He waded a few paces into the swamp, but found the standing water to be too brackish for drinking, and probably loaded with giardia to boot. He needed water that would not freeze all the way through once winter hit.

He followed the outlying scrub of black spruce for several hundred yards before turning into the forest to beat his way through the tangle of willow and alder. He pressed on until the brush thinned, and soon found himself in a narrow grassy glade with dead brown fiddleheads reaching up to his thighs, and a shallow stream trickling along its length. He looked in the direction that the clear water flowed from, and was pleased to note that it came from the direction of the parking area where his truck sat buried.

5

His team was mostly made up of two litters, both descending from the same lines which had produced Uncle's old gentleman leader Golo. A rangy group of yearlings for the most part; thick furred, rawboned and filled to the brim with youthful energy. So far, there were three seasoned leaders in the bunch, Titan, Legend and Halo, but he was hoping to train more as the season progressed. He watched them now, all waking up and stretching their long legs. They looked fast and tough, prideful creatures with not a spare ounce of fat to be found anywhere on their bodies. He could go anywhere with these dogs, and he greatly looked forward to doing so.

Sweating as the sun climbed to its zenith and shone down upon his labors, The Boy unloaded the cargo from the flatbed and hauled it into the bushes off to the side of the parking area. He dug and slopped mud with a wood handled spade until he was able to crawfish under the truck far enough to wrap heavy chains around the rear tires, then dig a channel to further let the muddy water out of the lagoon. It took a long grinding of the starter to get the engine sputtering to life, and when he applied gas, the tires spun and shot the chains into the trees. Cursing while he went to retrieve them, he got them back on, but found that the battery was dead when he leaned into the cab and cranked the key. He stood there, muttering obscenities until he could think of no more. He fumbled with muddy hands to pop the hood, but it refused to open. He stared at it for a while, not knowing what to do; the highway and Trapper Creek were twenty hard miles back the way he had come, and there was little hope of summoning a tow to this wilderness remove.

A truck engine could be heard rumbling in the distance, coming from the direction of the highway about two miles off. He reckoned that with the shape that the road was in that it might be as much as ten minutes before they arrived. He fished around in a battered green ammo box that served as his tool catchall until he found several long screwdrivers with which he started back to work on the hood. After digging around for a few minutes and twisting and tearing at the metal bracket holding it shut, he managed to mangle it open with a dull screech of tortured metal. He had the hood propped up and the jumper cables out when the truck drove into view at the end of the parking area; a battered reddish brown Ranger with oversized mud-tires and two dark shapes silhouetted in its interior.

The driver of the vehicle hesitated upon spotting the Chevy in his path, than gunned around in a rooster tail of brown water and gobbets of muck. The Ranger sped off toward the open swamp country without slowing. The Boy watched them go, and then turned back to where his dogs sat panting in the shade. He was offering them fresh creek water in their dishes when he heard the rumble of the Ranger's engine returning. He walked back to the truck and rummaged out his fixed blade from a pile of dirty clothing on the seat. Listening to the engine growling its approach, he carefully threaded the holster through his belt and secured it around his waist, making sure to shrug into his shirt and let the tail fall down over the cutter. He leaned in, and pulled the bulk of the .41 Magnum out from its hiding place behind the seat and put it up on top of the vinyl covering where he could more easily get his hand on it. He pulled a soiled rag over it as the Ranger came back into view and stopped about a hundred yards away.

The truck sat there idling for a long while. The Boy could make out the dim shape of a rifle hanging from a rack behind the vehicle's occupants. Minutes ticked by and the smell of cigarette smoke drifted on the light breeze. As if on cue, the driver and passenger doors suddenly popped open and two big men stepped out. They were both bearded and wearing faded army surplus, and one of them had a big pistol in a shoulder rig. The other, the shorter of the two, chugged the last of a can of beer and tossed it to the ground. They both came strolling towards him, and then halted about fifty feet off. Now that they were closer, The Boy decided that the shorter man was also armed, but kept his piece pushed around to his back.

'Hey, Pirate, you know you're blockin' the road?' the taller one called. His eyes were little and piggy and food was crusted in the tangle of his beard. He wore a bush hat pulled down low that made his ears stick out. His friend, shorty, started to drift over towards the dogs.

'Yes, I know. I ran into some trouble,' The Boy acknowledged.

'The only trouble I can see is that you're blockin' the road.'

The dogs were all standing and had their hackles up. They sensed their master's emotions, and all of them suddenly erupted in a furious barking frenzy which startled Shorty nearly out of his muck boots.

The Boy half turned towards Shorty, making sure to keep the open door between himself and the other man doing the talking.

'Mister,' he said. 'It doesn't seem like my dogs like you much. Maybe you should back off.'

'Obscenity your dogs, man!' Shorty snarled, backing away from the tether line with his hand at the small of his back.

'Truck's in the way and your dogs are a menace!' the taller man said, his tone holding loud amusement.

'Maybe you guys should just get a move on,' said The Boy.

'You're sticking awful close to that truck, Pirate. What you got in there? A gun? You got a gun in there, Pirate?'

The Boy shook his head. 'What do you guys want? I'm kind of busy here.'

'It doesn't look like you're too busy, kid. It looks like you got your thumb in your rear to me.'

'What do you want?' The Boy repeated. Shorty was drifting further around to his blind side which would ensure that he could not watch them both at the same time. This was beginning to make him very nervous.

'We want you to get your obscenity of a rig out of our way. Pirate.' said the taller man. He put one greasy thumb to the side of his nose and blew a long green streamer of snot onto the ground. 'Hey, you want a beer?' he suddenly offered.

The Boy turned slightly, tracking Shorty. 'No, I don't want a beer,' he said. He started to slide the Magnum out of its holster under the rag, gently easing the hammer back to full cock. Neither man could see his hands, but they both froze just the same.

'I want you two to leave so I can get my truck out of the road,' The Boy said.

Shorty regarded him through bloodshot eyes and idly folded his arms and started scratching at his elbows. He began nodding as if The Boy had uttered something of the utmost profundity. He abruptly turned on his heel and strode back to the Ranger. The taller man smiled sadly and shook his finger at The Boy, then joined his buddy.

He turned with his hand on the doorpost. 'Hey Pirate,' he called back.

'Yeah.'

'What you doin with all those dogs?'

'They're racers. We're going on a circuit this winter. That's why we're here. To train.'

'Good luck kid.' They loaded up and turned the Ranger around in a tight u-turn and sped off across the swamp.

The Boy and his dogs watched them go and listened to the sounds of their engine until they could hear it no longer.

Chapter VII

1

THE Boy set up a rough camp in the woods below the parking area. A stripped pole of slender spruce tied off between the trunks of two birch trees, with a large blue tarp thrown over and staked at the corners, served as his shelter. He cut down armloads of shaggy spruce boughs and used them to plug one end of the crude structure, blocking it off somewhat from the elements. Just in front, he fashioned a shallow fire pit and lined it with large stones taken from the stream, making sure to build it high in the backside and leaving its face open to bounce heat back into the sleeping area. Over this went a blackened grill scavenged from some long abandoned barbeque. He moved the dogs down into the trees and wound their tether lines around several hairy trunks that would keep the worst of the wind and snow off of them. As he cut down extra boughs to use as bedding for the dogs, he kept one ear out for motors going by on the road, but heard nothing for the rest of the afternoon.

The day passed, and as the sun set, he got a fire going and made a pot of black coffee and heated chili in a cast iron skillet. He sat eating and drinking with his feet to the coals and the team quietly keeping watch, his wet clothing from the night before drying on a line. In the distance, he heard a great many dogs erupt in a din of barking. This lasted for a long while, and then subsided, and later his own dogs broke into mournful song. When he turned in for the night, he brought Titan and Halo into the shelter and let them bed down at the foot of his sleeping bag. Sometime in the hours of darkness, they both migrated up to the head and bracketed him with their warm furry bodies.

2

It rained through the night, and still a light drizzle fell from an early morning's slate-gray sky. All fourteen of the dogs were hooked up and screaming to go while The Boy strolled back and forth along the gangline with his steaming coffee mug in hand. Titan and Halo, brother and sister, were both in the lead and leaping into the air as far as their tugs would allow them to go. Legend was in the swing next to a young male named Caliber. The three older dogs had started out with him as yearlings, too, but were now battle hardened vets of three seasons tasked with the tough job of teaching all of the crazy yearlings how to behave. They were all attached to the Odyssey, a rugged little dune buggy crossed with a go-cart and converted into a sturdy fall training rig for the dogs to pull around before the sled season began. It had four fat tires and a steel roll cage encasing the driver and 250cc engine. It rode low to the ground, putting the operator in an uncomfortable sitting position at eye level with a dog's rear end, and his legs pointed straight forward into a thin plastic cowling.

The Boy took his time and petted each dog on the head and murmured soft words. He squatted down in front of the leaders and let each one of them enthusiastically bathe his cheeks and rub their faces against his chest. The energy coming off the team was like a crackling flow of electricity, and he did not want to let them go until they had calmed a bit. In his experience, he had found that this early cart training was some of the most critical work that he could do with his team to prepare them for a tough winter of grueling training runs, and teaching them all how to cool down and take things easy was one of the most important lessons that he could teach.

Once they had quit barking and patiently stood there for few minutes with their heads cocked expectantly watching him, The Boy climbed down into the Odyssey and released the parking brake. The dogs took off in a rush, but slowed down to a trot once they felt the light flutter of braking coming up the line, and by the time they reached the swamp they were well under control. With a dog team, it was easy to travel through the stew of mud and fermented tundra moss. Titan and Halo picked their way through to the shallower areas, and the Odyssey floated over the slop of muck he couldn't steer around. They left the swamp and entered a forest on the far side, and here the ground firmed to compacted mud and the occasional large rock. Shortly after, the trail forked, and he called *gee* for the leaders to take the right branching which pointed to the foot of the distant mountain range. The forest was broken with open fields and swamps, and soon they found themselves back into rutted bog. From up ahead came the sound of a diesel engine rumbling slowly along, surely a large generator. Once they cleared a thin line of scrub birch, he could make out a large log structure with a graveled parking lot and a number of rundown outbuildings.

The Boy called *whoa* and locked up the brakes and steered to the side of the road, careful to plant the front right corner of the cart on a large rock jutting out of the ground. The dogs fanned out and began marking their spots and chewing tufts of withered grass. Legend immediately began to dig at the ground like a beast, sending a storm of dirt clods flying from his hind feet to scatter the Odyssey's cab and occupant.

The Boy observed that the road forked again at the parking lot; one fork mounting a steep climb and disappearing into rugged hills in the direction of the Petersville Range. The other veered off to the left and dropped down into a deep ravine, both banks connected by an ancient bridge of rusted steel girders and creosote-coated beams. Water rumbled beneath, and on the far side the road could be seen climbing out of the gorge and winding its way up to the hill land in the south. To The Boy's left gentled a narrow valley of open grassy fields bordered by old forest, also extending in a southerly direction, its ending too far away to properly make out. A haze of wood smoke colored the air, and he sensed that the road he had passed earlier must trace its border. He had never before been in this country, but he knew something about it from hearing other musher's talk; there would be a number of kennels located that way, all hidden in the folds of surrounding forest. Up in the nearby mountains were an assortment of long abandoned gold shafts and claims from a bygone age, the Petersville gold mine being chief among them.

He tied off the team just behind the leaders and dropped all of their tug-lines, throwing each of them a chunk of raw hamburger in the process. He watched them as they all gulped it down and began frantically sniffing the ground for more. Once they settled down in the weeds, he trooped down to the lodge. Titan and Halo came with him, running free to describe loose orbits around his position as he walked. There were a motley crew of all-terrain vehicles pulled up in front, and when he entered through a heavy plank door, he found a low ceilinged lounge gloomy from shuttered windows and dampened light fixtures. Soft music was issuing from a jukebox in the corner, and cigarette smoke thickened the air. A rough looking group of men sat hunched and scowling from a table covered with dirty dishes and empty beer glasses. They stopped talking and stared at him. Behind the bar was a thickset woman in her middle years with trembling hands and hung-over eyes. She smiled at him when he chose a stool at the bar.

'So you're the one everybody's talkin about,' she said in a rusty voice. She shook a slender brown cheroot from a pack and lit it with a steel zippo, dragging deep and slowly letting out a long blue cloud.

'People are already talking?' asked The Boy.

'What did you expect, hon? Some kid leavin' his rig plumb in the road and settin' up camp like a hobo right there in the barrow.'

The Boy shrugged. 'My truck died. I'd be happy to move it if someone would give me a jump.'

'Those your dogs?'

'Yes ma'am.'

She studied him while she smoked. The corneas of her eyes were thick and yellow and he could hear liquid burbling softly down in her chest.

'Well?' she prompted.

'Ma'am?'

'Just what are you plannin' to do with those dogs?'

'I'm a musher. I'm training them up to go race on the Kuskokwim and along the Alyeska Pipeline.'

'A musher. Ain't you a little young to be on your own?'

The Boy shrugged. The woman didn't seem to care whether he replied or not.

'There's been dog mushin' goin' on in this country for years,' she said. 'My Mama used to run a trapline all the way to the Yenlo Hills and down into Skwentna, if you can believe it. The Old Man lives just a few miles back on the Trapper Creek trail. He's been mushin' since before I was born. Mama knew him when she was just a little girl, knee high to grasshopper, and she said when he first got goin' it had nothing to do with racin', it was all about freightin' gold and fur out of the hills. He didn't start the Great Race until he was way along on his career. He's the one as got Mama started into dogs herself. Mama's real old now, doesn't have much time left. Hasn't had dogs for a real long time.'

'Well.' The Boy could think of nothing else to say.

The woman's eyes refocused on him. 'Hon, you plannin' to set up camp for the winter?'

'Yes ma'am. That's the plan.'

'This is hard country. Especially for a boy.'

'I can take care of myself alright.'

'Yeah, hon? Tell me, why do you wear that patch?'

'I lost my eye when I was little,' he said. He started to slide off the stool.

'You hungry, hon? I can have the cook whip you up some bacon and eggs if you are.'

He shook his head. 'I don't have any money.'

'This one time it's on the house.'

He sat back down and the barmaid disappeared into the back. He turned on the stool to glance at the men who were talking to each other in low voices and giving him hard looks. They were a bearded, woodsy lot with heavy woolen caps and carhart bibs and mud-thickened work boots. One of them had roughly braided hair almost scraping the floor from where he sat. The Boy nodded to them, but was not acknowledged in return. When his food came, he ate with both elbows on the table and shoveled it into his mouth without ceremony. The woman watched with a bemused smile on her face.

'Well hon, no one is goin' to go accusing you of not knowing how to eat,' she said, lighting a fresh smoke.

'Thank you for the meal, ma'am,' he said.

She waved her cigarette in airy dismissal and moved on to the end of the bar and started to build a drink. He was on his way to the door when she caught him with her voice.

'*Hon, the ravens will show you the way.*'

He froze in his tracks, turned slowly back around.

'What did you say?' he asked through lips gone numb.

She was taking a long pull from her glass. She looked at him, puzzled by the look on his face. 'I said that after the cook is done I'll send him up to go get your truck started. Why, hon? You look like you just seen a ghost.'

He stumbled out to the parking lot, and for a moment as the door slammed shut behind him, all he could make out was a smear of gray light. His heart was pounding and breakfast felt like it was boiling up in the back of his throat. Sweat poured down his face and his knees began to buckle. And then Titan and Halo were there, one of them pressing into his leg and the other nuzzling his hand and slowly the world resolved itself around him. He squatted down and held both of them to him and buried his face in their soft neck fur.

It was the garbled sound of a raven cawing that made him look up. One lone raven sat not a hundred yards distant on a limb overhanging the road. Its eyes were dead black and it looked down upon him for one long moment, working its charcoal colored beak in a series of dry clicks. Suddenly, it burst into the air, seemingly without effort or premeditation, and even after it had disappeared to the north he could still hear its cries for a time until they, too, faded and were eventually gone.

3

The dogs were in a tangled mess when he made it back to the Odyssey. It was hard to say who the culprit was, but the gangline had been chewed at the midway point and the dogs were all wound tightly around the surrounding brush and layered with slobbery mud from their playful exertions. It took some time to sort it all out and splice the line back together, but The Boy got them all hooked back up and on the move again in short order. Titan and his sister were once again in the lead, and they allowed their master to guide them into the valley using only voice commands. They swung in a long arc and got onto the road headed back in the direction of camp.

When they made it back to the fork in the road, they followed the Trapper Creek trail which was little more than a rutted path through deep forest with the occasional brief glimpse of the valley low and to their right. It seesawed over a series of steep hillocks and foundered through a number of mud bogs latticed with corduroy bridging. Paths let off at intervals, and presently they came to a wide area, and The Boy could tell by the way the dogs' ears perked that they could hear something up ahead. They emerged into a clearing and found a rough township made up of small tarpaper shacks and yellow school buses seated on blocks and chopped along their sides to let out crude lean-tos of tin shingling and ragged blue tarps. There were dogs everywhere; some in lots, others chained to broken down automobiles and bits of ironmongery laying about in half overgrown profusion. A faded sign stood in the drive, one of its stands drunkenly leaning with rot, making the statement that 'The Old Man Drinks Hot Tang!' and beneath this, almost illegible with time, 'The Home Of Trapper Creek Kennels!' The picketed dogs made not a sound, but whipped about as their spaces would allow with heads and ears up and wild blue eyes blazing. A group of men in overalls and muck-boots stood in the drive, staring as he went by. One of the men raised a hand in solemn greeting. As he left them behind, he reflected that none of them looked particularly aged.

He followed the trail through the rest of the morning, and finally called a stop when the way was blocked by a swampy creek drainage too mucksome to cross. The dogs were foamed up and panting, eyes rimmed with grit and ribcages heaving with the effort of pulling the rig through the mud and slime. He strung the team along the side of the trail in the tall grasses and dropped their tugs. He released his three older dogs to run free, and built a small fire while they disappeared into the forest. He hung his orange rubber rain gear from an alder branch and reclined on the damp moss with his feet pointed to the flames. He dozed for a bit, only waking when the leaders came back from their exploring and curled up as near to him as they could get, each one vying for a spot on his lap to rest their heads.

They passed the day in this manner, and got back on the move pointed towards camp when the clouds thickened and an icy rain began to spatter down. When they passed the Old Man's encampment on the return trip, The Boy could see evidence of a great many dog prints and four-wheeler tracks coming and going from the driveway. The fresh tracks scarred the mud of the road and continued on towards the Roadhouse while he made his way back to camp.

There was a strange man standing next to the cab of his pickup when his team came trotting in. The man had a truck pulled up nose first to his, and both hoods were up with cables forming and umbilicus. The man stood there smoking and staring, large belly bulging out of soiled mechanics coveralls.

'You the cook from the Roadhouse?' asked The Boy.

'That would be me,' agreed the man. 'The lady back at the lodge sent me.' He jerked a greasy thumb at The Boy's truck. 'You're in here pretty deep. When this thing gets done charging, I'll hook up to you with the strap and get you out of there.'

'Mister, I can't tell you how much I appreciate the help.'

'Don't worry about it. We all need help at some time or other, don't we?'

The Boy nodded solemnly. Something about his skinny, mud spattered face made the older man burst out laughing. 'My name's Crazy Tom,' he said sticking out his hand. 'Just don't ask me why they call me that.'

4

As September passed, the weather remained fair and the days folded themselves into pleasant routine. The dogs grew bulky and strong on a diet of high powered kibble and buckets of blended fat. The three leaders developed a near telepathic connection to their master, and the yearlings metamorphosed from gangling teenagers to rock hard athletes who performed their jobs with speed, power, and precision. The Boy eschewed the orthodox methodology of out and back training runs, instead favoring all day mini camping trips where he would load the Odyssey with buckets of feed and dishes and take the dogs out for the day, sometimes exploring the hill country between the Roadhouse and the Petersville mines; other times traveling down the Trapper Creek trail looking for offshoots and new paths through the swamplands. He started running into The Old Man's handlers out training teams on three wheelers and old chopped-down Volkswagens, but mostly liked to avoid them because their dogs did not pass well.

One morning, a truck pulled up to the parking area while he was tending the morning feed. Titan and Legend were instantly at his side, looking intently up the path. They heard heavy footfalls, and then a man whom he recognized from The Old Man's camp strode into sight. He was short and stocky with a broad chest and ginger beard. His blue eyes were lazy and set close together in a way that made him look vaguely cross-eyed.

The man stood there for a moment turning his head in a slow circle and taking in the camp site. If he heard Legend's low growl, he paid no mind at all.

'I work for The Old Man,' he finally said, sending a stream of black chaw juicing into the fire pit.

'I knew that,' The Boy acknowledged.

'Been seeing each other on the trail, figured I better get down here and introduce myself.'

'Where's The Old Man?'

The handler shrugged. 'He's still down in the Valley, won't be up here 'til snow flies. I'm in charge of three other guys, and we're miling his team up for him til he can come up.'

The Boy nodded.

'You must be The Trapper's boy. I know your dad pretty well. I was working as a checker in McGrath when he scratched that year. That was one bummed out dog musher, I can testify. You running the dogs for him?'

'No, these are my dogs,' said The Boy. 'He's not my dad, just my uncle, and I run for myself.'

'Well.'

'What about you? What are you getting The Old Man's team ready for?'

The handler chuckled sarcastically. 'The Great Race! What else is there?'

'I'm doing mid-distance. I figure plenty of people think that's important too. The Delta K300 and the Pipeline race.'

The man's eyes popped. 'You're going to Bethel, and then to Copper Center back to back?' he asked, voice incredulous. He looked down and seemed to notice the dogs sitting at The Boy's feet for the first time, the .41 hanging from its harness above the tent's door opening. He took a moment to consider this, and then aimed another stream of chaw to hiss upon the fire.

'Kind of ambitious, ain't you?' he said. 'That K300 is infamous for tearing up teams. I wouldn't put a group in there for anything.'

'Racers race. The K300 is the biggest purse and best competition outside of the Great Race.'

'That so?'

'Aye.'

'And you're just going to stay in this tent all winter? You'll freeze your ass off.'

'I'll make it. This'll be good training.'

The man laughed harshly, and then turned suddenly conspiratorial. 'Actually, there's more to the story with The Old Man,' he said. He reached into a back pocket and dug out a tin of chew and planted a wad down in his cheek.

'See, he hasn't been coming up here much for the last couple of winters. Mostly, it's just me and the guys, and all of his lease drivers from France and Germany and such. Pretty much, he's just been coming up for a few weekends here and there and taking over right before the race. That team that got eighth last year? That was my team, my training. His dogs of course, but I picked them all out and made them what they were.'

'Why is he letting you do all of the work?' asked The Boy, assuming that the man was merely boasting. One thing he had learned about this business was that the world of professional mushing was filled to the brim with handlers who all thought that they were the sole reason that their patrons' teams could find their way from one end of the race season to the other.

'Hell kid, have you ever seen him? He's old like shoe leather that's been left in the sunlight too long, and there's some talk about his being sick and all. I saw him just a couple of weeks ago, and I'm telling you, he didn't look so good.'

'The Old Man is sick?'

'The Old Man is sick.'

'What's wrong with him?'

'Don't know for sure…some would say it's the cancer. He's not saying though, that's for sure.'

'What are you going to do with the team if he can't run it?'

A sly look came into the man's face. 'Well, maybe I'll have to take the team in the race for him. That could be.' He looked wistful for a moment. 'I'll tell you what though, that bastard is plenty tough. If someone can beat this, it's him.'

The Boy studied him for a while, and then shrugged. 'Sounds like you're going to have a full winter. Sorry to hear that about The Old Man,' he said.

'Yeah, kid. Be glad you don't have my job.'

5

High in the hills above the Roadhouse, he sometimes felt as if he were all alone in this vast country, surrounded by limitless sky and endless mountain vista, never seeing a single solitary soul during his adventures. The road in these parts was mostly firmly compacted dirt, gentle on the dogs' pads, and on some days he traveled deep into the canyon folds and went without trail or track until the rig could go no further. Far away from the world of man and mechanical contrivances, he would turn the dogs free to roam the brush while he gathered driftwood from the banks of dried-up gully washes and built enormous pyres to light the night and bounce their glow from broken coulee walls. He would make his sleeping arrangements against some solid abutment and lay on his back, looking up at the star washed heavens with the team gathered round and the Magnum within an easy reach.

On one of these mornings, he awoke to a world covered in white. No more bare dirt or screen of moose brush, just a soft and timeless blanket of snow seen through a shifting curtain of gauze. The dogs were an assortment of scattered lumps with steam rising from their nostrils, and the fire was out and long since cold. He lay there for a time propped up on his elbows with his body still in the sleeping bag. It was not yet dawn, but there was enough dull light to see if one looked from the corners of their eyes, and he did that now because something was going on out there, just beyond his range of visibility. Soft gulping and clacking from somewhere up on the canyon wall to his left, out of sight in the flurry. He strained to see, and so intent was he that he did not even notice the fine thread of blood leaking from his right nostril and glossing his pale lips with scarlet drippings. The sounds of wings thrashing came from the right hand side of the coulee, this followed by the harsh cawing of multitudinous throats, and then he could see for a momentary break in the snowfall. There were hundreds of black shapes lining the rim of both sides of the canyon, all jostling and clicking and gulping to one another in strange converse. He stared uncomprehendingly at this spectacle and as he did so, his juices seemed to cool in their windings throughout his body.

And then he heard his Mama softly singing somewhere further up the canyon. The ravens all fell silent and, one by one, turned their obsidian eyes down upon him. Slowly, like a corpse arisen from the grave, he slid from the confines of his bag and got to his feet, naked as the day he was born except for a mantle of freshly fallen snow wreathing his shaggy head and cloaking his shoulders. As he walked down the canyon, he felt nothing of the cold or the rocks under his feet, did not notice the blood coming in freshets now to paint his hairless chest and drool a long, horrible trail behind his passage. The dogs arose silently and formed an arc around his advance, wraiths in the morning's dim murk. He came to a place where the brush cleared and shapes loomed around, showed themselves to be a rundown collection of ancient buildings gone to waste decades past. A sluice box with the husk of its conveyor still perceptible extending into the dry creek bed; the shell of some living quarters built from old twisted logs rambling to his right with one door hanging open and creaking in the wind, plastic sheeting splintered with rot and hanging in tatters within the empty sockets of a pair of window holes. A crude spruce pole cache stood with sprung doors and looted interior; the rusted hulk of an ancient generator sprawled at its footings.

The Boy stood quite still while surveying this scene, his dogs silently drifting around him and amongst the constructs like a pack of wolves. He saw the sled turned over in the yard, still faintly visible under the covering of snow. It was an old snowmobile sled with a tow bar and iron runners and its belly pointed away from where he stood. He could hear his Mama's singing coming from the other side, solidly hidden from his view. Singing something that he couldn't quite make out, but it was sweet and warm, and now he heard a baby crying and a young boy trying to shush it, and the sound of this and the knowing of what it must mean brought him to his knees and forced his face into his hands. Even with his fingers tightly laced together, scalding tears and steaming blood ran from them as if through a sieve and melted the frozen ground where he knelt.

It was then that his dogs gathered close and Halo thrust her muzzle into his face from one side and Titan did the same from the other, and all the rest of the pack threw back their heads and howled from the bottoms of their souls. He would have died right there if it had not been for them, he knew that the moment he regained his senses. The fugue was draining him like a tide going out from the beach. There were no ravens, no abandoned gold claim; no sled; just he and the dogs and the lonely canyon with its load of new snow. He arose on legs that felt as flimsy as dandelion puff and hobbled back to where his possibles lay like a man a hundred years aged, and when he got back to his sleeping bag he crawled inside and fell insensate for a time, shaking and chattering and half dead from the cold. When he finally summoned the strength to creep back out, his skin was ashen except for where the blood had dried to a maroon shell. He pulled on his clothes and got the fire rekindled and put his hands as close as he could to the flames, and for a time he just hunkered there with his mind emptied of all thought or consideration.

The snow stopped around mid morning and the sky cleared like a vale being pulled from some priceless work of art. He got the team harnessed and hooked back into the gangline, and though they all stood subdued, the dogs had power enough as they dragged him and the Odyssey out of the mountains and back to the valley below. On the way down, they passed groups of hunters two and three together all decked in camouflage and riding three wheelers and some in chained up trucks. These men would all pull to the side of the road and stare as he passed them with the team chugging like a freight train and the Odyssey whipsawing in their wake.

6

Night was poised to descend, and the parking area was bustling with activity as The Boy and his team hove back into their parking spot.

The sky had gathered itself into a dull black eye, and now snow mixed with sleet spattered down in grim preview of a storm to come. Every person in the valley with a truck was there sweeping off windscreens and chaining up tires, lifting hoods and firing up engines. A number of snowmobiles idled with headlights pulsing to the beat of their 2-cycle motors, their spent fuel rising in a choking blue fog. The dark was coming on fast, and a shrill wind was picking up to whip the tops of the trees and send snow from their branches blasting in quick curtains to the earth.

He stood next to his rig with his clothing wet through the middle and crusted frozen at the edges, absolutely spent from the day's exertions. He watched dumbly as men hollered to one another and trucks rocked back and forth, looking for traction in the slop gathering about their wheel rims. The drivers of the snowmobiles throttled up their machines and departed in cocks-tails of thrown up snow mixed with loose mud and gravel. Headlamps and assorted flashlights began to come on, one by one, and the scene was rendered in stop-motion to The Boy as he watched the men getting into their vehicles and pointing them back down the mountain, towards Trapper Creek and the highway.

A shape came up to him in the dark, ginger bearded and snow covered.

'Hey kid, you all right here? Do you need any help getting your truck going?' asked this anonymous figure.

The Boy looked at him uncomprehending, hearing the man's voice as if it were echoing from the bottom of a well.

'Jesus Christ what happened to your face?'

Go away, The Boy thought.

'Jesus, are you hurt?'

I'm fine, go away.

'Kid, why don't you answer?' this accompanied with a rough shake that made The Boy's teeth rattle.

The Boy shook his head and felt some of the mist slip back a little.

'I'm fine,' he said, and his voice sounded impossibly small even to his own ears.

'Where is all the blood coming from?' the man asked. He sounded panicky. He had a flashlight and he shone it right into The Boy's face.

'Just a nose bleed,' The Boy murmured. He sagged back against the Odyssey and hoped this man could not see that it was the only thing holding him up. 'I bumped my nose is all. I'll be…fine.'

'Kid, it looks like someone shot a moose and it bled out all over your face!'

The Boy could think of nothing to say to this and the man stood there waiting, a silent shape in the dark.

'If you don't get your truck out now, it's going to sit here all winter,' said the stranger, finally.

The Boy leaned his head back and felt the wind rasp against his unprotected flesh.

'It doesn't matter,' he said. 'I've got nowhere to go.' He drifted off for a while, and when he looked again, he saw that the parking area was empty save for his own truck and boxes; dim shapes slowly disappearing under a blanket of snow.

The dogs were all curled up in their lines. Their heads perked up and their tails began to wag when they realized that he was unhooking them. Working very slowly, he pulled off each harness and let all of them run free, sitting down and resting from time to time while he did this. Once, he drifted and came awake to Legend frantically washing his face, the smell of the dog's rancid breath gagging him back to a state of awareness. When the job was finished, he struggled to his tent and collapsed in the dark, wet clothes and all, somehow summoning the energy to pull his sleeping bag around his scarecrow frame. His mind immediately faded into a black and troubled sleep of the most profound exhaustion he had ever known, and as he lay nearly comatose, the winds began to howl and the snow blew through the open front of his enclosure and covered him completely.

The three older dogs nestled around him as best they could and together they waited out the storm.

Chapter VIII

1

THE Boy lay in his hole for five consecutive days while the storm raged and thrashed and covered the world in its glacial embrace. He only crawled outside to throw the last of the chunked meat to his dogs for their meals, and stagger his way back on all fours like an animal. He got very sick after that first night, and his paper thin body was wracked by a terrible cough and bent nearly double from vomiting. It crossed his mind at one point that he might be dying; sometime later, he wished that he would. His dreams were twisted and terrible, and he was visited by any number of specters both good and ill.

He awoke on the fifth morning stinking and cold, weak as a newborn kitten. His stomach muscles ached from retching and his head spun in crazy parabola and he could not remember ever having been as hungry. Carefully, lest something break, he sat up in his bedding and surveyed his surroundings. His tent was filled with snow and there was white as far as he could see from the opening flapping in the breeze. It was midmorning, and a cheerless sun shone hard and yellow from the perspective of a distant horizon, turning the snow into a sea of sparkling crystals. He guessed that the temperature was well below zero, knowing that often times a storm was driven out by the presence of a high pressure system moving into the region and bringing with it a blast of super-cooled air.

The campsite was well trampled down by the activities of the dogs, and the fire pit was a dimple with several of the bigger rocks sticking out. He cleaned it out and got a fire going, and warmed his hands by the heat of it. Once he had his shaking limbs under control, he found a pot and began to melt snow. He dug a bag of moose jerky from the drifts and tried to chew some of it. When the water came, filmy with seeds and bits of bark, he drank it like a man come from the desert, feeling it spread to every furthest part of his body and awaken the numbed flesh like a new garden feeling the first touch of spring sunshine. When he was finished, he put on more to boil and began digging around for his food box. When he found it, he also found that it was nearly empty. A sack containing a few meager handfuls of rolled oats, a couple tins of sardines, and a dented can of beef stew. He rolled the lid back on the sardines and crunched them down.

Struggling through snow that reached his thighs, he made his way up to the parking area. The road had become a narrow snowmobile trail and he could smell exhaust and oil from the most recent of its travelers. His was the only vehicle still here, and it was but a hump in a sea of drifted white. He worked through the cold remainder of the morning and slowly uncovered the flatbed well enough to get to the boxes where he kept the dogs' dry food and some emergency rations for himself. With this chore complete, he brought a bag back to the campsite and prepared a wet meal for the team. Though the three elder leaders watched him in silence, the yearlings were frantic with joy at his return from the purgatory where he had slumbered. Their beds were iced over, but their bodies remained in good flesh despite the spotty care of the last week. While they gulped their meal, he carefully went through the group, one by one, checking them over for any signs of ill health and lavishing each with affection and love. The rest of the day was spent gathering fresh spruce boughs for their bedding, and by the time the sun was riding low in the west and the long shadows of evening twilight were upon the land, he was fully exhausted. Before sleep, he prepared hot water for the next morning's meal and left it in coolers with kibble to soak. He crawled into his sleeping bag without eating any dinner for himself. His rest was long, black, and dreamless.

2

It was time for sled training. From all of the days spent dragging the Odyssey, his team had become almost too strong to properly control. For the first few runs, he split the group in half and ran seven dog teams to all of the places he had earlier explored by cart, and then repeated this with the second team. After several days of this, he had them sufficiently calmed to entrust his life to a fourteen dog team, and when he did so, it was like riding atop a magic carpet while the wild and majestic scenery fairly flew past to either side. Now that it was winter, mushers and dog teams began to show up nearly everywhere, coming into the main trails of Trapper Creek and Petersville Road from many of the offshoots that he had noted earlier in the season. Most of this traffic was coming from The Old Man's camp, though The Boy had yet to actually see The Old Man himself. Mostly, it was his main ginger bearded handler and droves of foreigners driving leased teams.

The Boy came back to camp after one such day and found Uncle and Middle Cousin waiting for him. Uncle was on a new snowmobile dragging a heavy freight sled filled to the sidewalls and covered with a thick tarpaulin. He stood next to his ride, a scarred and gaunt man with glacial blue eyes and a killer's bony hands. Middle Cousin had a group of dogs tied out in the trees and his sled, too, was loaded for camping; it was he who approached his older cousin, and the look that wrote his face was a mixture of fear and supplication. Not a word was spoken. The Boy studied the two of them for a long while with his heart beating too fast in his chest and a strange species of terrified anger burning low in the coal bed of his belly. Finally, he swallowed hard and nodded, then went about the chore of unhooking his team. As he tied the dogs at their pickets, he heard Uncle fire up his snowmobile and drive away. He could hear the sounds of Middle Cousin feeding his own team, and then they grew quiet and a little later the sounds of boots crunching down the path.

3

Middle Cousin helped him get the fire going and they sat together on upturned buckets and watched the flames dance. From Uncle's sled came a sorely needed restocking of foodstuffs, both perishable and canned. The Boy tore open a half frozen package of lunchmeat and roasted it on a stick. The first cocoa he had seen in months bubbled on the grill and the smell of it filled the cool night air. They reclined in companionable silence for a while, and it was the younger of the boys who spoke first when the words finally came.

'Looks like you were about out of food,' he observed.

'Plenty of dry food for the dogs, but I was running pretty lean for myself,' The Boy agreed.

'Why didn't you shoot something?'

The Boy smiled and poked at the fire with his stick. A fine filigree of crimson sparks spattered away and faded into the dark. 'It's not like it was back on the river,' he said. 'Around here in the civilized parts of the world they call what we were doing poaching. They got laws against it.'

Later in the dark, tucked side by side in their bags with the fire pit softly glowing at their feet and painting the insides of the shelter in weltering shades of burgundy, the boys talked about all of the things that brothers often do, and it was not until later that Middle Cousin told him why he had come. The Boy had nearly drifted off to sleep when he heard his cousin whispering.

'It rained all over the valley, then froze up. It's just one big sheet of ice down there. You can't even walk without chaining up,' the younger boy said.

'So he sent you up here to train his dogs.'

'It's not just for him. I get to take the best of them into the junior races. Everybody's looking for snow, and this is where it's at.'

'Why doesn't he stay up here too?'

Middle Cousin was quiet for a long time. 'Mama can't be without him,' he said finally. 'And he can't be away from her. You know he doesn't like camping out.'

The Boy laughed at this.

'What's so funny?'

'This is a heck of a business to be in for not liking to camp out, I was thinking.'

'That's not the only reason. He doesn't say, but I think he's still pretty messed up about what happened. You know, between the two of you.'

'Still? I didn't know he was messed up in the first place.'

'Are you?'

'Are I what?'

'Never mind. I just think it's kind of weird that you're up here all by yourself in the middle of nowhere living in a cave.'

'You're here too, I've noticed. How else was I going to get my team trained?'

'Are you still planning to go out to the YK Delta? Papa thinks you're crazy.'

'He does, does he?' The Boy shrugged. 'I guess there are a lot of differences between how me and your dad look at things.'

They were silent for a time, just laying side by side and feeling the cold on their faces.

'Did you hear about The Old Man?' asked Middle Cousin.

'What about him? I thought he was supposed to be up here training his team, but all I've seen so far on the trails are his handlers.'

'He's in the hospital. Sick, or something. Word is, all of his family has come in from the bush to be with him, afraid he isn't gonna make it.'

The Boy was stunned. Even though he had already heard some talk of The Old man's condition, it had never occurred to him that it might be true. He had never once laid eyes on the old gentleman, but had heard so many stories growing up that The Old Man constituted a living legend in his mind, and he literally could not picture the world without him in it.

'Is he going to get better?' he asked stupidly.

'Nobody knows. Papa doesn't think so, but I'm not sure how he would know. Papa doesn't exactly hang with that crowd, if you know what I mean.'

'Yeah, I do know,' The Boy acknowledged. He was silent for a time, and then changed the subject when he finally did speak. 'Hey, tell me about your team. Are you excited to be racing this year? Have you got any cart miles on your team?'

'Not very many,' Middle Cousin admitted. 'We started in late August, but the brakes went out on the rig we were using, and then it got too warm once we had them fixed. I just started again when the rains came in and screwed everything up.'

'You have plenty of time to get them miled up,' The Boy said reassuringly. 'It's not ideal, but you can do it. How are they looking?'

'Papa thinks it's the strongest group he's ever seen. And I am pretty excited about the race. I was hoping that you could give me some pointers on what to expect and all.'

'You want my advice?'

'Well, yeah,' said Middle Cousin, a note of admiration creeping into his voice. 'I mean, what you did over the last three years in all of those races, people are still talking about it. And they weren't even the good dogs that you were using, just Papa's cast off's. He still can't believe how you got them to perform.'

The Boy considered this. 'Well, the first thing that you need to get through your head is the fact that he was wrong about those dogs,' he said. 'They were some of his best, he just didn't know it. See, that's the thing about running sled dogs, they don't perform exactly the same for each person working with them.'

'But how did you get them to do it? They wouldn't even pull a lick for Papa, no matter how he tried to make them.'

'That's just it. I don't make them do anything; I just let them do what they were born to do and got out of their way.'

'Are you for real?'

The Boy sighed. 'Just get some sleep,' he said. 'And try not to freeze off anything that you might need later on in life.'

4

Trapper Creek was known for its snow, and now it showed the children why. The sky turned the color of ash and proceeded to dump piles of wet snow from its belly for days without end or relief. As the two boys went about the daily routine of gathering firewood, preparing feedings and training their dogs, the snow came down and buried the world in a slow avalanche. Their tent became a wind tunnel through which the elements had their way, and nothing they tried could keep the drifts from piling in. Soaking wet from their exertions during the sunlight hours, they would crawl into their sleeping bags and tremble miserably cold throughout the long reaches of the night, afraid to get out their clothes for fear of finding them frozen and un-wearable by morning. The sun hid its face during this period, never so much as lightening a single narrow patch of sky so far as they could tell. And though Uncle made periodic trips to check on his son and bring basic foodstuffs, the two boys maintained on the ragged edge of starvation during their time at camp. Especially The Boy, who hated to impose on his cousin for anything. Middle Cousin had to force him to take the most essential of supplies, often becoming righteously angry in the process.

The rank hunger of poverty was nothing new to these two, and they went about daily tasks with the grim efficiency of men much older.

The trail was a constant soup, buried by snowfall and drifted in by a constant light wind. The Boy trained with a large team and only a light load of basic camping supplies and extra kibble in his sled. He had spent some of the last of his remaining dollars to convert his runners from iron to plastic, and as a consequence, his team flew through the mountains with a surplus of power. He found it quite strange that everyone else seemed to be stuck in the old groove of forcing their dogs to walk by pulling massive loads on sleds with iron runners, and in some cases like the teams from The Old Man's camp, bicycle rubber encasing the metal. One day he approached his cousin as the boy was about to leave with one half of his team on a short out-and-back run. His cousin's sled was an ancient freighter, and it was laden with two hundred pounds of sand in burlap sacks. In addition, there was a sixteen inch truck tire chained to drag a few feet behind the ending of the runners.

'What are you doing?' he asked the younger boy.

'Uh, running my dogs?' answered Middle Cousin with a suspicious look on his face.

'You're not training them to run. Just the opposite. You're training them to walk.' The Boy said.

Middle Cousin scrunched his narrow little face in consternation. 'I'm not following you, I guess,' he said. 'This is what we've always done.'

'I know. I used to do that, too. But listen, do you still want my advice? I really want to help you out here, if you'll let me.'

'So help.'

'Have you noticed how I don't drag a tire, or pack my sled too heavy? Do you know why that is?'

Middle Cousin shrugged. Behind him, his ten dog team stood, harnessed up in apathetic silence without a single ounce of pressure on the snowhook line. 'No, I don't know. It doesn't make any sense to me,' he admitted.

'Sure it does. I keep the load down and the resistance dialed back, especially in crummy trails like we have out here, so that the dogs can stretch out and really run. If you always make them grunt these heavy burdens, always make them plod around during training, then how can you expect them to stretch out come race time?'

'But Papa says that his team always goes fast early on, he can't barely hold them back when he's in a race.'

'Listen,' said The Boy, very seriously. 'I'm not trying to say that he isn't a good dog trainer, because I know that he is. No question about that. But he doesn't really do that well in races, especially against the real tough teams, like The Norwegian-

'That's not fair! Nobody can beat The Norwegian!'

'Not yet,' agreed The Boy. 'But listen, that's not the point I'm trying to make here. The point that I'm trying to get through to you is that the only reason that Uncle is getting some speed early on in a race is because they're overjoyed to not be dragging that godawful tire around anymore, so of course they lope. But that kind of speed burns off real fast, and when it's gone, the dogs are all burnt out from using muscles that they weren't trained to use. You know what I'm talking about, you know that his team always walks into Nome, or whatever he's racing in.'

Middle Cousin didn't answer, just stared at his boot tops with sullen eyes.

The Boy clapped him on the shoulder. 'You do whatever you want,' he said. 'I'm just telling you what works for me.'

Later, when he was preparing to hook up his own team, he noticed that his cousin's tire was disconnected and leaned off to the side. A perfect set of runner tracks with dog prints in between showed leaving the parking area.

This made him smile.

5

The Boy found out that is was Thanksgiving morning only because he came across a tattered dashboard calendar shuffled in amongst the detritus littering the floorboards of his truck. He was looking for any scrap of food he may have missed from searches prior, and when he found the schedule, he sat back on the frozen vinyl and just looked at it like a man trying in vain to decipher some foreign script. He got out and walked back to camp where Middle Cousin was struggling to light a fire with ice encrusted kindling and a damp book of matches.

'Hey,' he said. 'How long have you been here? Do you remember?'

Middle Cousin stopped what he was doing and rocked back on his haunches. 'I don't know. A month maybe? Maybe more. Feels like forever,' he said. His small face was pale under a mask of smoke grime and his eyes were like brown almonds. The Boy supposed that they both stank, though he couldn't tell. He looked around the campsite, but he knew that no matter how much he wanted it to be, there was no more food to be found. All that was left was one package of frozen bologna still in its wrapper.

'How long has it been since he was up here?' he asked, meaning Uncle.

Middle Cousin shook his head. 'Over a week, but he told me he would be here before Thanksgiving. I was hoping that Mama would send up some of her potato salad and maybe some turkey. Wouldn't that be good? And pumpkin pie. Man, that's all I can think about, and it's driving me crazy.'

The Boy silently showed the calendar, and the other child noted it with a dull lack of surprise.

'I've got an idea,' The Boy said. 'Let's take the day off, maybe go down to the Roadhouse and get something to eat.'

'We could do that? You think we should do that?'

The Boy ruffled his cousin's greasy hair. 'Of course we can,' he said. 'Let's go right now. We'll just hook up a little team and take one sled.' He took a lot of pleasure in seeing the other boy's face light up.

They found the Roadhouse parking lot deserted; though a generator could be heard whooping in the shed and Christmas lights twinkled around the window casings. The rich aromas of holiday cooking nearly drove them both mad with hunger. Inside, the main hall and dining room were dark and empty but for the sounds of revelry coming from the closed off room behind the bar. The two boys hoisted themselves onto stools and sat dripping and gawking at the walls adorned with all manner of exotic mining knick-knackery collected from the back country. Finally, The Boy realized that nobody was coming. He leaned over the polished wood surface of the bar and craned his neck, but could still see nothing, though he heard an intensification of laughter and silverware scraping against glass. The smell of turkey and trimmings were all but overpowering. He noted a small brass ringer, and this he smacked with the palm of his hand. The sounds in the back suddenly quieted, and after a moment, angry footsteps approached. It was the barmaid he'd met earlier, and her face was closed and hard.

'What do you want?' she snapped. 'Can't you tell we're closed?'

'No ma'am,' said The Boy. 'There was no sign or anything. We were just hoping to get a meal.'

She stared at him. Her eyes were filmy and she smelled so strongly of alcohol that it made his stomach clench. She had drawn her eyes with a colored pencil and slathered a thick coating of foundation onto her cheeks; the effect was ghastly.

'Ma'am?'

'I said we're closed. The kitchen is closed. Now why don't you two just get to wherever you came from and quit ruining my dinner?'

The Boy looked over at his cousin who was very close to tears, looked at the convenience rack on the wall behind the woman.

'How about a candy bar?' he asked, beginning to grub around in his pockets for some change.

'You don't understand English? What part of being *closed* doesn't seem to make sense to you? Were you raised in a cave or something?' This last display of wit actually made her bark laughter.

The Boy nodded and slid off of the stool. He grabbed his cousin by the jacket sleeve and pulled him along. When the door swung shut, he heard the lock clank and the woman cussing them in a harsh, boozy voice. They rode back to camp in silence, and when they pulled in, Middle Cousin went back to work on the fire while The Boy unhooked the dogs and let them run free. It began to snow big wet flakes that hit with a splatter.

That night, they sat on buckets arranged before the fire pit while the snow melted from their trash sack ponchos. They roasted the last of the bologna on sticks held over the flames, and ate it while it still hissed and spat.

6

The boys awoke the next morning miserably cold and weak from hunger. The Boy left his cousin to kindle a fire while he checked on all of their dogs. His legs felt too long for his body, and his knees trembled underneath his weight. He walked up to the parking area and stood passing discolored water in the middle of the trail while Titan, Halo and Legend frolicked around him like pups. When he finished, he stood there with a faint surf pounding in the back of his skull, feeling more like an empty shell then a person of flesh and bone. Slowly, he turned to all points of the compass, noting the sky clearing in the north and a cool bite to the breeze coming from the east. His sleeves were frozen to the elbows, his bibs up to his thighs, and he clanked like an old suit of armor when he moved. He gazed down the path where he could just make out Middle Cousin squatting in front of their hovel with a thin plume of smoke rising skyward before him. His mind moved like a rusty piece of long neglected machinery, and he gradually came to a decision.

He pried the door to his truck open and leaned the seat forward. Behind was a saddle scabbard bundled in a thick towel which he carefully withdrew. He laid it on the seat and unwrapped it. Inside was a .32 Special lever action carbine and cleaning kit. He stripped it down and sprayed its parts with lubricant, and then put them back together.

He polished the stock with an oily rag and recharged the magazine. Middle Cousin looked at it when he came walking down the path, but didn't say a word. The Boy leaned the rifle against a tree and pulled out his cutter and began sharpening it on a whetstone the size of a deck of cards.

Middle Cousin watched him, and then held out his hand for the stone once the older boy was finished. The younger boy's knife was a small folding model which he sharpened with the simple economy of effort one attains only from long hours of practice. 'So, where do we go looking?' he asked, once finished.

'I've seen signs all over,' said The Boy. 'I think we'll go up towards Petersville and cut off into one of the side valleys. Shouldn't be too much trouble.'

'Ok.'

They were in the process of harnessing a small team and hooking up the sleds when they both heard a snowmobile's engine droning. They stopped what they were doing and just listened as it drew near. Eventually, it came into the parking area and switched off. The Boy looked at the man in the snowsuit sitting astride the machine and could almost recognize him.

'I'm the cook from the Roadhouse,' the stranger said, seeing that the boy did not remember him. 'Crazy Tom. I'm the one who got your truck going back in the fall, remember?'

The Boy smiled. 'Of course. I've seen you go by a few times. You have a place off the Trapper Creek trail, past The Old Man's camp?'

'Aye, that I do. Me and my wife moved back down in there must be twenty years ago.' He rummaged around in the carry rack mounted behind his seat and pulled out a thermos and a small paper bag. He tossed the bag to Middle Cousin and began pouring steaming black tea into paper cups. He distributed these to the boys and stood there rolling a smoke and watching them gulp it down.

'My wife figured you two to be a little undernourished,' he said with a smile. 'When's your Pa comin' back?'

The Boy shrugged. 'My uncle was supposed to be back here yesterday. Something must've held him up.'

'Aye, I see. Well, seeing as how you two likely missed out on a holiday feed yesterday, I was thinking to invite you boys back to my place for Thanksgiving leftovers. My wife, she's just an awful good cook and she made enough food to feed an army, and there is no way that we can eat it all, so you would really be doing us a favor if you came by.'

'Well, I don't know…' started The Boy. He glanced over his shoulder at his cousin who looked about ready to bolt for the hills. 'We're doing pretty good here and we wouldn't want to impose or anything.'

'Oh, I wasn't trying to imply anything,' said Crazy Tom hastily. 'You two look like young men who can sort out their own problems without any help from an outsider, I can see that. It's just that we hardly ever get company where we live, and it would do my wife and me and our little girl a world of good to have some visitors for a change.'

The two boys looked at one another, and The Boy turned back to the older man. 'That would be very nice,' he said. 'What time should we come over?'

They settled on a time, and Crazy Tom fired up his snowmobile and putted back the way he had come. The Boy watched until he was out of site, and then withdrew the .32 Special from his sled and replaced it behind the seat in the truck. He found his cousin pawing through the contents of the paper bag that Crazy Tom had left behind. Two foil wrapped turkey salad sandwiches, a pair of bananas, and several slices of apple pie.

'It's like there's a party going on in my mouth,' Middle Cousin moaned happily.

They spent the day cleaning around camp, gathering firewood and freshening dog beds. The Boy turned all of his dogs loose and took them out to the swamp and let them swarm in a frenzy of good natured activity. Titan, Legend and Halo never strayed far from whichever space their master occupied, but the yearlings were want to chase one another and end up as specks on the horizon. In these instances, Titan, who was the fastest running of the three older dogs, would blaze after them and chase them back like a Border Collie herding sheep. As The Boy watched, he no longer even thought to remark on the fantastic array of prismatic colors leaping and winding from the dogs' activities like a rainbow coming loose at the seams and bleeding its threads in wild profusion. To him, these phenomena had become a common occurrence to be taken utterly for granted. When he looked upon his dogs moving thus, he saw in them the one thing that made his heart swell with pride and fierce joy.

The day passed slowly, and though they would never have admitted to it, they were both very excited at the prospect of a home cooked meal and some strange new company. No matter what else, they were still just boys.

7

At the appointed time, the two boys hooked up a small team with Halo in single lead and six dogs behind, The Boy on the runners and Middle Cousin tucked down in the bag. The dogs felt the boys' excitement and they flew over the trail as if they had wings. It was settling into dark when they reached the place where Crazy Tom's driveway cut off of the main road and wound its way down through thick forest into the narrow end of a gentle valley. The cabin was a simple log structure fashioned into an A-frame with broad front windows trimmed with lights, and a second story balcony overlooking the vale to the east. The sounds of a small generator came from behind somewhere, and the smells of burning birch mixed pleasantly with those of cooking in the well groomed dooryard. The boys unhooked the tugs from the dogs and secured the front of the mainline to a stout poplar.

Crazy Tom stood on the porch with the light from the windows at his back. 'You boy's about ready to eat?' he called down.

It wasn't until they were both seated on a low plank bench at the hardwood table, with a full banquet arrayed before them and the woman of the house sitting and staring at them, that the two of them realized how profoundly filthy they both were. Their clothing was shiny and stiff with layers of grease worked into the fabric, and their hands were nearly black from all manner of accumulated grime. They bowed their heads during the Lord's Prayer and tried their level best to make their hands as small as possible later while eating.

Crazy Tom's wife was a full blooded Athabascan with broad shoulders, thick hands, and a mouth that looked solemn even with a faint smile touching it. She spoke not a word while they supped, and the child sitting at the foot of the table was as taciturn as she in a pretty checkered red and white dress and long dark hair all twisted into a fancy braid. They were dressed in their holiday best, and this, too, embarrassed the boys for their own shabbiness.

Crazy Tom carried the dialogue, asking quick questions and then leaping straight to his own tales before they could so much as answer. This was fine by the boys, for all they really needed to do to facilitate their own end of the conversation was occasionally grunt in all the right places while filling their faces with turkey, stuffing, candied yams with marshmallow, and giant helpings of cranberry sauce to go with all of the trimmings. He spoke of back before he came to Alaska, when he grew up in Montana and went to school in Missoula with plans of becoming a math teacher; hunting elk, white tail deer, and big horn sheep in the Rocky Mountains; guiding back packers in Glacier National Park and Yellowstone country. How he had decided everything was getting too crowded with city folk and weekenders, and packed everything he owned in the back of a white Ford pinto and drove it all up the Alaskan Highway (of course back in those days twasn't much of a highway, no sir, more of a pot-holey gravel road as much as anything.) He'd been looking for wide open spaces where a man could be himself without all of the pressures of modern civilization pressing down upon him, and boy did he find it.

'I started out fishin' for an outfit out of Seward,' he said whilst rolling one of his many smokes. 'Didn't take long to tire of working the fisheries, I can tell you boys. That's how I met my wife.' He smiled at her from across the table and covered her hand with his own. 'Isn't she just a caution, boys? Why, the way she cooks it's a wonder that I'm not a big fat guy.

'Of course, that's where The Cowboy is from, you know, down in Big Sky Country. Heard tell he's got himself a nice setup up in the mountains, runs beef and horses and whatnot. He's won the Great Race a time or two hasn't he?'

'Yessir,' agreed The Boy sitting back with a stomach fit to burst. 'Back before The Norwegian showed up. Nobody's won since that.'

'Ah. The Norwegian. That's all anybody can talk about, how he's taken the crown back to his homeland four years running now. Everybody laughed at first, said he just got lucky and caught those boys a napping with his blitzkrieg strategy, but that didn't hold water after he won it the second time, and now nobody ever even sees him on the trail after Nikolai he's so much faster.'

'No, not faster,' The Boy corrected. 'Steadier. He's not really any faster than everybody else, his dogs can just do it on a lot less rest.'

'You reckon?'

'I do.'

'Then how do you beat that? He's taken the best The Cowboy and The Woman and all of the Alaskans can throw at him, and made it look like he was taking money from first graders to boot. People are saying it's unnatural.'

'Somebody's going to have to bring a better team and outmaneuver him I suppose.'

'Maybe you, one of these days?'

'Maybe me.'

Crazy Tom lectured in that vein for a time, about the state of mushing and how nowadays folks were only in it for the sponsors (Not like it used to be back in the days when it was all about trapping and running freight and hauling passengers); how the Great Race was starting to turn into a big money race and such; how word had it that The Old Man was still sick and getting sicker by the day; The Tinkerer's bizarre new sled and The Outdoorsman's outspoken disdain (Now there's a real man, mark my words!) for said conveyance; how The Woman (The only damn driver in the entire country who maybe had what it took to contest that Scandinavian devil! Didn't she run him pretty hard last year while everybody else just let him go? Did you boys know that she was also a runner of marathons and triathlons? Yeah, that gal can pretty much do it all!) was going to steal the show this year and send that Norwegian back to his homeland nursing a royal butt kicking. And always back to The Norwegian, how he seemed to never get cold, or tired, or really felt the same as most other folks did. Word had it that he descended from Viking stock and could trace his ancestry back to the time when Leif Erickson crossed over and discovered Greenland, and that some folks from his homeland had taken to calling him Beowulf (Only half joking mind you!) on account of his mushing heroics.

It was the tail end of the evening and there was a lull in the steady stream of words when The Boy got up the nerve to ask about the metal box sitting in the far corner under the stairwell leading up to the loft. It looked like an oversized toy box with its top open, except for the latch being on the inside of the lid and it being made all of burnished steel.

He had spotted it upon entering the cabin, and the strangeness of the thing had lurked in the corner of his vision throughout the evening's pleasantries.

The room got really quiet and Crazy Tom looked at him strangely, and then over at the box. 'Yeah, that,' he said slowly. He was smoking, and his cigarette was nearly down to the butt and he ground this out in a little glass ashtray sitting on the edge of the table. 'That's for our daughter to hide in. Sometimes she has to get in it. It locks from the inside.'

'Oh. Ok,' said The Boy. He looked away from Crazy Tom to his wife who was looking back at him with eyes gone utterly black and still. The little girl was staring down at her plate.

'Ma'am. That was a wonderful meal,' The Boy said, breaking the silence. 'The best I can remember having. I wish we could stay, but we really have to get back and feed our dogs.' He looked over at his cousin who was sitting there opened mouthed, and motioned for the boy start moving with him towards the door.

While the two of them were getting the team straightened out and pointed back towards camp, Crazy Tom's wife packed them a basket filled with leftovers from the table. Crazy Tom brought this out to them and handed it into Middle Cousin's lap where he sat in the basket of the sled.

'Thanks for coming over, boys,' he said. 'If you two ever need any help, or want to come back for another meal, don't think twice.'

They thanked him profusely, but all three of them knew full well that this would be their one and only sup under Crazy Tom's roof. They bade him well and made their way into the night.

8

It was pleasantly cool, and fat flakes of snow drifted softly from the darkened sky and covered the trail in a gentle blanket. The dogs were eager to run, and the only sound that they made with their passing was a steady panting of breath and jingle of snaps jostling against collar rings. They travelled through a shallow well of light thrown from a solitary headlamp beam atop The Boy's brow, and the world all around was as still and thoughtlessly dreaming as a child's snow globe. Middle Cousin dozed where he lay in the basket, hypnotized by the flurries, and The Boy lolled on the runners, half drunk from second hand smoke and a shrunken belly overfilled with rich fare. They climbed up to the Trapper Creek trail and the lights from The Old Man's camp glittered in the distance and they moved that way as surely as if mounted on rails. The Boy was starting to doze off himself when they ran into the wall.

At first the headlamp showed nothing but the blackness at the end of its meager reach; the dogs were the surest tell, because they stopped in their tracks and frantically fanned into the deep snow on either side of the trail. Then there was some immense silhouette in their midst, and Halo was shrieking in pain and The Boy was yelling and off the sled, and though he could scarcely believe it, Halo came flying through the air above his head and disappeared into the black, and the shape lowered its head nearly to the ground and hissed at him, eyes set impossibly wide apart and glowing against his light, yawning reach of its antlers sweeping and catching two more dogs and pile driving them into the bank.

He was fumbling with the pistol, but not fast enough, not nearly, and now it was he who was tumbling and down on his knees as a wall of bristling brown hair and muscle and rage swept past him and caught Middle Cousin as he was frantically clawing his way out of the sled. The little boy never made a sound, just crumpled in on himself and disappeared inside the wreckage of the sled as the beast spun and began to stomp and bellow. As if in a dream, The Boy was back on his feet and the ugly steel bulk of the .41 lay naked in his hand, and when he put it right up against the side of the beast's head and squeezed the trigger, it barked like heavens own thunder and knocked the creature around as surely as if it had been hit by a truck. Twin streamers of blood spun from flared nostrils the size of coffee mugs, and the great creature staggered off of the trail into the deep snow and its life's blood described a gory arc as it heaved and plunged and worked itself back onto firmer ground. It shook its body in a furious motion, and once again came at the sled, paying not one whit of attention to The Boy as it passed. He stuck the barrel of the pistol into its armpit, and in the moment before he fired, he realized that he could smell its rank musk; then he shot it twice through the lungs as fast as he could pull the hammer back and squeeze the trigger, and again the beast was staggered from its path. It stumbled back from the trail and sank down to its knees. Its eyes rolled madly and bubbles of pink froth exploded in steaming splatters from its mouth. It tried again to rise, and with a terrible effort succeeded, then gave it up and slowly settled back down and rolled over onto its side. It lay there; staring into the dark with scarlet running from its ears and muzzle, and the sound of its panting was like the bellows in an ironworks.

The Boy turned from this spectacle and drove the .41 back into its holster. All around him the dogs were a whining mess and some were groaning and whimpering in pain. He could hear Halo yelping out beyond the reach of his headlamp, and he was afraid of what he would find when he opened the sled bag, but he opened it anyway, and he was right to be afraid, because what he found was something no boy should ever have to deal with alone in the dark and the cold.

He fell to his knees and, crying his name over and over, pulled the little boy's moaning, broken body out of the sled and into his lap and cradled him there in the middle of the trail while the snow fell thick and covered the scene entire.

Chapter IX

1

T HE Boy waited for word that his cousin was in stable condition in a hospital in Anchorage, and then fled deep into the mountains. He filled his sled with meat and camping supplies and made Halo as comfortable as he could. He saddled the team and climbed throughout a day the color of iron, until the Roadhouse was a speck seen below and the mountains reared and hulked all around. His team marched until the trail ended, and then they broke their own way into the vast untracked wilderness of the Petersville Range. As they traveled, The Boy's eye was blurred and he lost track of all time and took no notice of the wolves which emerged from the forest to join his travail. He clung to the handlebar like a man to a life preserver, and the images that occupied his mind in its entire were best left untold.

He came back to himself at the gates of a mighty canyon, the jaws of which soared to either side until their craggy peaks were lost in the clouds. Down its throat, the far off landscape took on the aspect of a heat mirage, and he thought to see the plane of some great lake simmering in the distance. He rubbed his ice encrusted eye socket like a man awaking from a dream, but still the vision held. An unkindness of ravens spun like flakes of ash between the canyon walls and their harsh cries came faintly on a stern breeze that knifed through his thin clothing and chilled him to the core. A metal signpost thrust from the ground to his right, strangely incongruous with the surroundings. It read PETERSVILLE MINING CAMP 4 MILES. He stared at this uncomprehending for a long time, until the sun slid behind the western escarpment and long shadows played across the land. His dogs looked back at him from where they stood within the traces, eyes wild and grins toothy. Halo was a silent bundle, and for a moment he thought that she was dead, until she stirred slightly and gave a feeble panting moan.

They continued along a snow covered road through folds of rough hill and tangles of alder and moose-brush, until they reached the eastern wall of the canyon, and then there was only gray stone on one side and a long silent drop down to the valley floor on the other. They crawled across this wall on a road cut from the living rock and no wider then a single set of wheel ruts; in some places the cliff folded in on itself to form crude funnels where spring freshets no doubt flowed during the warmer seasons. In these areas, wind blasted snow gathered across their path and formed slick side hills where he had to heave the sled over onto one runner and drag with all of his might in order to keep the whole mess from skating outwards to oblivion; if ever once the dogs had faltered in these places all would have been lost. Though this thought did occur to The Boy, he cared not one way or the other as to the outcome. He mushed on and kept his mind to its simplest routines and the dogs dragged him through the pass like some kind of elemental locomotive.

They reached the far side where the canyon gentled and the mountains slumped away. Here was a wide plateau several miles across and creased by numerous gullies and washouts and furred with low stands of brush and not one solitary tree. Behind him, through the canyon, could be seen a dark slice of sky and the first stars of night coldly burning their distant watch signals. Ahead lay a rude collection of abandoned buildings and rusted machinery, gaunt and leaning in the strange twilight.

He guided the team into the central area of this unlikely township and called then to a halt in the lee of a long corrugated steel Quonset hut with boarded up windows and long drifts of snow trailing from its downwind side. He anchored the team front and back and shone his light from one end of the building to the other, until he found the entry way, and this he forced open with several savage stomps from his boot. Inside was a dry, dark cavern, spacious enough to house multiple pieces of heavy equipment, metal girders lacing together high overhead like rusted wishbones. He walked into this space and his footsteps stirred old dust on the cracked concrete flooring and shivered the stagnant air with a muted series of echoes. There were senseless drifts of crumpled newspaper scattered about, and one of these he stooped to pick up and it was a paper unfamiliar to him with a date already years gone by. He gazed for a while at the grinning, age yellowed face of some politician he almost recognized, and then let it fall from his gloved fingers. He turned his headlight from one end of the room to the other and his light was nearly swallowed up in all of that blackness. At the far end was a section which had been walled off for offices, or maybe living quarters. He found a hollow core door with a faded calendar shot of a naked women tacked to its surface at eye level, and this he opened and found on the other side a large room with sprung file cabinets and bunk beds lining one wall and a potbellied stove cast from pig iron mounted in the corner, its skinny black chimney disappearing through the false ceiling. A set of warped cabinets were arranged along the other wall and a brief glance told him they had long ago been emptied.

He knelt to examine the stove and was pleased to find it intact and with a full wood box bristling with dry kindling. He shucked his gloves and set to work building a fire in its belly; at first it would only gutter and belch choking clouds of smoke into the room, but soon it was gasping for air and sending great gouts of flame shooting up its vent. He closed the door and adjusted the damper and flue. When he had the settings where he liked them, he donned his gloves and went back outside. He led the dogs one by one into the Quonset and set them to run free, then let Legend and Titan into the living quarters and carried Halo's mewling form bundled in his sleeping bag. As gently as possible, he laid her in front of the stove where the orange glow from the damper covered her with its warmth and the embers refracted in the lenses of her eyes. He pulled a mould spotted mattress from one of the bunks and flopped it to the ground and laid himself down upon it, the fires heat penetrating into his wet clothing. He lay there for a long while listening to the sounds of the dogs breathing and the wood popping and crackling, until he finally dozed off.

He jerked awake during the darkest hours of the night with his mind feverish and thinking of the picture of the women's nude body, and this in turn made him think of that long-ago girl and the wanting of her in this manner both exhilarated and shamed him all at the same time. He groaned aloud and got to his feet, threw open the door and pulled the calendar loose. He considered it for a moment, then tossed it upon the flames and went back to sleep.

2

He surmised that this had at one time been a thriving township. In the morning, he set out to explore his surroundings and turned the dogs loose to do the same. There were four of the Quonset huts arranged end on end, and across a wide expanse of parking lot from them was a machine shed with blackened windows followed by a long train of cabins with tarpaper sides and skinny chimneys jutting from their steep pitched metal roofs. He went through the buildings one by one. The first two Quonset huts were much like the first, but the fourth was loaded with mostly empty fuel drums and stacks of wooden pallets. The bare innards of a diesel generator hulked in the corner, and The Boy could see from the caked oil pooled below its casing and shingles of rust coating its exposed parts that it had long since quit running. He found an empty bucket and salvaged some fuel from one of the drums, enough to slosh around in the bottom and make his hands reek of kerosene. He set this outside the door, and then began to drag pallets outside. He quit once he had a large stack, and then made his way through the thigh deep snow to the distant machine shed. The doors were boarded up too securely for him to force, so he pried the cover from one of the windows and busted the pane.

Inside was as dark as any cave, and he was obligated to switch on his flashlight. The floor was oil soaked and littered with all manner of debris. There was another generator in here, this one smaller then the first one he had found and in much better repair. He thought that this one might actually work if it had fuel in its tank. Mostly, there was little of interest in here, but he did find a tool cabinet bolted along one wall with an open padlock hanging from its hasp. He opened this and saw a wall with a number of dusty tools hanging from pegs. He selected a square nosed shovel with a short handle and a double bladed axe with a duct-taped handle. The head wobbled on its mount, but he thought that it seemed serviceable enough. He carried these to the window and pitched them out, and was about to climb through himself when something caught his eye. It was an overturned file cabinet with shelves flung open and contents spilled loose. He crouched down before it and pulled a gleaming object from the floor. It was a silver locket on a long chain. He opened it and looked upon the countenance of a lovely women with strong features and hair all in a long braid. The inscription on the facing side of the hasp read 'My Corilina, my love', and reading it sent a chill skittering down his spine. He dropped the locket as if stung. He stood up too quickly and was alarmed at the stars swarming across his field of vision. He stumbled blindly to the window and heaved himself through and fell face first into the snow outside.

The next building was a combination mess hall and office, a portion of its low roof caved in from a previous winters snow load. The floor inside was ankle deep with drifts of sugary fine powder. Long rows of benches and plastic cafeteria tables lay overturned, as if some angry melee had taken place. In a gutted kitchen, he found a drawer still in its shelf that held a full set of cheap tin place settings and a stack of plastic trays. Underneath this was a stack of pots and pans and a long tube with a rubber bulb on one end, a turkey baster, he remembered from some Thanksgiving past. He took the largest of the pans and the baster and set them aside. The office portion was secured from the weather, but he found little of interest here except for several paper tubes packed full with topographical maps of the

immediate region and the Susitna Valley to the west. He took these
and a handful of pencils bound together with a thick rubber band
which he stuffed inside a parka pocket.

Outside, he stopped and looked up at the sky. It was a pure, lazy
blue, untracked save for a distant contrail already breaking apart in
the stratosphere. Aside from this, there was not one sight or sound to
suggest that he was not the lone human being ranging about the face
of the planet. It was long in the afternoon and already shadows darkened the canyon to the south. He cast about for the dogs, but they
were nowhere to be seen. When he got back to the Quonset which
he had stationed as his quarters, he found them all gathered inside
and curled in various spots on the floor. The dogs leapt to their feet
as a single unit and came to him as soon as they noted his presence.
They pressed in from all sides and would not let him alone until he
had thoroughly petted and loved each one, and even then he had to
fight his way through the pack.

Inside the bunkroom, the fire was banked low and Halo was
lying on her side and softly whimpering. She tried to get up when
she saw him, but was unable. Her once shiny coat was now dull, and
she had become as skinny as a rail. Hating to hurt her, he gathered
her in his arms and brought her outside and set her down in a clean
patch of snow. Her hind end crumpled beneath her own weight and
he had to hold her upright while she passed water, and he could not
help but see that it was dark and shot through with blood. She turned
her head to regard his face and he could clearly see the capillaries
breaking up in her corneas, and when she tried to lick his cheek, her
breath held the stench of decay. Murmuring tenderly, he scooped her
up and brought her back to the fire and covered her with a blanket.
He made a thin broth of melted snow water and strips of moose meat
in the pot he had taken from the mess, and this he trickled across her
cold blue gums with the baster. Some of it made it down her throat,

and some of it she coughed out, but he kept at it until the broth was all gone, and then he cradled her head in his lap until she passed out again.

Outside, he took the axe and chopped the pallets into kindling until the sun gave out. While he did this, the team skirted his work area and stayed well clear; they were filled with a restless, nervous energy, and they wondered why their master had brought them to this place. After dark, he went back to the bunkroom and got a pair of kerosene lanterns going with the fuel he had salvaged, and by their flickering light flattened out the topo maps and poured over them for the rest of the evening. Titan and Legend came into the bunkroom, even though it was clearly too hot for their liking. They both took turns fussing over their sister and finally curled up together in a far corner and softly whined their displeasure.

The Boy studied the maps until he could no longer keep his eye open, and then he, too, curled up on the floor and fell asleep.

Sometime in the long hours of darkness, Halo came to a brief lucidity and quietly dragged her ruined frame out of the bunkroom and into the cold and laid herself down under the stars. She had been terribly afraid, but was no longer. Now she just gazed up at the sky pulsing with a display of northern lights which almost seemed to reach down and caress her body, brighter then she had ever before seen them. Her last thoughts were of running for her master, and it was his hand that she felt touching her with love and compassion as all sense of the world faded away.

3

There was a storm coming. The Boy could see it building in the wedge of sky beyond the canyon like a dark bruise slowly engorging with blood.

He had known from the moment that he awoke and found

her gone what had become of Halo. It was, after all, the inevitable conclusion he had expected, and the culmination of his flight into the ranges. He found her body stiff and cold and surrounded by her teammates, all of them gathered in a loose semi-circle and silently watching. A line of ravens rimmed the roofline of the Quonset hut, and when he turned to look around, he was unsurprised to see that not a single roofline, guy-wire, or structure remained uncovered by the host. Completely silent, they, too, only watched the spectacle as it unfolded.

The sky lowered and began to fill the air with stinging grains whipped on a rising wind, and though the temperature turned savage, The Boy worked with his parka off and sleeves rolled up past his elbows and sweat gleaming on his naked hairless chest. His Mama called to him and sang, and his little baby brother cried, but he ignored them such was his concentration. As his labors continued throughout that strange day, it became dark much too early and great billows of freezing snow raged from out of the canyon like the cold breath of some mythological beast. He worked like a machine, a singular engine, the axe rising and falling, harder and harder, faster and faster, crushing and splintering and throwing up constellations of white hot sparks as it fulfilled its obligation as a tool of great purpose—and still he continued like a mindless automaton.

He came back to his senses such as they were and took the fact of his surroundings for granted. A great deal of time had passed; the too early nightfall and the blizzard and already enough new snow to come up past his knees; the wind shrieking so loud that any rational thought seemed nigh impossible; the pyre of splintered wooden pallets the result of his day's labors, so immense that two dump trucks working together could not have hauled it all away. There was a hole through his middle and he knew not whether it was because of an empty stomach or a fractured heart. He let the axe slip from his blistered and bloody fingers. The smell of raw diesel fuel assaulted his nostrils, and he saw that he had taken drums of fuel and held them over the pyre until their contents were fully drained. He heaved a long and weary sigh, his head bowing forward and long shanks of frozen hair occluding his face. His was the profile of a man tired beyond all reckoning. When he raised his face, he saw that Halo was laid out to rest at the place where the stack of wood formed a rough bed, and already her body was being blanketed by freshly fallen snow. The dogs were dim crouched shapes at the periphery of his vision, hunkered low and silently waiting.

A spark of light suddenly caught his eye, out of place in all of the dark. He gazed out to the distant canyon and at first saw nothing, and then, just as he decided that his eye had played some trick, it came again, a brief flash from high on the east face of the canyon wall; come and gone in an instant. As hard as it was storming down here in the encampment, he knew that up in the pass would be much worse, perhaps even impassable. He watched for a time, heedless of the pain of his freezing flesh. The light blinked on and off, on and off, and gradually resolved itself as a long yellow tunnel. From the way it moved, he knew it to be the headlamp of a dog team and musher. It took an eternity to travel the length of the canyon, and at times The Boy even wondered if the musher had been stopped, and that would have been terrible indeed, for he could not think of a worse place to be forced to a halt. But no, the musher and his team made progress however glacial and after a time cleared the rim of the canyon and dropped out of sight below the plateau.

The wind slowly subsided and the snowfall intensified, and soon a dim light painted the brush and tops of the buildings of the encampment. Titan and Legend took up posts to either side of their master and the rest of the team came to silent attention as long shadows sprang from the crest of the plateau and raced ahead like a herd of silent horses. A moment later, and the new team became visible. The musher's headlamp was a star above the handlebar of an immense freight-sled and his dogs were trotting calmly and the sounds of their breathing and the jingling of their tack was clear even from a quarter mile's distance.

The Boy crouched and laid a striker to the pyre, shaving a quick flurry of sparks into the fuel and tinder until the whole thing went off like a brush fire, lighting the area as if a blazing sun had set itself down amongst the abandoned structures. Quick tongues of flame lapped at Halo's fur, and then hungrily ravaged her. Within moments, her form was hidden behind a wall of smoke and swirling sparks and these sparks leapt into the night sky like a crackling shower of meteorites.

The stranger's team came into this well of firelight and stopped just short. The driver was a small man dressed in a knee length parka and mukluks and his face was completely hidden from view behind a thickly wrapped scarf. This stranger anchored his sled and slowly made his way along the team, dropping tugs and patting dogs on their heads, muttering words of thanks and praise. The Boy could almost recognize his voice. At last, the stranger finished his chores and approached the fireside, un-wrapping his face and letting the crusted scarf dangle from his gloved fingers.

The Boy and he just looked at each other for a long moment without either saying a word.

'I was wondering when you would show up,' said The Boy finally.

4

The man was very old, his face seamed and creased with a roadmap of wrinkles. He was freshly shaven and his eyes sparkled and seemed to smile even though his countenance was solemn.

'This is a night that was made for mushing dogs,' he said now, and his voice held the odd combination of youthful vigor and ancient frailty.

'Aye,' The Boy solemnly agreed.

The old man gazed into the fire which was starting to die down. He stooped and reached into the embers and selected a glowing coal the size of an egg. He handled it gingerly, and then carefully placed it back.

'You were the one who started all of this, this mushing thing,' The Boy said.

The old gentleman smiled and shook his head. 'No, I didn't start mushing, not at all. At best, I had a hand in getting the Great Race going, but that is all.'

'Ah. How did that happen to come about?' asked The Boy. His vision blurred, and a wave of exhaustion washed over him, profound in its intensity.

The old man chuckled. 'It was many years ago back when I had just left the Army. I had a job mushing freight in and out of a big gold claim out Holy Cross way. That was back in the days when dog teams were commonplace in the bush, like airplanes are now. One day, it sank in that I was the last one hauling by dog sled, that at some point the people of the villages had given up the husky and had started using snowmobiles. At first these were just a novelty, these machines, only one or two people in a village might have one, and those ran poorly. I lost my best friend, a woodcutter from Grayling, to a snowmobile accident. He was miles from home when his broke down and he died attempting to walk back. A ground storm blew up and he got lost, ended up in the overflow. We never did find his body, just his tracks going into the water. It never would have happened if he had been on his dog team, but of course he got rid of all of his dogs to buy that damn machine.

'It didn't take long for the machines to spread throughout

the bush, and the sled dogs disappeared in direct proportion. The machines were faster, didn't require the same level of year round care. It was just another way that western influence worked to subvert the natives' traditional values, or at least that's how it seemed to me at the time. There came a time when I would go through the villages on my team and the children would come out into the streets and stare in wonder at this oddity, and this fact alone was painful to bear. Finally, my job ran out and I went home to my family in the Valley, but no matter how far away I went I could not forget what was happening, that a way of life was ended and a page forever turned. It haunted me, got to where that's all I could think about, that I was one of the last people left in the world who still loved sled dogs enough to live with them and work with them on a day to day basis, and that when I was gone…they would be gone too. Those were the reasons behind my motivation to start the Great Race. I knew that an important part of our world was on the brink of passing away, and I simply couldn't bear to see it go.

'The how of starting the Great Race is its own story, and not the one that I came up here to tell you.' The old man stopped here and the two of them were silent, sitting side by side and staring into the flames.

Unaware that he had fallen asleep, The Boy jerked awake with his companion's hand on his arm, but it was a strange kind of wakening, for he felt as if glue were pulsing in his veins and his brain was wrapped in a bed of wet cotton. There was nothing left of the pyre save a bed of coals simmering in a deep hole and blackening of ashes around its perimeter. Of Halo, nothing remained but her memory.

'Listen,' said the old gentleman. 'Are you listening? I have something to tell you, something very important.'

Yes, said The Boy or maybe didn't, maybe he just thought it.

'I know who you are. It is no accident that I came tonight to find you. I came, because there are things that I need to tell you. I know what you have gone through. I'm here to tell you that it has just begun, and it only gets harder. Before your story ends, your suffering will be the stuff of legend. It will become the subject of tales told around a campfire on dark and stormy nights such as this one. I know what drives you, what pushes you to compete, why you rush to embrace dog mushing and also racing, how you are making your way through a series of trials just so you can be ready when the time comes.'

The Boy just stared at the old man's face, scarcely able to breathe.

'I know that you think that you are all alone in the world, that it is just you and your dogs, and you are mostly right about that, but not completely. There are others who will guide you. Your Mama remains, and you know this because you can still hear her calling your name, calling for you to come-

'Home,' The Boy whispered. 'She calls for me to come home.' He raised his hands and covered his face and the old man pulled him into his arms and held him there and said into his ear:

'I know who you are and how your story is going to end. I am here to tell you to not be afraid, that if you would make it home, you will have to be strong like few in this world are. You are a true son of the northland, and the land itself will hold you in its bosom when the time comes, when the moment of your ending is at hand.'

The Boy's mind fractured and began to break into splinters and shards of long faded memories. He sees his Mama's face as she leans down to pull him up off of the floor; her hair is held up by a checkered bandana and there is flour all over her cheeks. Now Papa is holding her in a loving embrace, and he is watching the two of them from a crib. Papa is whispering her name over and over because she has just told him that she is again with child, his baby brother; water spraying from the bow of a riverboat blasting along in the afternoon sunlight of a mid-summers day. Uncle sitting squint eyed and holding the tiller handle; dogs barking, first just one or two, and then dozens, maybe even hundreds, all of them joyous and ready to run; and now the river ripples and crunches with ice, and he is holding onto a set of handlebars and the dogs are ripping him down the trail at an all out run, and this makes his heart swell to the point of bursting. They run and run and a sudden wind sprays the trail with snow and grit and he can hear his little baby brother screaming in terror, the little guy just wants to go home, he doesn't understand what's going on and he doesn't want to die; and Mama is holding both of them tightly in her arms, and she knows that this is how it's going to end no matter how much she doesn't want it to be true, Mother Nature does not care what she wants, so her song that she sings is not one of hope, it is one of loss, and its only purpose is to calm her children in their dark and final moments.

'Listen,' said the old man, still holding him. 'The Northland is not fair or just, it does not even own or recognize either one of these concepts. These notions were invented by man to make his life seem more bearable. No, the Northland just *is*. When the time comes for you to go home to your family, you will have to accept this as truth, to let the truth of this live complete in your heart. That is the nature of your travail, to help you accept this. It will be your only chance. The Northland is a song, and if you would get to where you are going, then you will have to learn to sing with it and not against it.'

The Boy's mind convulsed.

'The Northland is a ballad, and you are a part of it. You must be a part of it.'

It is the wind that he heard blowing down the long empty corridor of his soul, and this was the last he knew of anything.

5

Dawn touched The Boy's face with a cold gray light. He sat up to
find that his companion of the previous night long since decamped.
The fire was dead, but still some heat emanated from its sifted ashes.
He crouched there like an animal, unable to marshal his thoughts
until the morning sun was well up and golden radiance had flooded
the plateau. At last, he gave himself a shake and stood straight up
and whistled for his dogs. They surged from the open door of the
Quonset hut and gathered round and he recruited them all into
the traces and pointed the sled back in the direction of the canyon
road. Before him were the slurred tracks of the old gentleman's team,
looking to have been laid in sometime in the pre-dawn hours. He
looked over his shoulder for a last survey of the Petersville Mine. The
collection of weather beaten and empty buildings seemed too apt a
metaphor for the landscape of his soul, and this bleak observation
sent a deep and abiding chill through the marrow of his bones. He
called the team into action and they leapt down the trail with Legend
and Titan side by side plowing through the occasional snow drift that
reached higher than the tips of their tails. They made it over the pass,
and soon the canyon was a distant blur to their backs and the day
was fair and warm as they descended back into the lower hills and
the land of men and civilization. It was late in the afternoon when
they finally arrived in the low country of the Shulin Lake trail system
and they found the parking area of the Roadhouse packed with all
manner of all-terrain vehicles, and even a number of small dog teams
unharnessed and tethered in a half hazard array.

The Boy noted a group of men at the entry way to the lodge, all
smoking and talking in low voices as if in the presence of clergy. He
noticed Crazy Tom foremost amongst them and he stopped and the
older man approached him.

'Hello there,' said Crazy Tom, holding out a big hand to be shook.

The Boy clasped his hand, nodded at the group of men and cluster of conveyances. 'Something of a get together, I see,' he observed.

'Aye, it's been quite a day, it has,' Crazy Tom agreed. 'The whole area has been all stirred up. Where have you been, lad?'

The Boy leaned over the handlebar and retrieved his canteen from the sled bag, un-corked it and took a long pull from its brackish contents. 'Up in the hills,' he said after slaking his thirst, jerking a thumb in the direction he had come from. 'I've been camping out at the mines up in Petersville for the last couple of days. I entertained The Old Man last night for some company, but other than that, I haven't seen a soul this past week.'

Crazy Tom stared at him open mouthed. 'You what?' he said at last. 'You've been up at the Petersville Mines?'

'Aye. It made for a lonely camp except for The Old Man showing up. I was able to shelter in one of the Quonset huts.'

'The Old Man showed up last night.'

The Boy looked closely at the older man's face, which was slowly becoming livid. He looked over his shoulder at the Roadhouse and could hear some woman inside crying loudly. 'What's wrong?' he asked.

Crazy Tom took a step too close and said in a low voice full of anger, 'I'll tell you what's wrong. What's wrong is some punk kid having me on at a time like this. You didn't see The Old Man last night, that's just bull and you'd better quit saying it if you know what's good for you.'

The Boy took a step back to give Crazy Tom some space and held out his hands. 'Look, I don't know what's happening here, and I don't really care,' he said. 'I think I'm just going to hit the road.' He bent down to yank the snowhook when Crazy Tom's voice stopped him.

'The Old Man died last night. He was in the hospital like he's been for the last month, surrounded by his family and friends, and they say he just died like a candle being blown out.'

The Boy slowly straightened back up.

'And that part about camping at the mines? That's crap too. That mine burnt to the ground twenty years ago, and they dynamited the road going into the pass to keep people from poking around the property.'

Crazy Tom turned on his heel and stomped off to join his friends, leaving The Boy gaping in his wake.

Chapter X

1

A week unattended had left the camp unrecognizable as such. It now lay buried under an ocean of new snow, the tent collapsed and the fire pit vanished. The Boy picketed the dogs back in the woods and spent the night in his sled, and every time his mind tried to bend back on itself to consider the events of the last few days, he would ruthlessly turn it in some new direction. The end result was a miserably sleepless night while a clown circus clamored for attention in the confines of his head.

Someone was kicking his sled, hard enough to jerk it from side to side even with the weight of his body holding it down.

'What the hell?' a rough voice asked. 'Are you going to sleep forever, or what?'

The Boy opened the frozen flap of his sled bag and peered out. It was still dark, not yet morning. A man's shape loomed over him and the rich smell of burning tobacco flooded his nostrils.

'Who is it?' he asked, working to free himself from his sleeping arrangement. The man did not answer, just turned around and walked away. Now The Boy could see that it was a small group of men standing together, talking in low voices and smoking. The tips of their cigarettes gleamed like red stars in the still, predawn air. He wondered how they were able to come upon him with no alert from his dogs or without awakening him from his fitful sleep.

'Who are you?' he asked again. He felt no hostility despite the rude awakening.

'Your camp is crap,' the man said over his shoulder. 'Typical white man. It's a wonder you haven't frozen to death before now.'

The Boy could think of no reply to this, so he shrugged and walked up the path to the parking area. The sky was gradually lightening, and he saw that the men had all arrived by dog team. There were five small teams pulled off of the main trail and parked slantwise like a fleet of motorbikes. He did a quick count, and came up with fifty dogs, all sitting in their traces and quietly staring at him. He didn't need to turn on his flashlight to see who's they were. He had been running into them all fall and winter driven by The Old Man's handlers.

'Yeah, quite a collection,' said the stranger who had followed him up the path and now stood at his shoulder. 'The Old Man asked me to come down and take them over. It was his final request.'

The Boy nodded. 'What became of the guy who was working his dogs?' he asked.

The man chuckled softly in the dark. 'Well, turns out that the fat little toad had designs on the team for himself, didn't even cross his mind that The Old Man might not let him just have them. He got pretty upset when I showed up and told him about the new plan, so I had to give him the boot.'

Though unable to see the man's face, The Boy could tell that he was smiling. 'So, why are you down here waking me up?' he asked.

'After I sacked the handler, it sort of created an uncomfortable situation around there, so me and my brothers thought we would find us a place to set up camp. Turns out this is it.'

'Ah. So what now?'

'I've heard a lot about you,' said the man. 'People have been talking about you all over the place. I wish I could tell you it was all good, but some of its pretty damn weird, to tell you the truth.'

This elicited a bark of laughter from The Boy and the man joined with him.

'They say that you're up here training for the Delta race,' he continued. 'That you're going to be the youngest man ever to run it, maybe even win it. I wanted to meet you, find out what all of the talk was really about.' The man jerked a thumb over his shoulder, indicating what was left of The Boy's camp. 'I gotta tell you kid, so far I'm not very impressed. You make things a lot tougher on yourself then you really need to. There's a better way to do things.'

'And I suppose you are going to show me this better way?'

'You're damn right I'm going to show you this better way. Living like this, about all you're going to accomplish is to freeze your pecker off, and a man of your tender age probably has big plans for his pecker. Or at least he should if he's got two testicles to rub together underneath his jeans. Be a shame to have your future reproductive cycle shut down early on account of sloppy camping practices.'

This left The Boy with nothing to say. All he could do was gape at this outrageous apparition.

'Now listen,' the man continued. 'We still have a couple of months to get you squared away and ready to make your big debut into civilization. You need the time to work on your camping and conversational skills, I need the time to retrain this sorry sack of problems that I've been saddled with. I mean, you wouldn't believe how screwed up that handler was training them, letting them learn just about every bad habit a group of dogs could learn. That little toad deserved a thumping just for being such a crummy dog trainer.'

The man's fellows all burst into harsh laughter at this last bit.

'So, what do you say kid? Me and my bro's need a place to set up camp, and you've picked the nicest spot around for miles. You into hanging out with someone who can teach you a thing or two about running dogs and living rough?'

'Well, um, I guess…' stammered The Boy.

'Good. That's really good.' The man stuck out his hand. 'Maybe you've heard of me. I'm The Whaler.'

2

The Whaler's mates turned out to be step brothers, four in all and the youngest not much older than The Boy himself. They wore an odd combination of traditional coastal gear; fur-lined parkas with small hood openings designed to cup the face of the wearer, and modern Refrigaware insulated bibs. The Whaler himself was garbed from head to toe in luxurious spotted sealskin devoid of any embroidery or beadwork. A short and powerfully built man, he was never without a long, bone-handled cutter fashioned from soft steel and strapped to a broad leather belt at his waist.

The troop's first order of business was to fashion accommodations for themselves. Working as a team, they excavated three large hemispheres all the way to the bare frozen earth, and then brought in huge armloads of the straightest willow poles that they could find, stripped and peeled and no thicker than a man's thumb at the base. They worked these into low domes, bases planted into the ground and tops bent and interwoven, lashed together with crude strips of some pliable animal hide. These strange cages were then plastered with mounds of wet slushy snow and sculpted and tamped down by hand until the walls were at least a foot thick and compacted to the point of becoming ice, leaving only a constricted chimney at the exact pinnacle and a low aperture at the front which necessitated a man to belly crawl upon entering, covering this with a flap of the same hide used to bind the peak. Inside were two bunks, one on either side of a narrow aisle, made from spruce poles welded into the walls and covered with tufts of dead grass cured over a fire. There was a small shelf built into the back wall and upon this was placed a wide pan with deep sides, into which was poured several quarts of some liquefied animal fat. A shank of porous fabric about a foot in length was dipped into this bath and one end left to dangle over the edge, and lit with a small yellow flame. The end result was a smokeless residence warm enough to disrobe and recline half naked while one's clothing dripped dry from pegs driven into the ceiling, and light enough to read a book inside.

This construction was started and completed before the sun had passed the midway point of its trip along the horizon, and to say that The Boy was impressed would be the understatement of the century.

The Whaler noted the boy's undisguised admiration and grinned. 'Your days of wearing wet gear to bed and freezing your tail off all night instead of sleeping are over. From now on, this will be your bunk,' he said, indicating the one across from his own.

'This is amazing,' said The Boy. 'I've lived in the bush my entire life, and never have I seen anything like this; not even close.'

'Well, you have now, and from now on you'll never have that excuse again.'

That night, shortly after sundown, they built a huge bonfire and took their ease on hide blankets flopped right down on the ground and The Whaler grilled The Boy on all of the trails hereabouts and up in the mountains. He looked at the younger man strangely when he related his experiences in the ranges, but made no comment. It was plain on his broad brown face that he knew that The Boy was holding something back from his recounting of events, but had no desire to press for more details. They passed hunks of whale fat and king salmon hand to hand and these were dunked in a jar of seal oil and eaten glistening and raw. The taste of the seal oil was new to The Boy, and the musky richness that flooded his tongue and clotted in his teeth nearly made him vomit. Somehow, with great effort, he was able to hold it all down and soon felt a new energy pulsing through his bloodstream, energy such as he hadn't felt in months, perhaps ever. The Eskimos all watched him intently during this process, breaking into huge grins at his obvious discomfort, and then looking solemn when he struggled with his gorge and won.

'Muktuk and seal oil are two of the best things that you are ever going to put in your mouth,' The Whaler told him. 'They give you energy like you can't believe, and work to keep you warm like no other food out there. A smart man never goes into the bush without these things, no more then he would travel without the tools for making fire in the cold, wet places of the earth.' His brothers all nodded in sage agreement.

The Boy lay back on his hide blanket and allowed the sensation of the rich new fare to settle in his stomach and the feeling of the fire warm his body. He was in the company of dog men, and this brought him to a level of well-being that he would have never supposed.

The Whaler pulled his cutter from its sheath and the blade of it was fully as long as a man's forearm. He began to grind it softly against a small whetstone produced from some inner pocket, and while he did so, he talked of all manner of things, some about living in the north, some about running dogs and hunting seal on the Arctic ice; mostly, about the Great Race in all of its many manifestations. He said:

'I started running the Great Race myself when I was just a young man, right at the very beginning. The Old Man himself talked me into it, just like he did all of us. Of course, we'd all heard talk of his idea, even all of the way up in Teller and Shismaref and Kotzebue. But where I'm from, talk is cheap, and it wasn't until The Old Man himself showed up in town one day on the back of the strongest looking group of huskies that I've ever laid eyes upon that I started taking it serious. He had traveled all the way from Knik in the Matanuska Valley, stopping at villages along the way to lobby for support and stir up interest. See, he was working on two things that he needed to accomplish which were vital to the success of any bush race, one of them being really in your face obvious; drivers to fill a roster. Can't have a race without racers, right? The second was something it took everybody else a long time to get, and even now a lot of folks still don't; the support of the people in the villages. The Old Man knew even before the beginning, that without the villages, there would be no race. It would be up to the villagers to house the mushers and all of the necessary race personnel, because the race and everybody attached to it would be guests on their property. And it would be the villagers who would clean up the mess once everybody was gone on down the trail without a thought as to what they'd left behind, and boy let me tell you, white folks know how to make a real big mess.

'So, The Old Man shows up to talk me into racing. He's on his way to Barrow, and I'm just as impressed as all hell. I'd been driving dogs since I was a baby, and even I never knew that someone could go so far on the back of a dog sled. His dogs looked amazing. They'd been on the go for a month and they still looked like they had just jogged over from Nome, fat and silky coated, bright eyed and full of energy like you wouldn't believe. But not out of control mind you, not at all. The Old Man could just look at them, and it was like he had some kind of telepathic bond or something, they would all just pipe down and watch him for their next command. If he told them to sit, he did it in almost a whisper and the dogs just did what he told them. If he told them to get up and get ready, it was the same thing, just a murmur of a command, but the dogs would leap to attention and start hammering the line as if he'd shouted through a megaphone.

'He really opened my eyes, and of course I was in. I was just hooked. Death couldn't have kept me away from his Great Race. He went through that entire winter motivating mushers and dog men, getting drivers out of the villages and mines and gold fields, and about the time that people back in Anchor town and the Valley were saying that the race wasn't going to go because there just weren't enough mushers left in the world to fill a roster, whole droves of us showed up from all walks of life and all points of the compass and pledged our entry. I tell you what, the press didn't even know what to say for about a week, and then they all jumped on board and acted like they had been supportive all along.

'We were all just a bunch of loggers and trappers and bush men back in those days, a pretty rough looking crowd I can tell you, all except for The Woman. She was just a sprat all in braids and freckles, like a pup following The Old Man around. She was a handler for him, and she was going to drive a group of his yearling's right along with the rest of us rugged manly men. Damn if she didn't turn out to be about the toughest and smartest of all of us! The Outdoorsman, he was just transplanted from the states and he took a real shine to her, offered her a job if she ever got sick of living in the Valley and running The Old Man's puppies. Who knows what he offered her, but they were friends for a while until she got her own team together and started whipping his tail, and then their friendship turned into one of the great rivalries of the sport.

'We came down out of the hills that March and it was just as much to be a part of this thing as it was for the gold waiting for us in Nome. The gold, twelve thousand dollars worth, and put up by The Old Man himself. He wasn't a rich man by any stretch, but he put up all of his savings and land holdings as collateral for that first purse, and if the race had fallen through he would have been made a pauper. Not that any of us knew it at the time, mind you. That much money back in those days was a really big deal, hell, it's still a big deal today. It might not be basketball, but it sure encouraged the mushers to put in as much effort as any Olympic athlete, I can tell you that much. Nobody knew what they were doing, though. Not the mushers, not the race organizers or the trail breakers. Well, the trail breaking fell to the Army to oversee, and it goes without saying that they didn't know what they were doing. Those guys nearly ruined us. But the rest of us, that was our first experience doing something with dogs other then working them in the back country. As the years went by, we all got better and more professional about how we cared for the dogs and covered the trail, the race sped up almost a week over the first four years, but I remember that first night after we started the first race like it was yesterday. I'm here to tell you it was a real circus.

'Fist off, hardly anybody knew what a headlamp was back in

those days, and we were all afraid to travel at night because of it. Plus, realize that those fools in the Army couldn't find their butts with both hands and a flashlight and three of their buddies helping, so you can just imagine what kind of crummy trail they put in. They didn't mark intersections, and would only put in one piece of lathe for every ten miles or so of trail, and then the numb-nuts wouldn't stick them in the snow the correct way and they would all fall down. Or tip over if it so much as blew on them. So, those of us leading the pack pretty much just followed their snowmobile tracks, and this was a pretty messed up plan because if it was snowing or blowing their tracks disappeared awfully quick, and even if the weather was steady, those guys didn't know where they were going most of the time either and they were always getting lost and having to backtrack ten or twenty miles on a regular basis. I was the first one to reach the Big Su that year, over by Susitna Station, and I got lost like you wouldn't believe. It was just coming on dark, and there were a couple teams right on my tail, and instead of making overland for Skwentna, I just blew it and followed the Army's snow-go tracks headed up the Susitna where they'd already gone and turned back the day before.

'It was too dark for me to see where they'd went a few miles and turned around, having realized their mistake, and I ended up going all the way to the Parks Highway in Willow. I had to leave my team and walk down the highway to a little bar and grill I could see lit up in the distance, and boy were they surprised to see me walk through their door! After they told me where I was, I about lost it, almost scratched right then and there. So, instead, I had a few drinks, and then went back to where I had left my team and brought them into the pub's parking lot and spent the night camped out back of their propane tank and tool shed and listened to semi's go past on the highway until it was light enough to see. Some old lady running the kitchen took pity on me and brought me a whole case of out of date bread to feed to my dogs, and the owner of the place had one of the local drunks run home and fetch me a bag of his pet dog's kibble.

'After getting lost, I was all scared up about travelling in the dark, so I planned right then and there to do most of my racing by the light of day when I could see what was what, and camp during the night, at least until I got back into country that I knew, like on the coast up to Unalakleet way. The next morning, I got going and made it back to the confluence of the Su and Yentna well before the end of the day and found that everybody else had had problems during the night, too, not just me. It had been The Cowboy and The Outdoorsman who had been following me onto the river the night before, though I didn't know this until later, and they'd followed me all the way up the Su until they lost my trail and got turned off in some slough and got up to their butts in a nasty patch of overflow. While they were drying themselves out on the banks of the river, there about forty more teams came limping in, all following their tracks. A really big mess, and by morning, that whole group was not much better off than I was. I caught the whole pack just as the front runners were getting into Rabbit Lake and calling it a camp for the rest of the night. I couldn't believe it. By the next morning, I was back out front and leading the whole darn mess.

'That first race was like the blind leading the blind. By the time we had reached the Alaska Range and climbed up to Puntilla Lake, nobody really wanted to be in the lead anymore. Usually that just meant that you'd be the first one to get lost, or run into overflow, or have to build a bridge over some open creek only to have everybody else come whooping along and breeze right across just after you got it done. And the Happy Valley and the Dalzell Gorge, don't even get me started. Let's just say that by the time we got down into Rohn, there wasn't a sled in the race that hadn't been broken twice or more. The Old Man came into Rohn with both of his runners broken off right behind the rear stanchions so that he had to run along behind; and The Preacher had skewered his sled on some old stump and blew it apart like a bomb had gone off in the bag. The both of them sat in Rohn for almost a week rebuilding their sleds, while the rest of us continued on to McGrath and Takotna, and they still caught up to us because we all ran out of trail in a storm and were out in front of our teams snow shoeing to give the leaders a track to follow, moving about as fast as a herd of snails. The Old Man passed us up and was the first into Iditarod, the halfway point. We all stopped there and had a big party. None of us could believe it that we'd made it that far.

'There were all kinds of problems. It was tough to find food for ourselves and the dogs. Nowadays, the race sends out our food drops way ahead of time and makes sure that there's plenty of straw for the dogs and fuel for our cookers, and they tried to do that back then, too, but they didn't have the logistics of it down. We would run into food and supplies every few hundred miles, and when we did, we'd all load our sleds fit to burst, all of us afraid that we'd run out if for some reason the planes couldn't fly, or maybe just sent our food to the wrong place by mistake. That was how The Outdoorsman got his big jump that year. While we were all waiting in Iditarod for the planes to arrive, he snuck out and started off for the Yukon, about a hundred miles away. None of us thought he'd make it. What we didn't know was that he'd brought over extra food from Ophir, and when he ran out of that on the way to Shageluk, he just staked his team out and went hunting for a moose to blast. I was the next one out behind him, and as I was going over those big hills on the way to the river, I reckoned I'd come up on him holed up somewhere looking for a handout. But when I came across that butchered carcass off to the side of the trail, I knew that the race was over, that the sonofagun was at least a day out front, and with a sled full of moose meat. I didn't know whether to laugh or cry.

'We got out on the Yukon River, and I can tell you none of us, man woman or child, was ready for what we ran into there. The wind was steady coming out of the north and just blasting us in the face, and it was cold like I didn't know it could get. Visibility was down to nothing, and most of us stopped in Anvik for a few days, hoping it would blow itself out. One of my buddies, from upriver in Grayling, came in to see me, told me that The Outdoorsman was still there and hunkered down just like we were, so I didn't mind waiting, Grayling only being about twenty miles up the trail. By the time I got there though, he'd been gone for a half a day or so, and I was hoping to whittle that down on the coast.

'But by then, me and a bunch of the other guys were all learning some real hard lessons about traveling long distance by dog team, and in such large groups. The dogs, not just mine, but mine were bad enough, were all starting to get sick. Some intestinal bug that made them go off their feed and blow what little they did eat back out their rear ends like brown water. And they were all just tired, mostly from lack of adequate training and over running earlier on. By the time we got off of the Yukon, most of us could walk next to the sled and still keep up with our teams. I never did catch The Outdoorsman, he was just too tricky. Every time I made some kind of move, he would somehow get word that I was coming along and he would get going, too, and all I'd find was a long cold camp with his used toilet paper blowing in the wind. So to speak.

'The Old Man and a few others passed me up and ran off and left me by the time we got to the coast. The Preacher actually almost caught The Outdoorsman on the last run into Nome, but ran out of trail before he could do it. In the end, only about thirty of us made it to the finish out of the fifty or so that started from Anchorage, and it took the fastest of us almost a full month to do it. A month, if you can believe it. Nowadays, the slowest most underprepared group of dogs can get there in two weeks. Nowadays they would lock you up for poaching if you popped a moose out of season just to feed your team.

'Things are different now.'

The Whaler stopped his long oration and gazed solemnly into the fire, as if some sad new thought had occurred to him.

3

The Boy hated to interrupt the older man's reverie, but could not help himself.

'You've almost won the race so many times. You've been the closest anyone has ever come to beating The Norwegian, at least since his rookie year.' Here The Boy fell silent. He had a question, but not the language to properly articulate it.

The Whaler nodded, but said nothing; he tested his blade with the pad of his thumb, and must have approved of what he saw, because he smiled a little and replaced the cutter into its holster. He looked at The Boy then, and the expression on his face was strange, partially hidden by a sudden column of smoke.

'Back in those early days,' he said, 'you could almost take time to run a trapline and still make out pretty good in the competition. That gradually changed over the years as the competition heated up and sponsors started picking up teams, and pretty soon there was a lot of side money getting laid on the table. The stakes were going up, and the way most drivers approached the race changed to make these accommodations. The Woman and The Tinkerer were the first to really understand the commercial aspect of the race, and they were soon the ones with the most powerful kennels and the ones dominating the pace.'

'But you competed with them, beat them often enough. Did you have a big kennel, or lots of sponsorship?' The Boy interjected.

The Whaler grinned and shook his head. 'Nope. Not a lot of sponsorship money being tossed around where I'm from. No, I just got by on toughness and wits, and the fact that nobody knows the coast like I do. Money can't buy you a victory in the Great Race. It just helps a lot.' He paused there and took a foil packet out of his parka and withdrew a stubby little cigar from it. He reached into the bed of coals at the periphery of the fire and selected one and held it between his naked fingers, placed it to the tip of his cigar and puffed until it was lit. He replaced the coal as if it had its own unique place in the fire.

'The Norwegian,' he said. 'Nobody understands him, least of all me, and I've been the closest to competing with him of anybody over the last few races, except maybe for The Cowboy. Let me tell you a little story. This happened last year. The Cowboy comes up to me right before the race, and he tells me that this is going to be his year. He's been doing well in middle distance and his team was of a seasoned age, and he has these two dogs that were brothers, Anik and Pluto. They were the best leaders that he'd ever run and they were both at their absolute peak. And that's saying something, because The Cowboy is legendary for having some of the best leaders. I'd raced against him with those two in the lead of his team, and I was plenty impressed. Anyway, his thought, and most of us agreed with this, was that The Norwegian could only make these epic pushes like he did because his leaders had tougher heads, for some reason, then the rest of ours. Now, what he was doing was no secret. I mean, he would just start the race from the word go and hardly ever stop, we knew that after the first time he whupped us. But what the big mystery was, was how the hell he was getting away with it. I mean, the rest of us tried to push even a fraction as hard as him, and believe you me a lot of folks tried, our teams would crack up and maybe not even finish.

'Well, The Cowboy figured that he had his number and had finally trained up a team that could race like he did. We were having ourselves a little huddle right there on 4th Avenue, minutes before the race start, and he told me that when the timer said go, he wasn't going to stop until Skwentna, and then only long enough to get some food into the dogs and then light out for Finger Lake. Him and me, we'd always been friends, and I guessed he was telling me because he wanted some company out there. But I didn't like the idea because the way I train dogs, I always like to come into a race real conservative and then build a head of steam as I go. So, I tell him so and he smiles and shakes my hand like he always does, and away we go.

'And he does just like he told me he was going to do. By the time me and some of the other guys are pulling into Rabbit Lake that first night and getting our bearings, there's word comes back to us that The Cowboy's already in Skwentna, in front of even The Norwegian. And that's the last we see of either of them, at least for a while. Of course we're all rooting him on. What he's doing is just plain ballsy, and you couldn't help but admire him for it. Of all of us, The Cowboy is probably the most aggressive, and watching him take on The Norwegian like that made even his fiercest rival proud. See, that's the thing. It had got to the point that we almost couldn't even picture racing with that bastard.'

The Whaler fell silent and just sat there puffing on his cigar, eyes unfocused and staring into the flames. He kicked at a crackling log and sent a shower of sparks skirling skyward.

'We'd come into those early checkpoints like Puntilla Lake and Rohn, and those two would already be gone,' he continued. 'And the word that we were getting through the grapevine was that The Cowboy's team was looking even stronger then The Norwegian's. That's all anybody could talk about. How that maybe after three years holding the crown, The Cowboy would be the one to make him cough it up. One thing was for sure, they were both pushing the pace harder than it had ever been pushed before. Then he started dropping dogs.

'Up until the Yukon, they both still had full teams. But after Ruby, The Cowboy's team started to dwindle. I was the runner up coming along almost eighteen hours behind those two, and I wasn't exactly taking a lot of rest, if you know what I mean, and when things started to fall apart for him, well, it was just painful to watch. Right there on the banks of the Yukon, right there at Ruby, I put on my own push and I caught up to him pulled over in Kaltag, and I knew right away that something was wrong with him. He was off; his eyes were all teared up when he came out to greet me. He pulled me aside and told me that he had dropped Pluto a couple of days before, had been running his brother Anik in single lead all the way up the river trying to keep up the pace.

'And Anik had quit. Plumb gave out; wouldn't go another inch. Running like he did just wore his head out. When I had a look at the dog, I could tell that it was over. He looked like a bad taxidermy job, eyes all listless and glazed over. I asked The Cowboy if he had anybody else to put up front, and he about broke down, said no, they were all used up.'

The Boy stared at him, transfixed by the account.

'See, that's the hell of it, kid. The Cowboy has one of the biggest, strongest kennels I've ever seen; he's maybe the best driver in the country, and trying to keep up with that bastard from Norway just about killed him. He had to sit there in Kaltag for a solid day before he could even get the team moving again, and then all he could do was limp along to Nome. And The Norwegian, he just took his best shot, the best shot any of us have given him so far, and shrugged it off and trotted into Nome a day in front of the next one of us to come along like it was a walk in the park; his fourth in a row, and each one of them seeming to be easier for him then the last.

'No, I don't understand him at all. I've never seen anything like him in all of my days.'

The Boy had never heard such talk; it filled him both with a feeling of strange longing and ominous dread. His mind grappled with this talk of legends and mythos.

The Whaler was staring at him, his almond shaped eyes practically glowing with the light cast from the flames. Orion's belt blazed just over his head, and Sirius pulsed a bit to his right; together, they formed an electric blue halo of sorts.

'You've got a few years yet,' he said, voice soft. 'Right now, maybe you're thinking that you'll be the one, the one who comes along and breaks the spell. Lots of rookies think that, trust me. Here in a couple of years, you'll go toe to toe with him, and then you'll see.'

Then I'll see, thought The Boy. *Then I'll see.*

Chapter XI

1

THE season contracted and the days of winter passed. The Boy took the Eskimos and their teams into the backwoods and the surrounding hill country, showing them the network of trails and discovering new ones in the process. At first The Whaler's group of dogs couldn't keep up, and then after several weeks of reconditioning, he was matching The Boy's team almost step for step. The Old Man's dogs were not nearly as disciplined as The Boy's, and when he asked The Whaler why he had taken them on, his new mentor just smiled and shrugged.

They were deep in the mountains, parked on the spine of a ridge overlooking the Susitna Valley to the east. The Yenlo Hills slumped in sullen retreat along one corner of the horizon, while the arterial path of a pair of rivers lay below their vantage in frosty silence. The two of them were taking their lunch, and The Boy commented that their time in Trapper Creek was nearly over, that it was about time to pack up and start heading out to Bethel in preparation for the big race. The Whaler looked back at his assortment of shaggy black dogs and slowly nodded. He looked at The Boy.

'Yeah, that's about right,' he agreed. His parka was open at the collar despite a cruel wind, and his broad face was split in a perpetual grin. 'I don't know how these guys are going to do out there, but I'm going to find out one way or the other. I think we should take them on one last big trip to toughen them up. What do you think?'

The Boy considered his own dogs. No matter how hard he ran them this year, he had yet to see them tired. Yes, one more run, one epic journey to test them and see. Looking down upon the distant, winding watercourse that would lead him back to the Susitna if only he followed it far enough, he knew just where they should go.

'The Delta race isn't like the junior stuff you've been running,' The Whaler was saying. 'It's not nearly as fast, and the trail is just awful. You've never seen anything like it, I can guarantee you. If you tried to go as fast as you did last year in the Junior Great Race, you would just burn up. It's an endurance race, plain and simple. It gets won by the team that can go with the least rest without caving in and can handle the worst weather you can imagine. Sometimes, I think that the Great Race should be a qualifier for it.'

Though he had never been there, The Boy knew of the race's reputation for miserable conditions and legendary competition. The Delta K300 was the second most important distance race in the world after the Great Race. Hunched on the noses of their sleds, they ate the remainder of their meal in silence but for the susurrus of the wind, two be-cloaked agents from some long dead wilderness empire.

'Do you think I'm crazy?' The Boy asked the man who had come to be his teacher.

'I know that you're crazy,' The Whaler said with the smile of a savage who finds humor in the very idea of civilization.

'That's not what I meant.'

'I know what you meant, and I still think you're crazy. Anyway you're meaning it.'

The Boy sighed. 'Do you think I'm a fool?'

The Whaler said nothing, but his grin remained.

They turned the teams around and headed back to camp as the day wound down into darkness.

2

The Boy and The Whaler recruited their teams before daybreak and turned them away from their tethers. They knew these trails, dogs and men alike, and there was no need for light. The sleds were loaded full with the necessities of a long trip, and the pace was brisk on a trail packed slick. They crossed the bridge below the Roadhouse with the atonal whomping of the lodge's diesel generator reverberating through the steel girders and shivering the rotted planking beneath their feet. Later, the sun blistered the horizon and found them pulling hard up the shoulder of the Petersville Range, and when they looked back, they could see specks moving about in the Roadhouse parking lot, and further on, a smudge of hazy blue and a plume of smoke that represented their own campsite at the edge of the swamp.

They climbed over a mountainside blown down to crusted ice and tufts of tundra with chunks and shards of lichen spotted rock sticking up, and down into narrow gullies filled with loose powder and thickets of pucker brush. This country alternated at intervals, and in all of the places where the snow collected the sled's runners punched through and the dogs were forced to apply a herculean strain against the mainline; the drivers loped alongside and struggled through drifts that came up to their waists. As they ascended through this country, the wind located them and tore at their efforts and forced them to buckle down and squint their eyes against a hail of splintered ice and dirt, and when The Boy risked a look over his shoulder to make sure that his traveling companion was still with him, he saw that The Whaler had pulled on his whalebone visor. The side hills became so steep that they were forced to roll their sleds nearly over on their sides and heave them along in a crab-like walk, and by the time they cleared the boulder strewn summit, their legs trembled and their lungs plunged and the blood of their bodies pounded in their ears. Legend and Titan stood together in the lead where lesser dogs would have failed at the task; they were survivors abandoned at sea, cleaving to one solitary rock outcropping and gazing down upon a land that lay like some great elemental tapestry spread out to all points of the compass in a haze of charcoal and blue, shot through with a winding of monochrome arterial spray and pocked with blotches and pools of purest ivory.

They began their decent from that lofty perch and, for a time, the pass into Petersville glowered to the north and the sky between its mighty jaws showed darkly thunderous; then they were below the point where anything could be seen but the vasty landscape of the Susitna Valley and all of its tributaries. The mountain loomed over them like a grim sentinel and cast their advance into the footprint of its shadow.

They reached a place where two ridges came together and became a funnel of rock and dirt, and still they dropped, and when they came out of this gorge they found that the sun had hidden its face and they were no closer to the tree-line then before. Thick clouds hurried across the sky, and though the wind had lain down, a fine spray of snow was now beginning to fall. They pitched a fireless camp at the foot of two boulders the size of automobiles, and positioned their sleds side by side where the stones came together and formed a crotch of sorts, sheltering them from the worst of the snow and the wind. They fed the dogs raw and themselves the same and hunkered with a tarpaulin pulled over their heads and watched as the snow came down.

Morning bloomed gray and silent, and the snow still fell. When they saddled the teams and made their way from the mountain plateau, they found drifts that reached higher than the dogs' heads. For this stretch, all twenty seven of the dogs were combined into one team and the sleds hooked in tandem; the two mushers each took turns snow-shoeing a trail in front of the leaders. This progress was very slow, and they passed the day in this manner and the night caught them still on the open steppes. With little desire to camp in such a place, they snacked the dogs and continued on, and their headlamp beams hunted and flashed and rendered the dark in a bizarre montage of half seen images. Sometime in the early morning hours, they fetched up at the end of a box canyon and were forced to a halt, the dogs half asleep on their feet and the drivers utterly exhausted. They stopped right in their tracks and bedded down in their sleds until it became too cold to lie still, and then they got the teams up from their ice holes and turned the whole mess around and backtracked until it lightened and they could see their way out of the maze of folds and mountain gullies.

The sky cleared and a three quarter moon passed across its face and they at last came into a forest of thickly grown black spruce and squat stunted birch mixed with willow and alder. The land gentled somewhat, and here the snow had thawed and refrozen enough in recent days that it now held them aloft. They arrived at this place shaking and tired as the sun was sinking into the west, and were obliged to set up camp to make themselves and the dogs a proper meal. Dead spruce trees were hacked down and lit ablaze, and soon they had a terrific fire shooting sparks into the darkening sky. They pushed their cooking pots into the flames and worked to build a thick pallet of green spruce boughs for their own sleeping arrangement. While they did this, twenty seven pairs of eyes watched them with solemn approval.

They bedded down as the constellations slowly revolved and the moon hid its face. Somewhere, not too far away, a pack of wolves began to howl. Legend and Titan were quartered at The Boy's feet, and now they stood to attention with raised hackles and fierce stares into the wood, and soon they and their brothers were accompanying the host. As they sang, the northern lights slowly bled out from the pores of the sky and pulsed with the beat of some celestial engine; thick rivers of color roiling and swimming from one side of that sky to the other like a chariot race of the gods.

Overcome with exhaustion, the two men fell asleep beneath that cold majesty, and while they slept, Legend and Titan remained watchful with the aurora borealis lighting its eldritch fires deep in the wells of their eyes.

3

Dawn came hard and cold and the sun crept into a sky the color of roughened slate. A thick layer of frost cloaked man and animal alike and when they decamped, their every movement was accompanied by a shower of frost and the clanking of frozen material. The dogs emerged from their melted holes and took a long time at stretching and passing their water, and when hooked into the gangline were slow to warm to the job.

They wound through sparse forest until they reached the border of an immense open plain, humped and folded with gullies and thickly blown snowpack that would hold for several steps before caving in. They leapt and plunged over this landscape, at times working cross-grain over the depressions and, at others, down their winding length. The sky steadied into a dim, hammered blue, and it gradually grew so cold that the air became like syrup in their lungs. They again found themselves in a stunted mountain wood and were soon weaving their way around and over downed trees and thickets of heavy brush; the dogs working as hard as The Boy had ever asked them to. Legend and Titan plowed through the worst of this as if telepathically connected to their master, and though breaking trail, easily outstripped The Whaler's team. They arrived at a place where a deep ravine crossed their path, steep sides plunging down and out of sight to some valley floor, and here The Boy called his team to a halt and waited for his companion.

When The Whaler arrived, his parka was open and sweat gleamed on his face and chest despite the cold. The two of them anchored the teams and tossed all of the dogs' snacks of frozen salmon and marbled beef, and then built a quick fire to warm their hands and prepare a meal for themselves.

'You sure you know where you're going?' The Whaler asked.

'Pretty sure.'

'Pretty sure? We'll never make it back up that mountain if we have to turn back.'

'No, there's no turning back,' The Boy agreed.

'Where are we? Are we getting close to Skwentna?'

The Boy slowly shook his head. He looked back the way they had come where the mountain slumbered in a bluish haze. 'I reckon we've come maybe fifteen, maybe twenty miles from the Roadhouse. No more than twenty. And we're not shooting for Skwentna. We're going to drop down into Lake Creek, about twenty miles below it on the Yentna. I figure Lake Creek can't be more than fifty miles all told from the Roadhouse, so, say another thirty miles or so.'

'Thirty miles of this? That'll be a long haul without a trail. I'm thinking we may have come twenty under our runners, but plenty of it was back tracking.'

The Boy nodded and sipped his tea. The Whaler leaned back on his haunches and fired up one of his cigars, and soon its pungent smoke filled the air.

'I'm thinking that we'll run into a trail pretty soon,' said The Boy. 'There's an old fellow from up in Skwentna that's been trapping this country since before I was born. He's got lines going just about everywhere, and I know he's got one that comes up this way. There's no way someone hasn't got a trail in somewhere around here. It'd be too much of a waste.'

'Aye,' agreed The Whaler, looking about in appreciation of his surroundings. 'How are your dogs holding up?'

'A lot better than I am. This snow-shoeing is about knocking my tail in the dirt.'

'Can't ask for better training though, eh?'

'Aye.'

They reclined for a time before saddling the teams and continuing on. They followed the ridge for some distance, threading the teams through savage growths of brush and dense copses of spruce and cottonwood, and their forward pace was glacial. It took them the rest of the day to find a place where the ridgeline folded into a steep runnel that let down to the valley floor in a series of shallow steppes, and once at the bottom, were able to make good progress on a narrow creek steaming with a fine sheen of overflow slicking its glaciered surface. The dogs trotted through this like a precision tuned machine, grateful to have something solid under their feet, even if wet. A fine scattering of stars appeared overhead and a thick bank of steam began to rise from the ice, and soon the mushers and dogs were cloaked in a frost that crusted their faces and sealed their eyelids nearly shut. They came to an area where a huge spruce tree lay across their path, long dead and shaggy with streamers of black moss, and this is where they set up camp for the night. They had dropped in elevation for many miles, and the land hereabouts seemed roughly sea level to the men, and from this The Boy surmised that they must be closer to the Yentna then he had originally thought.

They broke camp before daylight and left the smoking crater of their campfire winking along their back trail. They drove under a sky heavy with stars, witnesses to a full moon skulking just beyond the lip of the world. It was miserably cold, and The Boy ran beside his sled to keep his warmth up—but even with this effort, the air pierced his lungs and his toes rattled in their boots like stones in a can. His fingers became too numb to feel the handlebar, and as he wound his way down the creek, The Boy could sense the flesh between his eyes hardening and growing crisp. They left the creek around dawn and emerged into an open country terraced in a series of long marshes, and here they cut the blown-in ghost of a snowmobile trail, which in turn led them to a place where a great many more snowmobilers had come weeks earlier and scattered across the swamp in a multitude of directions.

As the first rays of a late January sun beamed across The Boy's frosted countenance, a feeling of exultation overcame him and his heart began to pound; the dogs felt this and began to charge. The woods at the borders of the swamp began to fill with movement, and the monochrome sky darkened with black spots, and all of the sensations of cold fled from his body. The world became a tunnel seen through a glazed eye, and all he knew of anything was the primal feeling of this strange power which sprang from his heart and blood and the matrix of his bones. He surrendered to it for a time, and he and his team ran locked into a rail that revealed the country in a dreamlike slur of bent images and fractured sound. The taste of rich copper that flooded across his tongue went unnoticed.

His vision cleared and he found The Whaler staring at him open mouthed. He was wearing his visor, and the white of it in contrast to the dark of his skin was eerily incongruous. The Boy slowly shook himself, looked around. The sun had climbed to mid-day and they were stopped in some kind of narrow slough, and he knew at once that they were very close to the river. He looked back at The Whaler. Both of their teams were standing at attention and were covered in frost and their whiskers stuck out from their muzzles like frozen spikes. His own dogs frisked and danced in their lines, and Titan and Legend began to scream and hammer their tugs. The power of this came back through the handlebar, and The Boy felt the tunnel start to close in around him again.

The Whaler stepped forward and seized his shoulder, digging his fingers in like a vice. He was looking all around and there was an expression of almost religious awe written upon his face. The Boy's dogs all picked up the chorus and the team hit the snowhooks hard enough to wrench them both a few feet through the splintered trail.

'Stop it,' said The Whaler and his voice came as a shout. 'I don't know what you're doing, but whatever it is, you have to stop it right now.'

The Boy refocused, and his companion's features swam as if viewed through a watery portal. The Whaler released him from where he dangled in his grip and he in turn sank to his knees and bowed his head to the trail and watched as a constellation of scarlet splattered the snow and ice, pools and whorls of steaming gore so dark that they appeared nearly black. The Whaler was kneeling at his side, and now his hand was steadying him, handing him some dirty rag to press against his nose to stanch the flow.

An image of the girl from Susitna Station's face shimmered in his mind's eye and oddly enough it was this thought that anchored him back to the earth. The bleeding slowed, and just like that, he and The Whaler were laughing.

'I never saw anybody do that before,' The Whaler said, rising to his feet and pulling The Boy with him.

'What did I do?'

'You don't know?'

'I had one of my seizures?'

The Whaler shook his head and this time when he touched The Boy's shoulder, his look was that of sadness. He said, 'I'm freezing my butt off just standing around. Let's get a move on.'

4

As The Boy predicted, they joined up with a trapline trail put in by a dual-track Alpine snowmobile. They followed it throughout the rest of the day, and as it grew dark, they found themselves emerging from the confines of the slough and confronted by the broad girth of the Yentna River. They camped on the bank where the two watercourses joined, and neither of them commented on the day's events as they dragged brush in from the woods and built their fire. It was very clear and very cold, and The Boy lay in his bag and shivered the night through, only sinking into a rough semblance of sleep in the brief hours before dawn; when he did find sleep, his dreams were troubled and strange.

Stumbling with a species of cold that was near hypothermia, both mushers were up and rekindling their fire shortly after the sunrise. They heated water for themselves and the dogs and stamped their feet in an effort to keep warm. As the sun rose from the terminus, a pair of coyotes could be seen standing on the river to the south.

'This is some serious country,' observed The Whaler over his steaming mug of tea. 'You grew up out here?'

'Aye, though I've been away from it for a time. Skwentna is north about twenty or so miles, and my family used to have a homestead on the Big Bend fifteen that way,' said The Boy, pointing to the south. 'We're on a real trail system now, and it's only about seventy five to Big Lake. We're almost done.'

'You're family. You mean The Trapper and his wife?'

The Boy shrugged. 'He's my uncle. He took me on when I was real little.'

'Well. Your uncle then. He's a heck of a good musher. I've ran with him quite a bit out on the trail.'

'He's one tough son of an obscenity,' The Boy agreed.

'He ever tell you about how you came to be adopted?'

'No, I just know that my real family had an accident out in the villages. They were schoolteachers out to Shaktoolik, and something happened. Uncle and Auntie never liked to speak of it to me.'

'Do you remember what happened?'

'Why do you want to know?'

The Whaler turned away and kicked at the fire, clearly regretting his decision to ask any questions. 'One year, I was running in the Great Race with your uncle,' he finally said, his voice sounding strangely pensive. 'Both our teams were sicker then the bejesus, and we were taking a little camp out of Unalakleet, at Old Woman. You know where I'm talking about?'

'On a map I do.'

'It's about forty miles before town, and a good place to stop if your teams is worn out, which both of ours were. So, we were parked there with our heads in our hands, commiserating with one another about our crummy fortune. And we got to talking.'

'So?' asked The Boy, dread slowly filling his arterial pathways like cold mud.

The Whaler looked at him, then away. 'He told me about your family in Shaktoolik, and how he was taking care of you for his dead brother.'

The Boy sat very still, terrified, but desperate to hear more.

'There was a problem with his story, though I never told him so.'

'You know about me? You know about what happened to my family?'

The Whaler nodded. 'Not directly, but you guys were fairly big news there for a while. What happened to you was kind of an urban legend throughout the villages, and there were a lot of stories going around. In fact, plenty of folks still do tell the story.'

The Boy was rooted to the spot. 'They do? What do they say?' he asked when he had caught his breath.

'You sure you want to hear this? It isn't good. I shouldn't have brought it up.'

'Tell me the story. Please.'

In the distance, the air rose from the surface of the river in simmering waves; the coyotes grew into distorted shapes with warped heads and feeble spider legs.

When The Whaler next spoke, his voice was pitched in a hush and he would not look at The Boy. 'The story has it that some dumb, liquored up white man, your uncle's brother, a schoolteacher if you can believe it, took his family out on the Norton Sound trying to get across to Koyuk. Their snowmobile quit about two thirds of the way across, and they got pinned down in a wind storm,' he said. 'The man made it on foot to the village, but he was all froze up and couldn't talk, and by the time the people of the village got the story out of him, the guy's family had been alone on the ice a day and a half. They went out there looking as soon as they were able and found them where he'd left them with the snowmobile and sled.'

'What then? Is that how I got back? They took me back with them?'

The Whaler looked at him now and began to shake his head.

'What happened?'

'They found the guy's wife and their baby, both frozen solid. But that's it. There was no sign of you at all. You were just gone, no tracks, no nothing. It was like the wind just took you and erased you completely. The villagers thought that the man was lying to them about a second boy, but he was adamant, started crying when they told him what they'd found. They called the sheriff's department to get the cops in on it, but he died of hypothermia before they got there to question him.'

'No. That can't be. No.'

'Like I said, that's the story they tell out there on the coast.'

'No.'

The Whaler turned away in dismissal.

The Boy came awake, the dream already fading to tatters; the explosive sound of someone hacking and coughing wrenching him back to a state of awareness. When he pushed his face through the flap of his sleeping bag and into the stinging morning air, the first thing he saw was The Whaler standing only a few feet away, simultaneously urinating into a snow bank and lighting a fresh cigar. The older man looked over his shoulder and smiled.

'You know, you talk so much in your sleep, it's worse than sleeping with someone who snores,' he said.

The Boy groaned and pulled his head back under cover. 'Get the fire going,' he croaked.

5

They struck camp at mid morning, after it had warmed a little. The sky was a pure, hammered blue, but a thick head of clouds could be seen building in the east and they both reckoned it was going to warm quick and maybe even snow. They were both correct. The sky soon scudded over with low gray clouds and a warm wind shot through with spicules of half frozen material caught them out on the open plain of the river, reducing visibility to a few hundred yards. The temperature shift was enormous, and the dogs ran with their mouths open and tongues dragging, eyes squinted and crusted against the veils of spume whipping into their advance. Fishing huts and small hunting shacks with nailed shut doors and boarded windows showed now and again on the high banks. The trail they followed was one of regular use, with a firm base except for where freshly fallen snow collected in shallow drifts. The track swung out from the bank and into the center of the river, and here they felt as small as ants marching their way through a series of hulking sandbars left exposed by winters freeze up. They mounted one of these and wallowed for a time through a sand trap that plunged the dogs to their bellies and made the sleds founder from side to side like boats on a squalling sea. When they emerged from this stretch, they found a place where the trail dropped back onto the river proper and flattened into a great open pan of savagely rutted ice, completely blown free of snow cover. It was a long sheet of overflow that had been mightily tracked up by a horde of snowmobiles while still steaming slush, and now lay refrozen into a serrated moonscape. The dogs stepped smartly onto this surface and trotted in a skittering half step while the drivers of the sleds fought with all of their power to keep the speed from getting carried away and to keep the sleds themselves from catching a runner and collapsing into wreckage.

They reached the Big Bend and the trail wound to the outside edge of the river, and all The Boy could make out of the creek mouth letting into the long abandoned homestead where he had spent his early years was a curtain of snow which rendered the distant flood-plain and sloping hillside into a foggy black and white photo; then they were past and it was at their backs, and he tried to think of it no more. Instead, it was the thought of the girl from Susitna Station that occupied his imagination, and he could scarcely control the beating of his heart as they struggled their way down river and closer to the last place that he had seen her all of those long years ago. The cracked and rutted ice persisted, and when he looked back, The Whaler had been reduced to a wavering dot. He looked ahead and shielded his eye with his gloved hand, saw the great rock outcropping which marked the ten mile boundary from the mouth of the Susitna looming ahead. At its craggy foot, the river had frozen into a rough series of broken pressure ridges, and the trail that wound through this landscape was over naked ice deeply scored and furrowed by previous travelers.

The Boy stopped his team and anchored the sled, and walking hunched into the wind, made his way up to the leaders. Turning his back to the blow, he hunkered down with the two brothers and hugged them to his body, and they were each happy to bury their faces in the warmth of his parka. He waited like this for a number of minutes, and slowly The Whaler and his team resolved from the ground storm.

'This is perfect training for the Delta race!' The Whaler shouted as soon as his team was stopped.

'How are your dogs doing?' The Boy shouted back.

'Great, but not as good as yours!'

The Boy grinned. Behind him came the harsh buzzing of an engine and he glanced over his shoulder. At first, he saw nothing. The wind was carrying the noise from a great distance. A few moments later, from between two curtains of wind driven spray, he could make out the dim shape of a lone snowmobile cruising upriver in his direction. As it got closer, the sound of its motor alternated between a tinny whine and a basso rumble, and soon The Boy could make it out clearly; one of the new breed of fancy racing machines called a Yamaha Phazer. It was pulling some kind of long sled from its hitch, a stack of two-by-six material easily as long as a wagon train and the driver seemed completely oblivious to their presence. He came shooting at them as fast as his machine could go, and it was only when the man was close enough to see into his helmet visor that The Boy realized that he was going to be run over. The driver of the Phazer had no idea he was there.

The Boy bolted to his feet and shouted and waved his arms and he heard The Whaler yelling behind him and it was like an electric shock ran through the snowmobiler such was his reaction. The man recoiled at these apparitions who had suddenly appeared out of the gloom before him and he half rose from his seat. He jerked the steering column hard to the left and he and his load left the trail only a few yards in front of The Boy's leaders. There was an instant of ghastly silence, and then the machine launched from one of the pressure ridges in an explosion of chunked ice and spewing snow. The train rolled over onto its side as it flew, and when it came down, the man was slapped boneless to the ground like a rag doll hurled by an angry child, and the whole mess came onto him completely and rode him with a terrific squealing of rent aluminum and shattered plastic. The Boy could only watch as the load of two-by material whipsawed past and the weight of it pushed the train for an impossible distance over that terrible field of overflow. Then both of them were running, and it was The Whaler who got to the man first, and The Boy didn't need to see his reaction to know that it was really bad, for he had already spotted the helmet flung clear and shattered like an eggshell, and of course the blood trail was hard to miss, too, and when he reached the scene and knelt at the snowmobiler's side, he found a man whose face was only the ruined caricature of such a thing and whose breath came quick and shallow from a chest crackling with horrible effort. The smell of blood and raw liquor rose from him in dizzying waves.

They did what they could to help keep the man from dying, and in the end wrapped him in sleeping bags and made him as comfortable as the circumstances would permit in The Boy's sled, and hauled him into the lighted yard of Susitna Station on the fifth evening of their epic camping trip.

6

The couple who owned and operated Susitna Station were exactly as The Boy remembered them; everything was the same.

The husband and wife greeted him and The Whaler with open arms and smiles, and the only darkness was their injured passenger whom they all worked together to hoist from out of the sled and bring indoors. The man had some background in paramedic work, and when he came from the back room where they had laid the snowmobiler, his hands were red and his face was serious.

'He's a mess,' he said now, as he washed his hands in a small basin his wife had filled with steaming sudsy water. 'He's going to live, though. We put a call in to Anchor town, and the hospital there is sending a chopper at first light.'

Outside, it had grown dark and a fierce wind whipped the yard trees. The small cabin was lit up, and a fire blazed in the corner hearth. The missus was in the kitchen with her apron on and covered with flour, a large wooden rolling pin in her work calloused hands and a counter top covered with dough. The smell of hot corn oil and simmering rice permeated the room. The Whaler was stretched with his feet out and his mukluks thawing by the fireside. The man sat across from him and they talked for a time, and it was good to be in a place of warmth and friendship and good cooking.

'You guys came all the way from Trapper Creek?' asked the man, incredulous. 'How the heck did you get over the range? I didn't even know there was a trail over there!'

'No, there wasn't a trail,' said The Whaler. 'We pretty much snow-shoed the whole way, at least until we got over the mountains and down into the lowlands on the backside.'

'I just can't believe it. I've heard tell of trappers and miners going that way, a few decades back, but not since. Heck of a trip any way you look at it,' said the man.

He looked at The Boy and smiled. 'You've grown some since last we saw you. We've been keeping track of your racing, and we're really proud of you. It's been good to see one of our own kicking some tail. What are you up to now?'

'We're finishing up training, and then taking the teams out to Bethel for the Delta K300 next week,' The Boy replied, with only part of his attention. The heat from the fire was lulling his tired bones to sleep, and he was trying to work up the courage to ask after the man's daughter.

The man whistled. 'You hear that, hon?' he called to his wife in the kitchen. 'Says he's heading to Bethel for the 300.' He turned to The Boy and gave him a considering look. 'That one has a pretty bad reputation for chewing up mushers and spitting them back out. Only the best of the best go out there, and word is plenty of them end up regretting it. You think you're ready for that, to race against those boys?'

'Hell, you should see this little obscenity out on the trail,' The Whaler cut in. 'I've been running with him for two months now, and I've gotta tell you, I feel kind of sorry for anybody who has to race against him. The way he runs dogs is just unbelievable.'

This praise made The Boy's cheeks burn, and he wished that he could disappear through his chair.

The man laughed. 'Yeah, I remember when we first met him as a little boy running traps out to Rabbit Lake. We knew then that he was going to be a tough nut to crack in the dog mushing scene, some day.'

The talk continued into the night like this, and most of it was The Whaler telling his incredible stories with the man only asking enough questions to keep it going. The Boy sat in a soft, high backed easy chair, nearly stupefied with food and drink. He kept looking around into all of the corners of the cabin and up the darkened stairs leading to the bedrooms in the loft, but he already knew that the girl was not here, and no amount of searching was going to change that. At one point, while passing through the room, the woman of the house stopped what she was doing and gave him a curious look.

'Honey, is something wrong? Are you looking for something?' she asked, drying her hands on a gray dish towel.

Someone, not something; someone. 'No, no,' he mumbled. 'I'm just admiring your beautiful home, ma'am.' His heart was struggling in his chest, and the sudden sense that the world was closing in around him was almost overwhelming.

He fell asleep where he sat, and only once got up in the small hours of the night to go outside and check on the dogs.

In the morning, the wind had lain down and the snowmobiler was still alive, though only semi-conscious. Word had come through on the family's wireless that the medical chopper was being fueled and would be on the way before mid day. The couple would not hear of sending The Boy and The Whaler on their way without bellies full to bursting with a hot breakfast and several pots of coffee. After breakfast, they watched in silent admiration as the two mushers recruited their dogs and lined them up to make the final push to the

end of the trail. There were tears in the woman's eyes as she embraced
The Boy. She said nothing, but did squeeze him a little too hard, not
wanting him to see her cry.

'You're only forty or so miles from Big Lake,' the man said gruffly.
'You'll make it there in no time.' He held his hand out to The Boy
and his grip was just as hard as he remembered. 'Good luck out there
in Bethel. I hope you do kick some tail. And I really mean what I
told you last night, that part about being proud of you. You've come
a long ways since we met you.'

At this, The Boy was struck mute. He merely nodded and
turned away with his heart hammering in his throat. He gripped the
handlebar of his sled and stooped to pull the hook. He stopped and
turned back and looked at the two of them. With all of the strength
of his will, he forced his mouth to open. 'Where is your daughter?'
he asked, and his voice came like a strangled croak.

The man's mouth started to frame an answer, and then he
stopped. He exchanged a puzzled look with his wife. 'Our daughter?'
he said, and the confusion on his face was plain.

The Boy turned away then, tasting bile and panic in the back of
his throat, sure that one of his spells was coming.

The man from Susitna Station spoke again, but The Boy did not
hear what he said. With the last of his will, he called to Legend and
Titan with a command that sounded more like a sob, and his team
took him away from that place.

✳✳✳

Someone was calling the count over the loudspeaker and the staging
area had become a chaos of darting flashlight beams and rushing
figures and screaming huskies. The Boy tuned this out, even though
massive doses of adrenaline were shooting through his system like
charges of nitrous. All thirteen of his dogs were harnessed and booted

and pounding the line hard enough to make the old truck rock on its springs; their combined energy was fearsome to behold. His fully packed sled was being repeatedly lifted from the ground and then crashed back down again, and it seemed as if the contents must surely burst from their confines and explode into the open. The teams were being led to the starting line in pairs, and it looked like a parade of legends in that train. The Whaler and The Woman, The Tinkerer and The Cowboy, the best of the distance drivers with the sole exception of The Norwegian who had yet to come from his Motherland to race on the mighty Kuskokwim River. All cloaked and hooded against the stinging cold as they stood their runners and their teams dragged them to the place where an epic confrontation was about to take place.

Then they were calling for The Boy. When he cut loose from the bumper of the Ford, his team slammed forward and dragged the snowmobile that it was anchored to onto its side, and a crowd of onlookers swarmed to set it right. He continued on as if he was being pulled by some great earth moving machine, and then all sounds become muted and it was only the breathing of that canine engine that filled his ears. Bright beams from the overhead floods illuminated each of his dogs in its own halo of frost and shattered ice particles thrown up from the action of their claws ripping into the surface of the trail. They surged in slow motion, and to The Boy, they looked like an avalanche of fur.

People were screaming at him that he still had a few seconds and stopping his sled at the line. He walked to the front of his team in those final moments before battle, touching each one of his dogs in communion. He didn't even notice that it was The Outdoorsman himself whom he shared the chute with, and wouldn't have cared even if he had. The wind had grown raw and hungry, and the Kuskokwim stretched out before him like a long, dark throat.

He looked back along the team from his leaders, the brothers Titan and Legend, and it was in that moment when the girl stepped from the crowd and came to him, rushed to him and crushed her body into his, and her breath was sweet and her lips were hot and she was saying his name over and over into his ear.

'I've been looking all over for you,' he whispered, starting to cry.

'I know I know, now you've found me, we've found each other,' she said, starting to cry herself.

'I've been so alone.'

'Not any more. Now we're together.'

He buried his face into the warmth of her long dark hair, and squeezed her so tight that he was afraid he would crush her. Then they were calling for him to come back to the sled.

'I have work to do,' he said, and the words came out in a husky rasp. She followed him to where he mounted the runners, and for a moment, it was he who was haloed in that uncompromising glare.

'I know,' she replied and pressed her hand to his face. 'Do what you were born to do. I'll wait for you to come back, and I will have roses for your leaders.'

The Boy stared hard into her midnight eyes and the sound of the countdown was an elemental pull in the tide of his blood.

'I will bear roses for your leaders,' she repeated.

The countdown screamed go and his team was an earthquake; a hurricane; a bolt of lightning from the god Zeus himself. The Boy and his dogs blasted into the dark, and the wind and the song of it swallowed them whole.

Balladeer

Chapter XII

1

THE Boy is now eighteen and nearly a man. He exists in a world composed almost entirely of black ice and grating wind, bone chilling sleet and flesh pounding hail. A place where the creatures of the sky gather overhead and the beasts of the forest caper under a gibbous moon; neither friends nor guardians, but grim watchers and strange companions instead, silent witnesses to his epic journey into the heart of obsession and, perhaps even madness. It is not that the world of man has rejected him, or he it. Indeed, each has been almost wholly oblivious to the presence of the other. The Boy has spent his life in a state of poverty and ignorance which he cares neither to address, nor to reflect upon. If someone were to summon the temerity to point these things out to him, to confront him with the issues of his squalor and social incompetence, he would be most likely to shrug and turn away, indifferent to his petitioner's plight or opinion. In many ways, this indifference sums up his thoughts on the rest of the world. Economies have spiked and then fallen; countries have struggled for survival and waged wars against one another; man has risen in some places, foundered in others; achieved great successes in many of the fields of civilization, and managed to disgrace themselves in as many others. Through all of this, The Boy has been a thrall to the Northland, a pilgrim without thought but for his own personal odyssey, a beast of burden grinding out the steps toward some grim destiny.

The world of man has done its work without him, and of this he has no concern.

His is a strange figure. At once dark and foreboding, with his clothes hanging loose and flapping about his lean frame, a fiercely localized storm seems to shroud his character. At other times, he seems frail and oddly vulnerable, as if the slightest touch could disperse him upon the breeze like thistle down. His face is a dim white oval of scars and twisting sadness. His lead dogs, Legend and Titan, are always at his side. They move when he moves, and when he stops, they stalk near to hand, ready to do his bidding. Together, he and his dogs have made themselves into a weapon. As night has fallen across the land, they have prowled the wastes. While storms have raged, they have hunkered like feral beasts under its fearsome blow, heads down and leaning into their tugs. They have been broken down to their components parts in the cold forge of the mighty Alaskan bush, and hammered on the anvil of the Arctic Northland. While many have slept, The Boy has been hunched and sweating at a great grinding wheel in the lonely reaches of the night, blade firmly held to the rasping surface and a gust of hot white sparks leaping and biting at his naked flesh, unseen, unfelt. When the time for racing has come, the time for deciding who will stand and claim their dreams, and who will stagger and fall, The Boy and his team have repeatedly swept down from the hills like the Mongol Horde, raging across the northern landscape and leaving their rivals shattered and reeling in their wake.

They have stamped their boot prints down upon every middle distance race trail in the state of Alaska; they are unbeaten. Only one race remains for them to conquer.

The presence of his family, his long lost Mama and baby brother, is nearly constant. They watch from the shadowed forests and whisper to him from where he lays. They call out to him, telling him that he is almost home and getting closer with every step. Sometimes he struggles to not think about what this means; he embraces it at others. Sometimes, while he is laying in the dark, The Girl comes to him and holds him in her arms. She smoothes his tortured brow and murmurs softly into his ear. This is the only softness that he has ever known.

In times of great stress or frigid joy, the world still bleeds for him like a rainbow made liquid, while the beasts of the northland crouch in watchful silence, panting and staring as the pain and madness bellow through the fragile shell of his skull like a cyclone of shattered glass.

He is now finally old enough to run in the Great Race. The time has come for him to begin the long journey home.

2

Very late in the afternoon on a day in March, The Boy's truck rolled onto an airstrip in the town of Wasilla, Alaska, with a knocking of pistons and the rattling death cough of an engine on its very last legs. A sickly cloud of ash gray smoke enveloped it as it pulled into its allotted parking spot amongst a long row of similarly appointed trucks; all with dog boxes covered with sleds riding atop their backs. The Boy killed the engine and kicked the driver's side door open, whereupon it nearly fell from a set of rusty hinges. He stepped out of the cab as the last of the afternoon sun flashed pregnant and golden on the western terminus, a brief flare of burnished effulgence washing across the sprawling township. This glowing nimbus lasted for only a space of heartbeats, and then long shadows began to accordion across the valley. On the distant highway, the Parks, taillights began to glow fluorescent scarlet streamers. The airstrip was a riot of activity. People were talking and yelling; a mob. Almost two thousand dogs were making their voices heard as their drivers began their final preparations for departure. Hundreds of vehicles rumbled and chortled, and exhaust climbed in thick columns to taint the air. The Boy breathed deeply, sucking in all of the sights, all of the smells.

The start of the Great Race.

With his boots planted firmly on the gravel surface of the airstrip, he stood like an island, a shadowed bulwark within the seething crowd of humanity passing by on either side. The minutes were counting down like grains of sand flowing through the neck of an hour glass, and he knew that it was time to unload the sled from the back of the truck and begin readying his team. As he did these things, the brightest stars began to spark in the blue dome of the sky and a long line of floodlights sizzled to life, one by one, around the perimeter of the staging area. The Boy's pulse began to quicken. He could feel all of his dogs' energies from where they strained at their boxes, all of them wanting to be set free to run run run.

People came to talk to him, some with pads of paper and pens, and some with microphones. *Will you sign this? Do you have a moment to speak? Can you tell us what it feels like to be a rookie coming into the Great Race? Didn't you just win the last three Delta K300's? Do you think that you can win here? How do you feel about The Norwegian?* Faces blurred together as he answered their questions and did his work, sounds blending and become a rumbling montage from which only fragments emerged.

Mushers! Bib number one leaves in thirty minutes! Thirty minutes until bib number one leaves the chute!

The sound of people hollering and dogs shrieking to be set free was nearly deafening. The Boy knelt down to where he had let his own furry teammates loose to mill about the truck, opened his arms and called them one by one into his embrace. When the brothers Titan and Legend came to him, he held them close and whispered into their ears.

The Girl knelt at his side. 'Are you ready, my love?' she quietly asked him. The brightest of lights was at her back, casting her lovely face into shadow.

'Yes. I'm ready,' he acknowledged.

'Are you afraid?'

'Afraid of what?'

'What lies ahead.'

'No. I'm ready.'

'Are you?'

'Yes.' He couldn't make out her face, but he could tell that she was smiling. She always knew when he was lying to her.

'Your powers are great; your dogs are mighty. I know that you are ready for the trail,' she said.

'But?'

'You've raced every good driver in this field, beaten them all in other races. I think that you can beat them here, too, even though you are a rookie to the Great Race.'

'I think so, too. But?'

The Girl hesitated, looked away.

'But?'

She turned her gaze back upon him. 'The Norwegian,' she said, her voice pitched nearly to a whisper.

'Ah,' he said. Now it was his turn to look away; at the very mention of this Scandinavian devil, the sky got a little darker, the air a little colder. The smallest thought of this man was nearly enough to suck the oxygen from the atmosphere.

'He has destroyed every team who has ever challenged him.' The Girl said.

'He has never had to challenge himself against me,' The Boy pointed out.

'Nor you him,' The Girl responded.

'Well.'

'Please, don't be upset. I just don't want to see you get hurt out there. I'm afraid of what will happen if you try to match him.'

'I didn't come here to match him.'

'Why then?'

'To see if he can match me.'

The Girl stared at him.

He ignored her, turned away and began to hook his dogs into the mainline. Within the space of a few minutes, all sixteen of his dogs were leaping and barking in harness. People in orange vests decorated with blinking red lights were telling him that it was almost time to make his way to the chute.

The great bearded figure of The Marshal was suddenly at his side, gripping his shoulder with a thick hand. 'Boy, aren't you forgetting something? Aren't you taking all twenty of your dogs?' he shouted in a voice like two big rocks grinding together.

The Boy shook his head from where he stood on the runners of his sled. 'No, I only have sixteen to go with,' he shouted back.

The Marshal's eyes widened. 'Only sixteen? You sure about this? You'll be the only one with such a small team!'

The Boy shrugged. He only owned sixteen dogs, and they were all here with him now. In front of his lead dogs, the first team was making its way to the starting line. He could see that it was The Preacher. Next was The Fisherman, and then it would be his turn. Soon, they would all be on their way towards each one's own wintery destiny. The handlers in orange motion for him to start moving up, and as he did so, The Marshal and The Girl took up positions to either side.

'Now remember,' The Marshal was telling him. 'This isn't like the Delta K300, or even the Pipeline Race. At those, if you screw up your team, you're only a few days out from the finish line. Here in the Great Race, if you screw up your team, you've still got a week to go, if you can go at all. Just take it easy on yourself, don't try to kill yourself by racing with the big boys. Give yourself some time.' With that, The Marshal was gone. The Boy knew that he had been given good advice, but he also knew that he would ignore it completely. His mind flashed to the first time that he met The Whaler, when the man from the villages had told him much the same thing.

His team was in the chute now, the nose of his sled right at a starting line sprayed in green fluorescent paint across the ground. The trail disappeared before him, bordered by two chest high walls of lathe and wire snow fencing, each holding back a throng of screaming spectators. The Boy clicked on his headlamp and strong yellow light leapt from the aluminum casing mounted atop his brow. His pulse was thundering in his ears and his mouth was suddenly dry with fear. All sixteen of his dogs were slamming themselves into their lines hard enough to twist the handlebar beneath his grip. Slowly, his mind muted the noises around him. He was only aware of the sea of faces and shouting voices in the most abstract of ways. Legend and Titan were looking over their shoulders, mouths grinning and teeth flashing. The lead dogs of the next team in line were gathered around the back of his sled, and one of them reached up to sniff his leg. The timer was shouting in his ear that he had ten seconds to go. In ten seconds he would be starting the Great Race. The Girl was leaning into him, pressing her face against his ear and trying to tell him something. What? He could barely hear her.

The timer shouted the last syllables of the countdown and the handlers frantically leapt away from the dogs and his sled. As one, the dogs heaved against the line and his final journey was begun. He left the chute behind like he was being shot from a cannon, and he felt sure that he would never see this place again. He also knew what The Girl had said to him, even though he might wish not to.

'*The ravens will guide you,*' she had said. '*They will show you the way.*'

Then this was gone from his mind. He and his team were flying down the trail.

His Great Race had begun.

Chapter XIII

1

IT took only moments to reach the Parks highway, where traffic was stopped and a parade of cars and trucks idled, backed up bumper to bumper for miles. The team blasted over the roadway and hurtled down the barrow pit on the other side in an explosion of vaporized snow and screeching sparks flung from the sled's dual brake tines. The trail was a shallow well, humped with moguls set so close together that the sled skipped from the top of each one. Behind them, the lights of Wasilla became a string of glowing beads. They traveled briefly through a screen of forest, and then dropped down onto the surface of a wide lake cris-crossed with a network of scrambled snowmobile tracks. The lights from homes clustered on the shoreline glittered in the new dark and the race trail stretched out before the leaders like a thin white thread marked with the occasional painted lathe. In front of them, a single headlamp beam searched the far shoreline and then disappeared. Behind him, several more headlights were descending onto the lake surface.

The Boy smiled. He murmured to his dogs and kept the heel of his boot solidly on the drag mat. The team responded by dropping down into a machine like trot and slacking their tug-lines a bit. Within moments, headlamp beams were painting his backside and drivers were catching him and calling for trail, and he knew that it would be like this for the next several hours, perhaps the entire night. He kept his own pace steady and wound his way from the lake and through more forest. The trail ran alongside another highway where slow moving cars paced them while they travelled along its ditch, and began to cross a series of gravel roads leading into the dark. At each of these was a throng of spectators shouting their well wishes, campfires billowing and beverages being handed out. They followed Knik Road for a time, and then dropped down a steep hillock onto a lake covered with vehicles and snowmobiles, people and more campfires. The trail swung into the icy slick parking lot of a bar and grill where a crowd of men and women gathered. One of them had a clipboard which he thrust at The Boy to sign. Someone shouted to him that he was doing great, his team looked great. With both feet planted on the brake bar, he scanned the crowd for the face of The Girl. He saw her in a brief flash, and then she was swallowed in the press. The dogs were stretched out and howling, anxious to be away from this mob of stinking exhaust and hollering voices.

He let off the brake and whistled to the leaders. The dogs leapt to action, and within the space of seconds, they were away from the checkpoint and into the peace of the bush. Knik Lake disappeared behind them, and they traveled through a thin forest of low black spruce. The sky was clear except for a deep orange glow in its eastern hemisphere, and a pleasantly cool breeze touched his face. When they reached a place where the trail came out of the woods and crossed a narrow marsh, he called for the leaders to gee off the trail and stop. He anchored the sled to a skinny tree covered with a thick layer of hoarfrost and pulled a bag of snacks from the sled bag. While he worked his way from Titan and Legend back to the wheel dogs, handing out chunks of frozen salmon, a steady train of teams passed by in a jingle of brass hardware and hiss of runner plastic. The Woman's piercing voice rang out from one of these darkened assemblages calling for her leaders to go on by, and right on her tail was a team whose harness and lines were all crafted from some lucent material that flowed like strange, silver water. One team pulled up alongside him, and the driver pointed a harsh yellow beam of light into his face.

'Isn't it a little early to be stopping, Boy?' called the rough voice of The Outdoorsman. His dogs spread out across the trail and began gulping mouthfuls of snow and pissing on the banks.

The Boy laughed. 'This is your big chance to make a move on me,' he called back, and tossed the bag of snacks into his sled.

The Outdoorsman chuckled, called his dogs up, and disappeared around the corner.

The Boy was in no hurry. He wanted to take the time to let the dogs know that there was no pressure on them, that this was going to be just like another big camping trip, nothing that they hadn't done a thousand times before. He patted each one on the head and carefully checked all of their harnesses and booties, and once they were all suitably calm, pulled the hook and began a slow steady jog down the trail. Their energy was perfectly cool and controlled, so he let off of the drag and began himself to relax. The night slowly unfolded, headlamps ahead and behind. The sky darkened and the stars shimmered and grew bright. A faint band of faded green aurora undulated over the distant silhouetted figure of the Sleeping Lady. As they moved, The Boy dug out his canister of seal oil and began eating scraps of salmon dipped into the liquid. The trail was hard and savagely moguled, and took them through country which alternated between low swamp and thick old growth forest and choppy hillock fronts so short and steep that the leaders were already cresting the tops before the sled could reach the bottom. They crossed a wide creek with steep cut-banks, the Little Susitna, and climbed from it back into open country, following a series of ruler straight seismograph lines until once again old growth forest gathered around and the flats were broken with a steady series of sheer drop off's with frozen streamlets at their bottoms.

Time slurred and became elastic, a flowing amorphous notion of half seen images and random fragmentary thought while the figures in the heavens slowly swung on their appointed rounds. Soon, he and the dogs dropped down the last steep hill, a free fall with a churning sand trap at the bottom, and found themselves on a broad slough which he knew would let on to the broad expanse of Flathead Lake. As he had expected, he saw a distant shoreline dotted with blue and yellow flames where a group of mushers had pulled their teams over for a brief camp and lit their cookers. The trail ran straight across the surface of the lake, which was packed hard and crusted with ice. A low fog sprang up to the height of his waist and coated him and his dogs in a fine layer of glittering frost. He swiftly closed the distance and found himself in the scrub on the far side; everywhere were dogs barking, people shouting, flashlight beams bouncing off of the tree tops. A tangle of tracks spread in a twisted snarl, each one occupied by a dog team pulled over for a bit of rest. As he passed, The Boy did his best to catalogue the group, all of them drivers who had passed him on the way out of Wasilla.

One of the teams was pulled over to the side of the main trail, and The Boy could make out the lean figure of The Cowboy illuminated in the backsplash of his own white LED beam. He was hunched over replacing booties and his dogs were screaming to go, furiously shaking the tree that his sled was tied off to. Right in front of The Cowboy with his team parked in the bushes at a ninety degree angle from the trail, was The Preacher. He was sitting on his cooler next to his old wooden freight sled, shoveling food from a steaming plastic bag into his face and doing his best to blind oncoming traffic with his 12volt headlamp. The Boy could tell from the way his dogs were laying down in tightly curled balls that he'd been here for a while. Then, he was past all of this commotion and his dogs were setting out at a steady clip for the banks of the Big Susitna. He had counted over thirty teams, most of who would sit here for a few more hours before continuing on. He permitted himself a rare chuckle.

They broke out to a wide open swamp, or dried up lake bottom, at least as wide as Flathorn, and here the dogs began to ramp up the pace. The Boy let the dogs build until they were just shy of a gallop, and then got back on the drag to keep them from going any higher. A crescent moon was climbing from the eastern horizon like a sickly orange grin and the air was cooling down and crisping his cheeks. Behind him, a white headlamp beam flared and he knew that The Cowboy was coming after him. The only sounds now were of snaps on collar rings and a steady hiss from his runners; sixteen panting throats. The trailing headlamp beam dwindled, disappeared. His own beam arced from the nose of his sled to a point just beyond the muzzles of Titan and Legend almost a hundred feet out in front of the brush bow, yellow effulgence dripping and splashing off of crusted snow banks and low overhanging bushes. The team moved through this lighted tunnel like stop motion phantasms patched together from silvered moon-beams and ebony thread. They left the marsh behind and wove through a stand of widely spaced birch with gnarled trunks, most of them spackled with wart like growths the size of basketballs. The trail funneled down into a narrow gully, and then fell away entirely, launching them onto the open width of the Susitna River. Here, the trail widened as a multitude of other snow-mobile tracks joined up with it, becoming soft and slightly punchy. Ahead, on the breast of an exposed sandbar, a number of headlamp beams shimmered in the cooling air. He noted these anonymous teams as he passed, thought one of them might be The Fisherman, then continued upriver and climbed the bank where the trail took off overland, bound for Rabbit Lake.

He turned back for a momentary last look upon his boyhood trails, remembering those long ago days when he had first came out to this country with his small team of scrappy trapline dogs. Suddenly, he thought of Uncle, The Trapper. He wondered where that man was in all of this benighted forest.

In the distance, he could see the buildings of Susitna Station lit up, and imagined that he could smell wood smoke from their fireplace. Further on, back on the Flathorn Swamp, a train of headlights could be seen bobbing like fireflies. These thoughts of Uncle and the rest of them nearly unhinged him for the sheer scope of the endeavor. He turned his thoughts away and noted that his were only the second set of sled tracks to mark the trail.

2

The route from the Big Su to Rabbit Lake was a fresh track put in special for the racers. It had been years since anyone had trapped here during the winter, and as a consequence, the trail had become a thin, baseless crust over bottomless sugar snow. The Boy and his team plowed through this at a pace slightly faster than a crawl, dogs heaving on their tugs and plunging through up to their bellies with every crabbing step. Ahead of them, The Boy caught the occasional spark of light flickering through the trees, noted Titan's head coming up and ears flicking forward, and knew from this that they were overtaking someone. As they mushed through this country, The Boy's mind was flooded with a kaleidoscopic spray of childhood memories like a deck of cards carelessly released to scatter across the floor. Each turn in the trail and each tree and stand of brush; every long unused marten set left to rust in the elements. He found his throat clenching and tears welling in the socket of his eye.

This is what goodbye feels like, he thought.

He caught the leading team as they both broke from the forest and emerged onto the smooth surface of Rabbit Lake. Ahead of them, on a narrow peninsula scrubbed with a thick stand of black spruce, lay the checkpoint; several hardback canvas tents lit from within by flaring Coleman lanterns. A number of flashlight beams wobbled and bounced, checkers guiding them into parking spots stomped into the deep snow.

The Boy halted in the narrow trench, plunged his hook into the snow and threw his sled onto its side. He made his way to the front of the team pushing dogs out of the way with his hip, and used his spare hook to anchor the front of the team. A small crowd of anonymous figures stood watching in the dark; officials, veterinarians, reporters. The Boy had a bag of meat snacks and he threw each of his dogs a treat, took one for himself and chewed it down while he unhooked tug-lines. Next came a bale of straw so dry that clouds of dust exploded from its flakes as he pulled them apart and made them into bedding. Moving swiftly, he lit his alcohol-cooker and filled it with snow, dug his cooler and bags of frozen meat and kibble from out of his sled bag. While the water heated, he went through the team on his hands and knees, checking feet and ankles, muscles and tendons. The dogs were all happy and fit; their eyes were bright and showed not the slightest sign that they were under any physical stress, and when he placed dishes full of steaming soup in front of them, they ate it like a pack of wolves, muzzles clanking the bottoms of their pans, bloody juice slopping over the rims. Only when these chores were done did he permit himself the time to look around and take stock of his surroundings.

The moon had set hours before, and now a thin sheet of clouds slipped across the sky. The Boy pointed his light over to the neighboring trench, noted the irregular sled and dogs in short tracking harnesses. He recognized The Tinkerer's setup immediately. So far, it was only the two of them in the checkpoint. He drank deeply from his insulated canteen, checked his watch. On the far side of the lake, several headlights sparked and the checkers began to shout. Chewing on a strip of dried salmon, he watched as a pair of teams came loping in, and more lights began to show behind them through the distant woods. He knew that within half an hour, this peacefully remote bush checkpoint was bound to become a screaming madhouse of activity. He sat down on his cooler, consulted his watch again. Behind him, his dogs were standing up and straining at their neck lines. Legend began to bark, and soon the whole team was joining him. As he watched, another team pulled up in front of the complex of tents. The driver was a tall silhouette striding from one end of his team to the other, and within moments he was gone, disappearing across the lake on the trail bound for Skwentna.

The Boy called to a figure slogging through the powder. 'Who was that?'

'Who was who?' the man called back.

'That team that just pulled out.'

'I think it was The Norwegian.'

Well. The Boy consulted his watch one last time.

The Tinkerer was standing at the rear of his sled and playing his headlight across the far shore. 'That was The Norwegian,' he said in confirmation. 'This is what he always does. He never stops here, just goes on until Skwentna, and then he only stay's there for a few hours before continuing.'

The Boy looked at him. 'Are you going to go after him?' he asked.

The Tinkerer shrugged, turned back to his chores.

The Boy thought about The Norwegian and wondered who, if anybody was going to give chase. He thought about how long a run it was to go all the way from Wasilla to Skwentna without resting. His own dogs were ready to go now, but he wanted to give them at least another two hours or so of rest. He switched his headlamp off and sat there in the dark, listening and watching. His dogs quieted and he dozed for a time, until his feet grew too cold and his nose began to burn. He got up and repacked his sled, hooked the dogs into their tugs, and got them back on the move. When he shined his light down upon the trail, he saw that there was only the one set of tracks in front of him; The Norwegian's.

'Take it easy!' The Tinkerer shouted after him. 'You're only a rookie for Christ sake!'

The Boy ignored this, and soon Rabbit Lake disappeared behind him.

3

He arrived in Skwentna shortly after a grudging, steel gray dawn. Warm wind gusted from the southwest, and the first fat drops of sleet began to spatter down as he pulled up in front of the checkpoint. The dogs fanned out and began to roll, some of the males marking their territory with long yellow ribbons of urine. A checker held out a clipboard for him to sign, and one of the race's veterinarians leaned in from the opposite side wanting to know how the dogs were doing.

The Boy planted a snowhook, and walked to the front of his team. He could see a veil of sleet advancing down the Skwentna River just beyond a line of parked bush-planes, and one solitary musher outfitted in a sky blue suit hunkered down in a snow trench, putting booties on his dogs where they lay curled in the straw.

The Marshal was there and he now approached. 'Where do you want to be parked?' he asked The Boy.

'How long has he been here?' The Boy asked, indicating the musher in blue.

'That's The Norwegian. He's been here about an hour, maybe an hour and a half.'

'He's already getting set to go.'

The Marshal shrugged. 'Where do you want to be parked?' he repeated.

'I'm going on through. Where are my bags?'

The checkers went running, and while he waited for them to bring his food, The Boy examined booties and harnesses. The sleet was coming down now in a steady shower, almost a rain. Where it hit, it instantly soaked through and within a space of moments his entire suit was sodden. A checker came back with his poly bags, both of them stenciled with his initials and swollen with food and extra supplies for the dogs. He took one of the bags and began to lash it to the top of his sled bag. His dogs felt this and began to howl and pound on the lines. The Boy looked up to where The Marshal stood with water running down his face and dripping from the tangled mat of his beard.

'Anybody out of here yet?' he asked him.

'Nope. So far, you and The Norwegian are the only ones here. If you leave now, you'll be first over the trail.'

'How's the trail to Finger Lake?'

'It's supposed to be good until you get to Shell Lake, about halfway, lots of local traffic keeping it packed all winter. After that, it's going to be about twenty four miles of punchy garbage.'

The Boy stood the runners and called out to Legend and Titan to get ready. At the sound of his voice, the entire team surged forward and nearly dragged the snowhook from the ground. He noticed the tall figure of The Norwegian come erect and turn to stare.

'No one's ever been out of here in front of him before,' muttered The Marshal. 'At least not since The Woman a couple years back.'

The Boy pulled the hook and let the team go. After one brief sweep of the slough, the checkpoint was lost in the mist. The trail followed the watercourse for less than a mile before completing a broad sweeping turn and pointing at a river bank thick with tangled underbrush. At the foot of the bank was a wide stretch of gray over-flow, into which his leaders dove and promptly disappeared, emerging from the other side in a spray of water and slush. When his sled went into the mess, he leaned forward across the handlebar and kicked his feet straight back. The sled foundered and began to roll over, forcing him to slide off and plunge into the water up to his crotch. His boots slid out from under him, and he and the sled tipped over on their side and began to drag through the alder bushes on the bank. He called for the dogs to stop, but they ignored him. Something lashed his face and drove a swarm of stars across his field of vision. He hit something unmovable, heard a rending crack. He pulled himself forward with pure brute strength and struggled to twist his hips, fighting to get his feet planted so that he could push himself upright. They came to a sudden, explosive stop that knocked the breath from his lungs and left him reeling on the ground. When his vision cleared, he scrambled to his feet, saw the sled wedged into a tree stump, the dogs lined out and barking to go. With all of the power in his body, he yanked the sled free and jumped onto the runners as the team took off, only noticing that his bag of food was missing from the top of his sled bag after they were speeding away. He stomped on the brake and looked back; saw the poly bag sprawled in the middle of the trail. Cursing, he made sure that his snowhook was firmly connected to a nearby birch tree, doubled up with a heavy piece of rope laced through his sled's bridle and lashed around the trunk for extra security. Even with the team so securely fastened, every fiber of his body cried out in protest as he loped back to retrieve his bag. He reached down to grab the top of it, and as he swung it up and over his shoulder, a sharp shriek of pain bolted up his arm, so unexpected that it almost caused him to black out. Panting, he ignored this, turned and ran back to his sled. As he bent down to retie the dog food to the top of his sled, his dogs suddenly fell quiet and he knew that a team was approaching. He looked up just in time to see The Norwegian come swarming around the corner, dogs lined out like a freight train, fierce blue eyes frowning from above a rain slickened face muffler. One brief image, and then he was gone.

It was only a matter of moments to finish securing the bag, but in that time, The Boy knew that he was in serious trouble. His left wrist was already purpled with swelling, and when he tried to rotate his hand, the pain of it nearly made him vomit.

4

They traveled through a morning the color of ash while a heavy wind prowled the treetops and drove curtains of freezing rain slantwise across their field of advance. The dogs ran with their heads lowered and ears flattened, The Boy illustrating a stark figure leaning into the runners with his face turned down to his shoulder, trash sack poncho wildly whipping about his skeletal frame. The country rose around them in a series of gentle terraces, open marshland with the occasional twisting portage through dense fringes of spruce and birch. The Boy caught the infrequent glimpse of The Norwegian's blue suit on the ends of some straight stretches, but he never seemed to get any closer.

A barren promontory loomed out of the fog, and the trail described a long arc around this lone peak until it had revolved to a point at their back, dwindled and was lost in the clouds. The smell of wood smoke and motor oil scented the air, and eventually the trail emptied onto a drifted lagoon and became bottomless. A cabin showed on the opposite bank through a screen of misted rain. A long line of bush-planes with their cowlings muffled with blankets and secured by heavy bungie cords were anchored below it on the flats. A crowd of people the size of ants clustered in front; the Finger Lake checkpoint, gateway to the Alaska Range.

The Boy was greeted by a gang of excited people who had been waiting all through the long night for the first teams to arrive, and they parked him in a trench stomped out next to The Norwegian's. He ignored their comments and questions; it was all he could do to keep from passing out while he did his camping chores, bedded the dogs and got their food going. He crouched next to his sled with his arm enfolded in his lap, hand dangling like a broken flower stalk. He noted the two shattered stanchions with a dull lack of surprise. He reached into the sled bag and retrieved his repair kit, a long satchel packed with lathe splints, steel hose clamps and tape, nuts, bolts and various tools. He began the work of attaching the splints. He stopped when he felt the weight of a stranger's eyes upon him. He looked up and saw The Norwegian staring at him. His bearded face was utterly impassive, but his eyes were blazing with fierce intensity, seeming to arc out of their sockets to convey a sense of ferocious appraisal. The older man stood with his jacket off, oblivious to the rain soaking his

body. He stared right at The Boy's blackened wrist. When he saw that
The Boy had caught his eye, the streaming wall of his face curved
into a wide, slow smile.

The Boy stood. He pulled his bag of raw salmon from out of a
side pocket in his parka. He reached for his cutter with his bad hand,
withdrew it in one smooth motion and cut off a hunk of the meat in
a single gleaming sweep of the blade. He chewed this and swallowed,
holding the handle of the cutter and the strip of flesh together in his
crippled hand. His smile was a rictus of frozen muscles, addressed to
everyone and to no one.

The Norwegian's smile faded. His eyes cooled, became
thoughtful. He turned on his heel and walked away. When he was
gone from sight, The Boy crouched down behind his sled and ejected
the contents of his stomach in one brutal contraction.

Teams began filing in, and were arranged in spokes upon the
lake surface; The Outdoorsman and The Preacher, then The Woman,
followed closely by The Trapper and The Whaler. The Tinkerer and
The Cowboy and The Silver Fox, all coming in like a chain of rail
cars. As The Boy prepared his team for departure, the late afternoon
became filled with the sounds and sights of a busy checkpoint, drivers
doing their chores and talking with one another, dogs barking to be
fed and bedded down, petted and loved. Overhead, the sky was a
seething mass of thunderous clouds, and from it the rain still sizzled
down to turn the snow into a dripping gray slop.

The Whaler approached, brown face slick and grinning, stump
of a cigar clenched between his set of square white teeth. He frowned
when he saw the way that his young friend was holding his wrist.

'Getting tested kind of early on,' he observed. 'You going to be
able to work out your chores with that thing?'

'I can still control my fingers. A little,' The Boy responded.
'What about you? You about ready to get a move on?'

The Whaler laughed. 'Hell no,' he said. He leaned into The Boy's downwind side, cupping his hands to light his smoke. 'I'm going to be here for hours. That trail about wore my crew out. If I tried to push out of here, I'd just be walking.' He pointed up at the clouds, off in the direction of Rainy Pass, and pitched his voice low enough so that only the two of them could hear it. 'See what it's doing up there, Boy? That's going to be a real obscenity up there. I can tell you, when it looks like that, it's blowing and snowing like you can't believe. The last thing in the world that you want to do is hit that obscenity with a tired team. That's how you obscenity your race right in the obscenity before it's even begun.'

'You think that's snow up there? Not rain?'

'At that elevation? I know that's its snow. There's no doubt about it.'

The Boy nodded over to where The Norwegian was strapping on his headlamp. All twenty of his dogs were booted and standing silently at attention atop their straw beds.

'He's going to push straight through the Pass all the way to Rohn, doesn't matter about the weather to him,' he said. 'If you let him go now, then it's all over. You'll never see him again until the banquet in Nome.'

The Whaler slowly nodded. He took a long drag on his cigar; let the smoke out in long ribbons from his nostrils.

'What about you?' he asked.

'I'm all booted up. I'm making out for Rohn,' The Boy said.

The Whaler sighed and shook his bristling head. 'How long before you go?'

The Boy hocked phlegm, spat it out. 'I'm letting him go for maybe twenty minutes, then I'm going after him,' he said.

The Whaler sighed again. 'Alright, you obscenity,' he said. 'You've talked me into it. I'll be ready to go in thirty.' He turned away and strode back to where his team lay stretched in the snow.

The Boy watched as The Norwegian called to his leaders in a lilting voice. His team pulled away from the campsite with the controlled precision of a sewing machine. A number of pale faces turned from their chores to watch his departure. He heard the voice of The Cowboy, cursing.

This is it, he thought. *This is the race, right here, right now.* His heart began to pound in the framework of his chest. He looked over to where The Whaler was booting his dogs in the gathering gloom. He slowly worked his way up the length of his own team, fastening tug-lines and stroking muzzles. When he reached the place where Legend and Titan lay curled in tight balls, he crouched down and slowly petted them along their wet bodies. Water streamed from the seams of his snow pants where his knees compressed the sodden insulation. He waited until he saw The Whaler straighten and walk back to his sled, and then he walked back to his own sled and mounted the runners. One soft whistle was all that it took to put his animals on their feet, where they were suddenly transformed from a peacefully sleeping team of dogs into a howling pack of wild animals. His headlamp beam leapt from his brow like a beam of yellow fire and his team exploded from their trench like an eighteen wheeler with its throttle stuck to the floor. The team rounded the corner where the trail left the lake in a sideways spray of slush, and catapulted him up the steep cratered hill and into the night.

5

They ratcheted up through a series of steep plateaus surrounded by dense forest. The trail was a savagely winding roller coaster ride, and the twists and turns of it nearly shook The Boy loose from his one handed grip. The dogs coursed through this benighted landscape like a pack of wolves following the spore of some doomed prey, carelessly slamming the sled behind them like a weight at the end of a long chain. For a while, The Boy could make out The Whaler's headlight a few miles back and giving chase, but eventually this receded, and then faded entirely. The rain came down in furious torrents, slashing his face and blasting moisture throughout the meager fabric of his clothing. The wind was a howling creature, thundering through the night like an obsidian locomotive. As they climbed, the gale turned harsh and cold and the rain became sleet that hit like a spray of nails. His suit slowly froze, and then became armor plating from which his naked body trembled and quailed within. The world contracted to the size and depth of a halogen headlamp beam, shrank further still. Snow came in breath smothering loads, slapping his face and clogging his eye, covering the top of his sled bag in a sheath of crusted white.

A string of lights resolved from the turmoil, revealed a cabin brightly lit from within; figures hunched against the blow and scrambling to keep their footing. The Boy's dogs raged into a chute lined with overturned straw bales and began to scream and thrash against the mainline when he called for them to whoa. Even with both of the hooks planted, the sled jerked forward like it was connected to some piece of earth moving machinery.

'Welcome to Puntilla Lake!' someone shouted, thrusting a plastic covered clipboard at him.

'Holy smokes!' shouted someone else. 'Just look at those dogs!'

The Boy scrawled his mark across the sign-in sheet with his off hand, swung his light in a tight arc, and caught sight of The Norwegian's team just pulling into a parking spot.

'How long has he been here?' he asked, yelling. At the sound of his voice, Legend and Titan nearly jerked the sled out from under him. 'Whoa, dammit! Whoa!' he shouted.

The checkers voice came rushed and excited. 'Kid, that's The Norwegian! He just got here, he's just now pulling over. You made up a half hour on him getting over here!'

The Boy smiled at this. 'He's pulling over?' he asked.

'Yeah, we think he wants to wait until the weather calms down before he goes over the top. The freakin' temperature's dropping right off the chart! Where do you want us to park you?'

The Boy looked up to where the jaws of Rainy Pass waited for him in all of that storming darkness. The insignificant radiance from his headlamp suddenly looked like something that could be wholly swallowed into the belly of that rough beast. He started to laugh then, a crude barking sound so unexpected that everyone fell uncomfortably silent. He stopped laughing as suddenly as he had begun.

'I have a message for The Whaler when he comes in,' he said to the man with the clipboard. 'Tell him I was wrong.' With that, he yanked the hooks and passed out of the checkpoint.

The lights of Puntilla Lake spun beneath him like a collection of iridescent pearls circling a drain, became dim, vanished. The wind roared from out of the blinded steppes with a kind of bludgeoning madness, and the cold was like something from a nightmare, clawing and raking to get at the core of him. Unnoticed, his face was blasted into peeling strips and his teeth were frozen in their sockets. His heart thundered against his breastbone, charged with adrenaline, and his lungs sucked at air so cruelly frigid that it burnt going down like lit sulfur. Unbidden, an image of his Papa being erased by that long ago storm came into his mind, a tall and broad shouldered figure carrying their last bit of light into that hungry vast. The Boy's laughter was a thing of crippled madness, whipped away from his frozen lips before he could even consciously recognize its lunatic presence. And still they climbed, between granite snow capped peaks that raised yet further to pierce the bellies of the clouds, unseen in the dark, but felt like the existence of a great hulking creature ready to pluck them from the face of the world. The trail wound them through a sudden forest of standing boulders and the rough ridges of exposed feldspars.

Through slotted eyes, The Boy observed his dogs pitching into this maelstrom, ears flattened and stumbling, stroboscopic images of the brothers Titan and Legend earning their namesake as they plunged through the drifts.

And then the wind stopped, as decisively as if some mighty breaker had been thrown. They had won their way to the summit. They emerged from a tumult of driven snow into a world of utter still-ness, and The Boy's headlamp beam now flared across a moonscape of jutting rock and scoured frost, looming shapes rendered in dead negative. It was so cold here in this place that clumps and fragments of snow hung in the air without motion, dreamlessly suspended in time. Overhead, glimpsed between a pair of gaping granite jaws, a river of crimson undulated across an ocean of flashing stars.

And then they were dropping. At first a gentle slalom down a mild gradient, without trail or marking of any kind, and then steeper and steeper until they were nearly achieving freefall. The dogs shook themselves as they moved, sending up small clouds of steaming frost and fractured powder from their clotted fur. They encountered a ravine shot with a twisting streamlet and choked with dense stands of snarled alder, and it was here that The Boy began to doubt his ability to maintain control of the team. Trees and stumps leapt into his field of vision like props in a carnival ride through Hades, slamming him from side to side and necessitating the use of both of his hands on the driving bow, regardless of the agony bursting up and along the deli-cate network of his nerve fibers. The team crashed down the length of this tortured path with their throttle stuck wide open, faster faster and faster yet, and came out the backside of it like an avalanche of spiked fur and gleaming open mouthed grins. There was a moment of smooth trail, and then once again they were plunged into a savage maze that warped all sense of time and space, turned reality into a wrecking ball and whipped it through the panes of the world like a freight train derailed.

In this place, The Boy lost all sense of time and his body trembled and became weak, and the pain from his crippled wrist came to him like a news broadcast from a distant planet. They fell from the face of a precipice and at the bottom found themselves in a narrow rock walled canyon. Its sides were rough and bare, and its floor was furred with a forest of old growth timber. A viciously frothing creek, over which a number of hastily built snow bridges sagged, coursed its length; The Dalzell Gorge.

They snaked their way down this defile, jumping over gaping fissures and crashing across crumbling ice bridges, black open water roaring below them and the dogs' shadows loping ahead. They had reached the last of these bridges when the runner on the right hand side of the sled dropped into a crack in the ice and failed to emerge. Without hesitation or warning, the sled flipped onto its side and blew over the edge and into the chasm below. Even with reflexes honed from years of practice, The Boy could do nothing to stop what happened next. The world cart-wheeled in slow motion; the nose of the sled made contact with some solid surface and everything came to a sudden, explosive halt. The contents of the sled bag ejected, and The Boy was catapulted over the handlebar and flung into a wall. A moment later, he dropped boneless into ebony waters.

Shattering cold; air and water, sucked into lungs made from blown glass. Someone was screaming, and the dogs were furiously barking. The beam from the headlamp stuttered across the depths of a hole in the earth, half water, half ice. The light shorted out, and then came back on for a moment, just long enough to illuminate a capsized sled and a line of flailing furry bodies dangling from a precipice, went black once again. The Boy surged through a torrent which lapped at his chest, unable to feel his body below that point. Through the flickering light, he could see the mainline disappearing beneath the ice sheet; a trail of silver bubbles, twisting and glittering. Frantic, he began pulling with hands numb and slick with ice. His fingers hooked into a harness, and he wrenched Titan back into the open and threw him up onto the shore where he lay without moving. His light flared out, and this time he knew that it was out for good. Mindlessly, he groped in the darkness with water pouring into his mouth, pulled back on the next tug-line until his fingers clawed into another harness. The body that came back to him was loose, a furred ragdoll, all four legs senselessly adrift. Gibbering, he heaved Legend over his shoulder and fumbled his way back up and onto the bridge where the cold hit his suit like a sledgehammer. Gasping, sobbing, he knelt down, feeling for life with deadened hands.

Reality contracts to the size of a pinhead.

Chapter XIV

1

THE Boy had only brief memories of the last few miles coming into the Rohn checkpoint. A broken sled filled with silent heaps of fur, listing drunkenly from one side of the trail to the other; his headlamp shorting on and off, bouncing elongated shadows of the dogs off of the bank of thickening ice fog; himself, crippled over the handlebar, insensate from the pain.

Upon reaching his destination, he did all that he could to care for his dogs, then crawled into his sleeping bag and lay curled in a terrible state of hypothermic misery. People came to him and shined their lights upon his face. They talked in rattling strings of nonsense, some pleading and imploring, others commanding and advising. He ignored them all. Someone knelt at his side and stroked his brow. He could smell the sweet, summery scent of The Girl. Groaning, he pushed the hand away; the time for summer was over, if there ever had been a time for it in the first place. Later, The Marshal told him that seven of his dogs, including Legend, had been flown away to a place where they could be helped.

'They're all going to be alright; Legend is going to be just fine. Just not for this race. A plane could take you away, too. There is no shame in pulling out after all that's happened. You'll never make it to Nome after all of this.'

The Trapper stood over him, frowned and shook his head; walked away. The Whaler crouched at his side, smoking and grinning; he didn't have anything to say, but he was a comforting presence nonetheless.

The Old Man patted his shoulder. 'It is almost over,' he said.

His Mama dwelled somewhere just out of sight, softly calling to him.

Night and day swapped ends, flipped once again. The moon continued to swell.

2

The Boy sat upon the nose of his sled and watched the sun set. It looked like red ball of wax melting against the western horizon. He held his left hand in his lap, the only position that seemed to ease the pain. He tried to avoid breathing too deeply; the sounds and sensations of rib-ends grinding together were too profoundly disconcerting. His boots were off and his feet were resting on a woolen dog blanket. He gazed down at what has been hidden there, a species of grim horror filling the hollows and empty pockets of his mind like strange insulation. A number of his toes and large sections of each foot were a frozen ruin, glistening black under the beam of his light. He felt the ghostly touch of his Mama's arms around him, and was unaware of the tears streaming down his face. He pulled the boots back on and stood on feet rendered into anesthetized clubs. Working in a kind of daze, he slowly recruited the remaining nine dogs in his team, putting Titan in lead and hooking both tug-lines to the back of his harness.

The Marshal emerged from the dark, scowled when he saw what the younger man was about. 'You sure about this?' he asked.

The Boy stopped what he was doing. 'Yeah, I'm sure,' he said in a voice as faint as dandelion fluff.

'It's going to be cold tonight out in the Burn. Maybe fifty, sixty below. I think you should at least wait until morning. It's not like your racing anymore.'

The Boy turned unsteadily, searched The Marshal's face.

The Marshal shrugged. 'I'm just being realistic, Boy. All of the top drivers are long gone. You're a day and a half behind the main pack. There's no way that you'll ever see those guys again. I just meant that if you're determined to continue, then you might as well take it easy and enjoy the scenery.'

'Enjoy the scenery.'

'Yeah. Enjoy the scenery.'

'Where is The Norwegian right now?'

'He's way out in front, up in Ophir on his layover. He's due to pull out of there in a couple of hours.'

'Anybody chasing him?'

'The Tinkerer and The Woman are putting up a good fight, but their dogs don't look nearly as strong. The Whaler, maybe.'

The Boy turned back to his work. He knelt down and carefully readjusted Titan's harness and stroked the old grizzled head. 'Our job just got a lot tougher,' he whispered into the dog's ear. 'Can you do this without your brother? Can you do it for me?'

In response, Titan thrust his warm body into The Boy's embrace and began to shiver with excitement. A shock seemed to crackle though the mainline and touch the rest of the dogs, and they all began to bark and slam themselves against their tugs. The Boy stood up and struggled not to cough.

'Look,' said The Marshal. 'I know that there's something wrong with you, with your ribs, maybe your feet, too. We've all noticed that you won't come into the cabin to warm up. I can't just watch you kill yourself out here. I'm sorry, but I'm going to have to disqualify you. I'll get a plane in here in the morning and fly you back to Anchorage.'

The Boy shook his head. 'Why?' he asked.

'Because you're a danger to yourself. That's all the reason I need. I'm doing you a favor, dammit!'

With exaggerated care, The Boy mounted the runners of his sled. 'You ready boys?' he called to his dogs. The team responded by ripping the sled forward several feet and yanking one of the hooks out of the ground; it sang through the air and knocked a slab of bark from the trunk of a nearby tree. He looked at The Marshal.

'You disqualify me, and I'll just continue on down the trail anyway,' he said. He turned his light back to the outgoing trail. With his left arm wrapped through the driving bow, he yanked the remaining hook.

3

The dogs dragged him through tunneled forest so dense with scrub growth and tightly hemmed in that the trunks of small trees scraped against either side of his sled; up a steep ravine filled from bank to bank with creek water glaciated into terraced rivulets like frozen lava. The moon hung low in the sky and painted the dogs' shadows upon the ground in flickering black streamers. The Boy clung to the handlebar as the constellations burned across the great dome of the heavens, his mind smoothly disengaged from the work of managing the team and the primal cold coming from out of the very bosom of the earth. His thoughts, when they did come, somersaulted and drifted in a number of oblique directions, always returning to the central theme of his family lost, the strange homecoming rushing towards him.

They encountered a place where a great fire had once burned and reduced the trees to charcoaled poles. The snow here had blown completely away, and clouds of dust came back from the dogs' feet in choking clouds. Halfway across this burned waste, they started catching other teams struggling at the back of the pack and passed them all in silence, like darkened trains running on concurrent tracks.

It was still dark when he pulled into the Athabascan village of Nikolai, on the far side of the Burn. He fetched food and water and rebooted the team where they stood on the plowed central roadway, departing shortly thereafter following the banks of a small river while the aurora borealis paled the western sky. He stopped the team for a brief time in an open swamp rumpled with exposed knobs of tundra and tufts of dry grass; lit his cooker and stood shaking inside his suit while it blazed with clear, blue fire. The dogs ate well and napped on crisping straw beds; got up stiff and sluggish a few hours later in the gloom of the frigid predawn hours.

They arrived at the township of McGrath running between the

banks of a river nearly as wide as the Yentna, found a long collection of frosted buildings, cars idling on the sides of icy roads, and a small group of locals heavily muffled against the cold. He signed the sheet that was placed before him, a meaningless scrawl of graphite at the end of a very long list, dropped back onto the river, and put the checkpoint behind him. Swampland let into hill country and the team climbed throughout a long gray morning, the flashing beacon of a repeater tower showing through the tops of trees where the forest thinned.

He found Takotna still crowded with teams; all 'back of the packers', folks who were just struggling to make their way to Nome. He bedded his team down amongst them and slept on the straw with his dogs, and woke a few short hours later to feel snowflakes gently brushing against his cheeks. He sat up in the gathering dark and noted a warm breeze moving the trees. Hobbling and gasping from the sensations emanating from his footgear, he prepared a hot meal for the dogs and stood watching as they all gobbled it down. Shortly after, he hooked them into the mainline and pulled away from his trench of drifted snow and bedding.

Climbing deep into a landscape of rolling hills, almost mountains in and of themselves, he passed teams all throughout the night. Sometime in the small hours of morning, it began to blow moist and warm and a light snow whispered across the rutted trail. He drifted in and out of consciousness for much of this period, riding the sled with his right hand grasping the driving bow and left hand dangling swollen and useless. Once, he thought he heard his baby brother wailing from the folds of his sled bag, but when he jerked the lid open and shined his light within, there was nothing there but the jumbled mess of his survival gear. Gaunt and shuddering with exhaustion, he pulled into the empty ghost town of Iditarod in the early gray hours of morning while a fine snow sifted from the heavens like confectioners' sugar. He set about the work of camping and feeding the dogs, going through them by one, limb by limb. Before he could prepare a meal for himself, he pitched onto his face and rolled over next to his swing dogs. Titan came back to him and curled up and began to wash his face.

The Boy awoke and lay on his back staring up into the darkening sky with snow covering his face and melting into his shagged hair. He thought about the rest of the racers on the trail ahead of him; The Norwegian; the blood that came when he coughed and the fluid burbling deep down in his lungs; the lack of pain coming from his feet, or any feeling at all, and the sick pounding in the meat of his skull; what must come next. He started to laugh then, a rusted sound which froze the marrow right in the bones of those near enough to overhear. When he climbed to his feet, it was like watching a dynamited building reconstructing itself in reverse animation.

The dogs were all curled under heavy blankets of freshly fallen snow. He woke them and put dishes of food in front of each, and stood watching them eat. They looked as if they hadn't run a step; the meat on their sides and ribs was full and firm, and their hips were still round with a layer of fat. Just looking at them restored a certain measure of his own meager energy. He felt a presence at his side, and turned to regard an old native man with a face as dark as wood stain and creased like the shell of a walnut.

'Hello old timer,' said The Boy.

The old man smiled and this made the skin turn up around his rheumy eyes. 'You're the one everyone has talked about,' he said, his voice slow and methodical. 'The one from Shaktoolik.'

'That was a long time ago.'

'Not so long. You're almost back home.'

'Aye.' The Boy shrugged.

'You are strong. The people of my village say that you are the only one who can match that Norwegian.'

The Boy smiled and shrugged. 'I haven't seen him in days,' he said. He gestured around the quiet checkpoint at the handful of teams parked in the brush. 'As you can see, I'm pretty far back in the standings. All of the top drivers are probably nearly off of the Yukon by now.'

'No, man, no. That is not so. Listen. The Norwegian is in first place, that's true, but not as far ahead as you think. He just pulled out of Shageluk a little bit ago, only seventy miles up the trail. Listen. It's storming really bad out there on the river-flats, blowing like you can't believe. Those guys are moving like snails; stopping every chance they get. Believe it, man.'

The Boy shook his head, gazed off to the west.

'You're going to catch them, man,' the old man said. The Boy looked at him for a time, and then slowly nodded. 'Be careful, though,' the oldster continued. 'During your communion with the northland, you must remain anchored to the earth, or the ballad will take you away, will erase you completely and make you a part of it.'

'What?'

'Listen, man. The time of the ballad is upon you. Sing with it; use its power to fuel you. You've done this before. Just be careful to remain tethered, or it will take you with it to dwell forever in the wild places of the earth.' The old man smiled a toothless smile and his yellow gummed eyes burned right into The Boy's center. His wrinkled mouth formed more words, but all that The Boy heard of these was the whisper of snow coming from the belly of the sky.

4

The Boy left Iditarod in the first part of the night, and his nine dogs with Titan in single lead held the power of twice their number.

They traveled through a country of massive rolling hills on a track bottomless and barely as wide as a sleds runner stance. The flanks of these hill climbs were tangled with stunted forests of dwarf birch and misshapen alder, and the tops were crowned with caps of wind scoured tundra.

He arrived at the village of Shageluk on the floodplains of the Yukon on an icy roadway in the middle hours of the night, trotting between rows of shuttered, single story houses with billows of smoke whipping from their chimneys and the wind blowing his sled up against an embankment of snow. He halted in front of the handicapped ramp of the town's community center and anchored the team, strode to his lead dog with the checker scrambling after, tossing snacks to each dog along the way. The central parking area was filled to capacity with parked teams and anonymous headlamp beams flickering in the dark. He played his own light against the field, picked out the sleds and gear of The Fisherman and The Silver Fox amongst the group. Moving with a new burst of energy, he mixed a cooler full of feed from a spigot on the side of the building, rebooted his team and got them pointed towards the outgoing trail.

'Hey, Boy, is that you?' called a dark figure.

'Yeah. Who is that?' The Boy answered, jerking his face muffler down and exposing his face to the wind.

'The Fisherman!' said the man. 'How are you, buddy? We all heard that you were in a bad way back in Rohn.'

'I'm getting over it.'

'I'll say. How the heck did you catch up with us so quickly?'

The Boy shrugged and leaned over his handlebar. 'I don't know. It's nothing to do with me, it's the dogs. They're just out of this world.'

The Fisherman laughed. 'No kidding. Well, everyone has been talking about you. We've all been watching the time sheets, and watching the way you've been coming up through the ranks is like being tied to a set of train tracks and listening for a freighter that you know is bound to come along at some point in the near future. I mean, it's really kind of a relief to have it finally over.'

'Yeah. Well, I've got work to do.'

'Sure, buddy, sure. Good luck.'

The trail markers followed the icy road for a few hundred yards, then dropped down a steep embankment onto an open pan of swamp the limits of which were impossible to ascertain from the pathetic glow of his headlamp. Down here on the unprotected plain, the wind came fierce and hungry and man and dogs alike ran with their faces averted. The Boy loped alongside the sled in a halting series of spasmodic lurches, and where some stinging sensation from the concrete hard surface of the trail should have been transmitted through the rubber soles of his boots, came nothing at all.

5

Time skipped like a stone across a placid lake surface, touching down only for the briefest of moments and sending out ringing ripples of thought, sound, taste and memory.

A clearing sky, paling to the faintest patina of rose on the eastern horizon. A long series of utterly flat marsh pans with borders seemingly leagues apart and stands of dead brown grasses waist high and whispering amongst the desiccated stalks of their neighbors. Snow the texture of sand, hissing in quick runnels about the blurred feet of the dogs, spraying from the tails of the runners in twin rooster tails.

They came upon a man with his team anchored down in the scrub off to the side of the trail. The man stood staring, the handle of a battered, blue plastic cooler dangling from one hand, a dipper from the other. His beard was a solid mass of icicles and his eyes were wide and blasted clean of emotion. He was hunched with his back to the wind and his parka hung and flapped from his lean frame like a shroud. Behind him, his team of dogs lay curled in the grasses, skinny and wholly exhausted. In this manner, The Boy and The Trapper traded positions on the trail without so much as a flicker of recognition. The Boy did look once over his shoulder as his team pulled him away, and he was struck by the strange figure slowly shrinking into the freezing dawn, almost seeming to melt into the floodplain upon which he stood.

They encountered a river, the apotheosis of all rivers. The trail ran out to this blurred expanse like a twisting thread lost in a sea of rippling snow-spray. A sun the color of iron recently pulled from the coals steadily mounted a slate gray sky, and to The Boy, it seemed as if a great fire must be burning somewhere and filling the atmosphere with its exhaust. A trio of wolves came down from the far bank and watched his progress, standing as still as statuary as he passed. The sight of them and the tree line behind them beginning to darken with roosting ravens made the spit in his mouth dry and the fog in his brain recede like a blast of warm sunlight burning away a morning mist.

A bluff loomed ahead, a church spire thrusting skyward at its foot. Clustered along a high, crumbling shore were all manner of powerboats with outboard motors kicked up on their stands. Titan led the team off of the crenulated surface of the Yukon and amongst these strange relics of civilization in a blazing rush; they halted when villagers of all description gathered around, smiling and talking, some reaching to touch, others holding out bits of paper and tablature to be signed. The Boy bedded and cared for his team, and only sank down to the straw himself after the last of the chores was finished. A race veterinarian garbed all in green pocketed his stethoscope and knelt down next to the boy. His hands were purple and shaking from the cold, and when he spoke, his life's heat fled through his lips in ragged streamers.

'Why don't you go inside and thaw out?' the vet wanted to know.

'That's exactly what I don't want to do,' The Boy laughed, stuffing a cold brick of some tasteless material into his mouth.

'Well,' the vet told him, 'you're dogs look simply amazing, mate.' The vet spoke in a mildly Australian accent, and for some reason this really cracked The Boy up, though if pressed he could never have explained it.

'You're dogs look like you've just been on a walk to the pet park.'

'Thanks, doc.'

The veterinarian stood up awkwardly. He studied the kid sprawled at his feet; the patch, and the cheeks glowing radioactive with frostbite; the wheezing rumble of lungs laboring against a bath of fluid. He nodded as if searching for something to say. Finally, he pointed at The Boy's gnarled wrist.

'I see that you've gotten yourself all bunged up,' he said. 'You'd better get that thing looked at, or you might end up losing it.'

'Oh, that's okay.'

'Why would that be okay, mate?'

'Because I won't need it for much longer!' The Boy laughed, chunks of food spilling out of his mouth.

The veterinarian from down under turned and fled.

6

The Boy let the dogs sleep until afternoon waned into evening, then recruited them into their tug-lines and got back on the move.

The trail markers led them down onto the jumbled surface of the great river and hugged the north bank; the ice sheet had settled, and now sagged in a long side hill shot with gaping cracks wide enough to dump a sled through. The wind was savage and coming dead on from the north. The Boy crouched down behind the driving bow when he could, and ran beside the sled only when there was no way to avoid it. Titan moved with his head pointed at the ground and the pace that he set for the rest of the team was a ground eating trot just shy of a lope. The hours burned by in the blink of an eye, and suddenly the team was mounting the bank again and charging down a narrow plowed road into the village of Grayling. The Boy halted the team when they reached a small cluster of cloaked figures standing in the roadway stomping their feet in a futile effort to stay warm. He scrawled his mark on the sign-in sheet, told the checkers that he was heading right through, and bound for Eagle Island.

'Just how far is it exactly?' he wanted to know.

'A long ways, kid. Easy sixty five miles, maybe more. And it's blowing to beat the band out there, so be real careful.'

'How cold is it supposed to get tonight?'

'Real cold. Maybe forty below. Maybe colder.'

'Without the wind?'

'Without the wind.'

'Is there anybody out on the trail right in front of me?'

The checker consulted his sheet. 'Yeah. The Tinkerer and The Outdoorsman, about two hours ago. The Woman and The Cowboy are about two hours in front of those two, and then The Whaler. The Norwegian is in the lead.'

'How far out in front?'

A quick look at the sheet. 'Says here he got into Eagle Island a couple of hours ago, so, he'll be leaving there anytime.'

'Okay. Where're my drop bags and the water?'

'Right over there.'

The Boy dropped his snowhooks and walked up the length of the team, ladling out a soaked meal of kibble and chunked moose right on the ice in front of each of the dogs. He found his poly drop-bags and handling his cutter with his good hand, gutted one of them and spilled its contents under the harsh glow of his halogen beam. He fumbled through the assortment of smaller plastic bags until he had the ones he wanted; the ones filled with dry kibble and salmon cut into fat pink steaks, and one bulging with strips of frozen chicken skins. He packed his cooler and filled it with brackish water from a faucet in the mop closet of the community center, walked back to where his team stood waiting in the roadway with a cloud of steam pouring off of his survival suit. He loaded his sled, pulled the hooks, and got back on the move.

7

The cold on the river was primal; it rendered The Boy's failing body into a shaking pillar of agony from which there was no escape. The wind raged into his and the dogs' faces without remission or respite, flinging a constant curtain of granular detritus to clog their throats and ocular cavities, howling with ferocity like the backwash of some titanic engine. The stars burned hot and blue and hung almost close enough to touch, and much later, a three quarter moon glared from the middle part of the sky and washed the surface of the Yukon in waves of purest ivory.

At one point, when a bend in the river brought a slight slackening to the gale, The Boy stopped the team to check booties and feed from the steaming contents of the cooler. The dogs gulped the food and rubbed their faces on the ground to clear the crusted ice from their eye sockets. He moved amongst them like a wooden puppet with half his strings cut free, jerkily patting heads and stroking backs and using his own stinging hands to aid in clearing the icy buildup. Later, how much later he had no firm reckoning, a pair of yellow sparks showed at the end of a very long straight stretch to the north, perhaps as many as five miles distant. He followed these beacons for a cold eternity, watching in a hypnotic like state as they slowly grew and became long amber wells of light moving uncertainly from side to side as if searching for something lost. Without warning, the two lights suddenly resolved themselves as headlamps mounted atop the brows of a pair of mushers traveling end on end, and it was only after he had overtaken them that The Boy registered their identities. A sled with a chair mounted on the backs of the runners and a team of dogs walking in short harnesses, a seated figure with his hood up and body hunched behind the windbreak of the driving bow. The Tinkerer. In front of him, kneeling on his sled's footboards was the powerful frame of The Outdoorsman, his team diminished in size and moving as if through molasses. The Boy passed them both and left them behind to become distant sparks once again.

8

Eagle Island was a spare collection of white canvas hard-backed tents arranged inside the mouth of a narrow twisting slough which snaked away from the breast of its mother between steep banks of crumbling black topsoil. Columns of acrid gray smoke rafted away from slender black stovepipes jutting from metal collars riveted to the canvas rooftops, filling the air with the sharp odor of spent fuel. The wind laid down here and The Boy guided his small team into a trench off to the side of the main trail. He camped the dogs in beds of dry straw and covered them over with the extra flakes until they disappeared completely. He turned his light down the slough where the headlamps of two other drivers knelt at their sleds, preparing for departure. Just ahead of them, he noted two more parking spots, both empty but for flattened bedding.

The Boy was sitting on his empty cooler and watching the blue flames of his alcohol-cooker spiral skyward when The Woman came and hunkered down next to him.

'I saw you coming in,' she said. 'It's really amazing how your dogs look. I'm not sure if I've ever seen dogs at this point in the race looking so good. Barking to go, even after a straight up run from Anvik. Really amazing.'

The Boy could think of nothing to say, so he just sat there with a big grin plastered to his face and sweat running down his forehead. He hugged his arms around his shaking body, trying to hold himself all together. He started coughing, and a fine spray of blood flecked the snow at his feet. Each single spot of crimson sent up a tiny curl of steam.

'You, on the other hand,' she continued. 'Don't look so good. You're just about used up. The Northland is slowly erasing you.'

The Boy made it through his fit, hocked up a wad of bloody phlegm and spat it away.

'Oh, I know how I look,' he said in a husky voice. 'But believe me, there's plenty more where this came from.' Two lines of his life's water slowly began to leak from his nostrils, joined together at the point of his chin and splattered across the breast of his survival suit.

The Woman shined her light into his face and sighed.

The Boy chuckled, wiped at the mess with the back of his crippled hand. 'You know,' he said. 'I've never been accused of being the sharpest tool in the shed. But, I am a survivor. I survived when I was little, and just maybe I'll survive now. Just maybe I'll surprise all of you.'

'You already have,' The Woman said, her voice pitched so low that The Boy had to lean forward to properly hear her words.

He pitched forward, and in so doing, jerked himself awake. He had fallen asleep sitting on the cooler. His cooker had died out, and when he looked with his headlamp, he saw that there were now four empty straw beds.

9

He got the dogs up and back on the move in the cold hours before dawn. The wind had settled and was replaced by a still cold so profound that the air itself felt like liquefied glass going into his lungs and burst apart in shrill explosions of vapor on the way back out. They travelled up the great river in a strange, hushed silence, as if they were small creatures sneaking across the floor of an enormous cathedral.

He caught The Woman and The Cowboy at sunup. The Cowboy was the first, and he silently stepped on his sled's brake bar and halted his team when The Boy called for trail. He looked neither left nor right, nor did he speak, just stood on his runners hunched and beaten. The Woman was a mile after. Her dogs were lined out and looking strong, but she was traveling very slowly and The Boy caught her at a run and her shouted words of encouragement were lost in his backwash.

Late in the morning under a hard blue sky, he approached the village of Kaltag. The buildings of the township appeared through a haze of mixed smoke and mist; a collection of weather battered single story homes and small buildings of unknown usage. A number of locals motored about on the backs of snowmobiles and battered quads, and a group of men and women stood waiting for him in front of a small shack with a green metal door and stacks of mushers' poly drop-bags ringing its exterior walls. The Marshal stood to the side, his eyes cool and face hidden under a heavy growth of beard.

'Welcome to Kaltag!' someone said. 'What do you need? Tell us what you need, and we'll get you all set up. Where do you want us to park you?'

The Boy stepped off the runners and nearly fell over. 'I need my bag, and a bale of straw. I'm going on through,' he mumbled. He dragged his frozen face muffler down, looked at The Marshal.

'What's the rundown?' he asked the older man.

'You're in third place right now,' The Marshal responded, his voice gruff. 'The Whaler and The Norwegian are on their way to Unalakleet.'

'Who's in the lead?'

'The Norwegian. The Whaler is trying hard to stay with him, but his team just isn't strong enough. The Norwegian is untouchable.'

'Well. We'll be seeing about that,' said The Boy. He turned away and hobbled up the length of the team. His dogs were all bright eyed and standing at attention, wagging their tails and looking for food. He patted each one on the head, and stood still while Titan used his leg for a rubbing post.

'One more thing,' said The Marshal. 'The radar says there's a big mother of a storm coming in, should be hitting the coast sometime before you get to Unalakleet. Gusts up to eighty, 150 below zero temperatures, zero visibility, the whole bit. Some of the locals are saying that they're worried about it taking the ice out of the Sound. It's going to be clear and cold for the next ten hours or so, but when this thing comes in, it's going to stop a lot of folk's right in their tracks.'

The Boy limped back to his sled. 'Well, we'll just cross that bridge when we get there,' he said.

'Boy, that's exactly what I'm worried about. There not being a bridge to cross.'

10

The Whaler was waiting for him outside of the Kaltag foothills, at the foot of a lone peak jutting from the flats like a solitary granite tooth. There was an old cabin with empty sockets for windows and drifts of litter scattered across its floor set just off the bank of a narrow winding creek, and The Whaler now lit a bonfire from pieces of dry alder limbs and chunks of desiccated cottonwood.

The Boy finished the chores of caring for his team bedded down in a willow thicket behind the cabin, and now staggered to seat himself on a stump at the blaze's perimeter. He sat trembling with his breath coming in labored gasps and his hair hanging down in his face, not even caring that his mentor should see him so weakened.

'Where is this place?' he asked in a croaking wheeze.

The Whaler grinned around a lit cigar and his features were partially hidden by its smoke.

'This is Old Woman,' he said. 'We're about forty miles out from Unalakleet.' He took a wooden handled rattle with intricate ivory inlays from his sealskin parka pocket, began to slowly shake it. The moon was filled with orange radiance, and its glow now joined that of the bonfire to light The Boy's face. In the darkened forest, a pack of wolves took up their lonely song.

'You couldn't match him,' The Boy stated. There was no need to specify who he meant. His shaking was becoming almost uncontrollable, and his teeth clattered together like dice in a cup.

'Nope,' The Whaler agreed. He shook the rattle faster, and the sound that it produced was like the whirring sizzle of a timber rattler's tail warning of danger. 'That obscenity was just too much for me. He kept on going when I pulled in here. I'm bushed, and my dogs are all worn out.'

'He's that strong?'

'He's stronger. He only let me tag along with him as long as he did because he could tell that he had the power to shake me off whenever he wanted to. Mostly, I think he was just having fun watching me burn up in his backwash.'

'Well.'

'How about you, kid?'

The Boy spat on the ground at his feet. 'Not so good, I'm thinking,' he answered. 'I'm real tired. I'm just about all used up. I feel like someone could read a newspaper through me.'

'Yeah,' said The Whaler. 'It gets like that sometimes.' His grin slowly faded and his face grew solemn. The rattle whirred even faster, and over their heads in the surrounding cottonwoods, the limbs sighed and creaked under a freight of dark forms rustling their wings and softly clicking their beaks.

'My dogs are doing good, though,' The Boy amended.

The Whaler chuckled at this. 'After what happened to you back at Rohn, we never should have seen you again,' he said. He dragged mightily on his cigar and the tip of it glowed like a red star. 'Yeah, I gather that your dogs are doing good. It's not going to be enough, though.'

'No?'

'No.'

The Boy stared at the tip of the cigar as if hypnotized. The buzzing of the rattle filled his skull from ear to ear. 'What do I have to do?' he whispered.

'Oh, I think you know the answer to that.'

'They told me about the storm coming up the coast.'

'Yeah. It's going to be the mother of all storms,' The Whaler nodded. 'The most savage storm to ever hit while the Great Race was in progress.'

'They said that it might take the ice right out of Norton Sound.'

'That is a very real possibility,' agreed The Whaler. His face was occluded by shadow, but his teeth glowed from within; faster and faster, the rattle.

'You know, that's where my family died,' The Boy said. 'Out there on the Sound, during a big storm.'

'Yes, I did know that.'

'They all died. My Mama, my baby brother. My Papa. The wind just took them, ate them like it was hungry, and they were the only thing that could satisfy its appetite.'

The Whaler was completely hidden behind a swirling wall of smoke. 'You'll know what to do when the time comes,' he said, and it seemed as if his voice were coming from some great distance.

'Some people say that I died out there, too. That the wind took me into its bosom and carried me away, to be a part of it forever.'

'Is that true? Will you let that be the way that your story ends?'

The rattle shook and became a thunderous roar. The light from the bonfire wobbled, contracted, sucked down to a single oblique tunnel thrown from his failing headlamp. His dogs were arrayed in front of his sled, walking buckled down and struggling to keep their feet in the gale. Carved into the trail in front of Titan was a solitary set of runner tracks, left like the evidence of dinosaurs.

The Boy hunched his face into his collar and began to laugh.

The storm had arrived.

Chapter XV

1

THE Boy reached Unalakleet in the early morning hours, shortly after a gloomy sunrise that did little to illuminate a world completely hidden behind a swirling wall of wind driven snow. His exhausted brain held a vague memory of half seen buildings on a high bank; a long row of riverboats and bush-planes anchored and muffled against the weather; crowds of people with hoods battened and goggles covering their faces, all shouting encouragement; a polished apron of ice scored by snowmobile traffic beyond measure, and a series of lathe trail markers leading the way out of town vibrating so severely that they must surely snap. They had crossed a roadway scoured down to gravel, and on the far side found themselves in a thicket of brush so dense that is was not unlike being in a tunnel. Here, for the space of a hundred feet or less, was a momentary respite from the gale.

The Boy felt for the snowhook; fumbled it away. For a long moment he just stood on the runners, gently swaying back and forth. When he did step away from the sled, his movements were the lurching motions of an engine strangling on oxygen and gasping up the last ounces of its fuel reserves. The dogs stood apathetically, their tug-lines sagging and their heads down. He tottered along the line of athletes handing out small treats of frozen salmon; watched dully as each dog left the offering on the trail and got as far away from it as their lines would allow. He found himself on his knees next to Titan, leaning on the dog to keep himself from toppling over. He wondered where he would ever find the strength to regain his feet.

Overhead, an unkindness of ravens spun like flakes of ash. Through a gap in the bushes, he could see out to the Bering Sea, a flat gray expanse without limit or border.

Titan began to lick his face. The Boy stroked his old friend, pulled him into his arms and held him tight. He closed his eye and concentrated on sending energy out of himself and into his dogs. He stayed like that for a period of time without conscious measure, until he heard the first excited barking. Titan struggled in his arms and began to whine. The Boy opened his eye; all around him and occupying every conceivable space, a host of ravens had settled into the brush like strange black fruit, softly gulping and crooking to one another. The dogs were all standing at attention, ears perked and noses tilted to scent the air. Titan began to bark and pound on his line, and this had the effect of starting a brushfire; the rest of the team followed their leader's example and all began to howl with excitement. The Boy put his good hand down on the trail and pushed with all of his failing strength. For a long moment, he thought that he might remain forever locked in that position, but then he slowly unbent to his full height.

He hobbled back to the sled and pulled the hook. As a single entity, the ravens burst into flight, blowing apart in a muffled explosion of ebony pinions.

2

And they climbed, up an impossibly long flight of stairs, right up to the very rafters and ridge beams of the world. Reality dissolved around them as The Boy and his dogs made their stand in those coastal mountains; vanished into a perpetual fog of whipping snow and swirling vapor.

The Boy ran behind the sled with his hair hanging down across his face and his breath coming in strangled gasps. The dogs pulled with all of the power in their bodies, Spartans one and all. There was no sound in this place, other than the susurration of the wind and the pounding of ten mighty hearts; the creak of sinew through sheaths filled with synovial fluid and the flexing of muscles in their bellies. No thought, save for those of the world that was lost and all of the ones waiting to be found. The wind was a story, a song, a ballad, and it wrote over all.

They came out of the void without warning or preparation, as suddenly as if a veil had been pulled from the face of the world. They were crossing the brow of a barren, rock strewn mountaintop; an island. Above them stretched a sky so big and deep and purely blue that it made The Boy's heart ache just to look upon it. The sun stood pulsing with hot yellow fire, perfectly in the center of this glimmering azure expanse, and the feel of it touching his flesh was like the first kiss of spring. Here, the wind had lain down to become utterly still. Below the narrow wedge of mountain peak they now straddled, the land all around was hidden in a seething cauldron of storming shadow. Far off to the north and west, he could see Norton Sound, a flat black wall stood on its side and dominating the distant horizon.

Even at this remove, he could hear it muttering its primal hunger, an ominous resonation down in his bone marrow.

Ahead, less than a hundred yards in front of him where the trail descended back into the storm, the profile of a musher and his long train of dogs painted themselves across his field of vision. The sun pinned this new team in its glare, and for the space of a heartbeat, they were haloed in radiant gold. Then they were gone, sucked back into the bosom of the earth, leaving only a glittering trail of vapor to mark their passage.

The Boy turned his face to the sky and let the burning radiance wash his haggard features for a moment, and in this space he and his dogs were cast in stark relief upon the surface of the earth over which they trod. Then he, too, was plunged back into darkness and chaos, and it felt for the entire world as if a great shroud were being pulled over his head.

They dropped for a time both elastic and without measure, and at last came out of the hills and crossed over to the sea ice. Somewhere ahead, surely only a handful of miles, laid the village of Shaktoolik. The dogs moved slowly in the maelstrom, leaning their bodies windward and scrambling to hold their footing whenever the ice became too slick to stand and the wind blew them off of the trail. They followed some kind of embankment on their left, working their way over sloping shoulders of drifted sand and jumbled piles of driftwood like the bones of ancient beasts, and finally were stopped altogether, blown across an expanse of polished blue ice and into a stand of brush on the far side of a shallow lagoon. The Boy lunged from the runners and went down on his face; without his weight on the runners, the sled flopped over and the lid of the sled bag flew open and a mess of gear and supplies tumbled away. He flailed his way to his knees and crawled to where his dogs were tangled around a copse of alder.

Working in a near delirium, he freed them and started them back towards the place where he last knew the trail markers to be. It was of no use. The wind bellowed out of the north, picked them up and flung them around, drove them like dead leaves before a hurricane and dashed them against the shoreline. The Boy walked to the front of the team and hooked a spare tug-line to Titan's collar ring, and began walking along the line of coastal grasses and detritus with the team pooled closely about his feet, heading into the wind parallel to where he knew the trail to be. Without someone to steer, his sled crashed over once again. He ignored this and kept moving, head bowed and heart pounding. They travelled in this manner, minds smoothly disengaged, intent only on forward progress. The lagoon to their right tapered, faded away. The markers crossed their tack and headed over a flat of bare tundra and writhing grass. The air cleared in this region, for all of the loose snow had long since been launched away. Hovering in the distance was a long line of painted squares and rectangles and the glint of sun-struck glass. Directly in front of him were a musher and his team of dogs, all knotted into a rough ball around their sled.

The Boy released the snap from Titan's collar and returned to his own sled. Behind them, the way they had come was a surreal scene, a vibrating onyx wall of titanic proportions. He stood the runners and his dogs started to move once again, nearly flattened to the earth with their efforts. They detoured around the stranded musher, and when they passed him, theirs were the only set of tracks creasing the trail. The Boy looked back, saw the man floundering to get his team lined out, a fruitless effort because the team did not want to go. His leaders just dove back into the tussocks the instant that they were released.

The Boy stepped on his brake bar and brought his own team to a halt, whereupon all nine of his dogs began to bark with excitement, eager to continue. He lurched back to where the stranger stood with his hands on his head and his dogs laying down in crumpled heaps. The man was very tall, broad shouldered and dressed all in blue. His face was hidden by a frosted gator and heavy goggles. The two of them stared at each other for a long moment, and then The Boy pointed at the man's leaders, then back at his own team waiting a few yards ahead. The man's shoulders slumped and he nodded. He went back to his sled while The Boy bent down and grasped the double neckline dangling from his lead dogs' collars. He walked with them until the stranger's team was lined out and the leaders were standing on his own sled's drag mat. Still holding their neckline, he managed to pull his hook and get his team going. The resistance from the stranger's team sent a sickening shock of pain blasting up from his wrist, but he held on until both teams were moving steadily, and only then did he release the neckline. Behind him, the stranger's leaders trotted with their heads sagging and ears down, exhaustion dulling their eyes.

Ahead of them, the buildings grew in size, gained color and gravity, grew larger still. Then they were among them on a plowed road running between rows of weather-pounded homes and small shuttered buildings with four-wheelers and snowmobiles parked in their driveways. Spiky furred dogs on long tethers stood on many of the roof tops, all furiously heralding their arrival.

A large group of people clustered together in front of a long, orange metal building: checkers and race officials; reporters with long boom mikes and cameras; locals in parkas and brightly patterned kuspuks. People were shouting and children were racing about. The Boy brought his team to halt in a spray of powdered ice.

The Marshal emerged from the throng.

'Welcome to Shaktoolik!' he shouted. The reporters all gathered around, thrusting microphones close enough to catch every word. 'Look, just get parked and take care of your dogs. We have your food right here, and there's plenty of water and fuel. When you're done, come on into the Armory and get warmed up. We need to talk.' He turned to the crowd and held up his hands. 'Alright, everybody listen up! These guys are both off limits until they've had a chance to do their chores and gotten some rest!'

The Boy and his dogs were led behind the building and sheltered at the foot of an immense snow embankment with curls of loose spray coming over its top and showering down upon them. He did his chores moving in an envelope of numb silence, looking up at one point to gaze upon the stranger who also was kneeling in his team and doing his best to care for his own dogs. After the dogs ate, they were covered with blankets and extra layers of straw and only then did the two mushers stumble away to find shelter. Up a long ramp of iron grating and through a stout metal door, into a world of gabbling voices, warmth, and the smell of cooking food.

The narrow space was crowded with people sheltering from the storm. Window sills were covered with hats and mittens, and clothes lines heavy with drying gear sagged from the low ceiling. Voices crackled from a com's room behind a thin partition. The Boy limped to a long table covered with empty Styrofoam cups and pitchers of juice and coffee. He carefully lowered himself onto a narrow bench and pulled his gloves off. The stranger sat across from him, stripping away his goggles and hat, and only then did The Boy make that final connection.

The Norwegian shook his head and heaved a weary sigh. He

reached forward and poured juice into a cup, and The Boy watched in fascination as he put the cup to his lips and drank its contents in one long swallow.

Behind them, The Marshal could be heard snapping into a telephone receiver. Around the room, people talked and stared. The Boy looked at his own naked hands in dim confusion. They were very dirty, and bent like claws. The space was slowly revolving around him, and he knew that if he didn't do something to stop it, he was going to pass out right where he sat.

'I lived here when I was very little,' he croaked to no one in particular, and even to him, the words sounded like gibberish. He tried to pour some juice for himself, but his hands were shaking so badly that the fluid began to slosh onto the surface of the table. The Norwegian took the pitcher from him and silently poured a cupful, and handed it across. The sound of an infant sobbing for comfort came from somewhere in the back, and when The Boy started to get up to go check on it, The Norwegian's hand closed over his and his fierce blue eyes held him.

'Okay guys, I've got some bad news,' someone was saying. 'This storm is going to be worse than we thought. Maybe a lot worse.' Who's voice? What was he talking about anyway?

The Boy tried to focus, but the room continued to spin. That little baby sounded so sad. Where was his Mama? The Norwegian stared at him in silence, his eyes growing, growing. Someone was talking in a loud, gruff voice, saying that they weren't going to shut the race down, no way, but there were drivers scattered from hell to breakfast and pinned down all over. The Whaler was stopped back in Unalakleet. The Woman and The Outdoorsman were stuck on the way over from Kaltag. The Yukon was a freaking mess, no one was moving. How the heck you two made it over here in the first place is going to be the stuff documentaries are made out of.

All nonsense.

Has it really been fourteen years? The Boy thought. *If I went out that door and walked the streets, could I still pick out my old house? What kind of family would I find living there now? That Scandinavian devil is really getting an eyeful, what the heck is he staring at?*

'Some machines went out towards Koyuk, but they turned back. They said that there were no markers standing. Not one. The winds were terrible, near hurricane speeds, they were afraid that it might be blowing hard enough to take the ice out of the Sound.'

I was only four years old. Imagine that. I remember crouching down on the ice and holding my baby brother, while our Mama held the both of us and sang her heart out. Just like it happened yesterday. It was blowing then, too, just like it is right now. I can still see Papa disappearing into the dark, holding that lantern and getting smaller and smaller. Mama and Papa were school-teachers, but they sure didn't know much about being outside in the winter! I heard that they still talk around these parts, about what happened, like it was some kind of urban legend. Maybe that's why everybody is staring at me like this.

A feeling of sickly, stinging heat began to emanate from his foot-gear in pulsing waves closely linked to the beat of his heart. *Well, ladies and gentleman, that is my cue to go back outside,* he thought, though he didn't move. For some reason, his body simply refused to obey his wishes. There was some significance to the words of The Marshal, and the fact that he was sitting across from The Norwegian of all people, but he couldn't make his mind focus on what that was, what any of it meant.

3

He opened his eye. He could tell that some time had passed from the quality of the dim light coming through the window, the whispered conversation of checkers and other race personnel. Fighting the urge to vomit, he lurched to his feet and stumbled through the door into a chaos of blasting wind.

Tottering like a very old man, he made his way to the rear of the building where his dogs laid hidden under their bedding. Every step brought him closer to lucidity like a man struggling from the black depths of an abyss. He reached the back of his sled and sank to his knees. He looked out to the north, to the Sound, where the air writhed and shivered and tore a hole in the very walls of reality. Somewhere out there in that howling void was the end of the trail; the end of his trail. Somewhere out there in all of that beautiful madness, his Mama called to him and sang her sweet-sad song.

He looked up at a sky dark with circling ravens and knew what was required of him. Slowly, and with great deliberation, he crawled on his hands and knees and began, one by one, to wake his dogs. They stood quiet and solemn, and not even Titan made a sound when he stroked the soft fur between his ears.

The Boy made it back to the sled and sagged against the driving bow, empty beyond measure.

The Norwegian was standing at his side, and his face was written in lines of terrible anguish. He put his big hand on The Boy's frail shoulder and gently squeezed.

'You are a warrior,' he said, slowly and in broken English. 'Truly you are. I have never seen anyone of your kind before.'

The Boy stared up at him.

'But this thing you are doing, it is madness. You have beaten me. You have no need to go out there.'

'Yes,' whispered The Boy. 'I do.'

'There is no trail. You will not make it. There are no markers.'

The Boy straightened to his full height and pulled back on the sled. Titan was standing at attention and looking over his shoulder, and now he began to bark and hammer at the line. His teammates picked up the call, and all of them began to howl.

'I don't need any markers where I'm going,' The Boy said.

The Norwegian shook his head, and his eyes left trails that hung in the air like the tails of meteorites. 'You are a warrior, but you will not see Nome. I think that you will go to Valhalla, instead.'

The Boy started to laugh.

'Well,' he said. 'Either way, I'll be there waiting for you. Titan? Boys? Let's do this.'

No long speeches. No excuses. The dogs simply leaned into their lines, and in this manner, The Boy and his faithful team passed into the bosom of the Northland.

River rat.

Dog man.

Balladeer.

Epilogue

THE wind is blowing very hard and it has grown quite dark. I can't see anything, except for the occasional glimpse of my heroic team leaping and plunging through the drifts. I was very cold for a long time, and scared, but I no longer feel a thing. No cold, no pain. In fact, I'm starting to feel sort of warm. The sound of the wind was deafening at first, but now it sounds more like a whisper, someone whispering to me sweetly, softly.

Lie down, just lie down, it whispers. *You're so tired, if you just lay down and get a little rest, then everything would be fine for once.*

And damn, you know what? I am lying down! The dogs have all stopped and are gathered around the sled. I guess they've had enough, too.

The wind is whispering, and it kind of sounds like someone singing now. For some reason, an image of riding at the bow of a river boat springs into my mind. There is an outboard motor rumbling at the stern, and a musky spray wetting my face, and a fine golden light splashing quick spumes of fairy dust from the surface of the water. Life was good, no matter what anybody says. A quick fan of faces play across the screen of my memories: Uncle, standing with the Mini-14; Little Cousin on his hands and knees, desperate to get away from that bad dog trying to gobble him all up; Middle Cousin, his face shining and clean and smiling; Auntie; The Whaler; and now, The Girl.

She is kneeling at my side, and her slender arms are wrapped around my quaking body.

'The time has come,' she whispers. There are tears running freely down her lovely face.

Home at last, I allow myself to relax into her embrace. The dark and the cold and the wind enfold me, slowly work to erase me. It is my Mama's voice that I now hear carried in the wind. She is the one singing. This is the wind which has howled through the lonely corridors of my soul for as long as I can remember.

'Mama,' I say, not sure if my lips even properly make the words. I reach up and touch The Girl's face, look into her dark eyes. She smiles down at me, and I can feel her strong arms straining to lift me from the ground. Her face shimmers, becomes my mother's.

'Yes, my sweetest love?' she says.

I gaze up to her lovely countenance and know that I, too, am crying now.

'I have waited so long for you to come home,' she says.

'I have come a long way to get back here,' I say, and once uttered, these words leave me weightless.

'I know you have, baby. Shush now.'

'Mama,' I say. I struggle to sit and push myself from her arms. I ball my wounded hand into a fist, drive it into the ground. The change is immediate. The wind is howling and ravening and shrieking to get inside of me, and the pain of the cold is sudden and horrifying in its lunatic intensity. I climb to my knees, then to my feet. But for my dogs, I am utterly alone in the void.

'Mama!' I shout into the storm. 'I didn't come here to quit, Mama! That's never been my way. I survive, no matter how bad, or how dark it gets. I didn't come all this way to just lie down! Mama, I came to tell you goodbye. I love you, and I'm sorry about what happened, but I still have work to do!'

I take Titan's collar and turn myself to the north where I hope the far shore and the village of Koyuk to be. With steps slow and methodical, I begin to walk.

Maybe I will make it, and maybe I won't. In the end, it doesn't really matter. All that any of us in this world can do is make our stand against all of the forces greater then ourselves, and let the cards fall where they may.

Later, how much I could not say, I see a light in the distance.